Acquainted
with the
NIGHT
and other stories

Acquainted
with the
NIGHT
and other stories

Lynne Sharon Schwartz

1817
HARPER & ROW, PUBLISHERS, New York
Cambridge, Philadelphia, San Francisco, London
Mexico City, São Paulo, Sydney

Portions of this work originally appeared in *Banquet, Dark Horse, First Annual Fiction Supplement of the San Francisco Review of Books, Forthcoming, The Iowa Review, The Literary Review, The Ontario Review, Penmaen Press Chapbook 2, Ploughshares, Redbook, The Real Paper, The Smith,* and *The Transatlantic Review.*

"The Wrath-bearing Tree" and "Sound Is Second Sight" were syndicated by *Fiction Network.*

Grateful acknowledgment is made for permission to reprint:
Portions of "Terence, this is stupid stuff" from "A Shropshire Lad"—Authorised Edition—from *The Collected Poems of A. E. Housman,* copyright 1939, 1940, © 1965 by Holt, Rinehart and Winston. Copyright © 1967, 1968 by Robert E. Symons. Reprinted by permission of Holt, Rinehart and Winston, Publishers; The Society of Authors as the literary representative of the Estate of A. E. Housman; and Jonathan Cape Ltd, publishers of A. E. Housman's *Collected Poems.*
Excerpts on page 77 from "Gerontion" in *Collected Poems 1909–1962* by T. S. Eliot, copyright 1936 by Harcourt Brace Jovanovich, Inc.; copyright © 1963, 1964 by T. S. Eliot. Reprinted by permission of Harcourt Brace Jovanovich, Inc. and Faber and Faber Ltd, London.
Lines from "Sailing to Byzantium" from *The Poems of W. B. Yeats,* edited by Richard J. Finneran, copyright 1928 by Macmillan Publishing Co., Inc., renewed 1956 by Georgie Yeats. Reprinted by permission of Macmillan Publishing Company, Inc., Michael B. Yeats and Macmillan, London, Limited.
"Get a Piece of the Rock" is used by permission of the Prudential Insurance Company of America.

FIRST EDITION

Designer: Jane Weinberger

Library of Congress Cataloging in Publication Data

Schwartz, Lynne Sharon.
   Acquainted with the night and other stories.

   I. Title.
PS3569.C567A66   1984   813'.54   83-48815
ISBN 0-06-015307-5

84 85 86 87 88   10 9 8 7 6 5 4 3 2 1

For Tobi Tobias,
for all those years
when she asked for more

CONTENTS

Acquainted
with the
NIGHT
and other stories

THE AGE OF ANALYSIS

Paul had always had an analyst, ever since he could remember. It began long ago, when, after several days of kicking, screaming, and gobbling handfuls of soil from his mother's potted plants, he was carried by his parents, working in tandem, into the car and on to Dr. Trowbridge's office in a tall building on North Michigan. How old he was then—eight, ten, six—Paul couldn't recall precisely. But he did remember quite clearly that first sight of the analyst.

Dr. Trowbridge struck him as a comfortable, grandmotherly woman. She sat calmly in a leather chair behind a formidable wooden desk, smiling a friendly greeting as his parents dragged him in. She had short wavy gray hair, plump cheeks, and very thick glasses with pale-pink frames; she wore a cotton print dress with short sleeves. It must have been summer. He remembered they had no coats. Later on, in their private sessions, when she used to come out from behind her desk to stroll around the green-

1

carpeted office, he noticed that she wore black oxford shoes with laces, old-lady shoes. Her ankles were thick.

Once he was in the office that seminal afternoon, he ceased his kicking and screaming. No one knew exactly why. He was distracted, perhaps, by the new surroundings, by the abstract mobile of colorful shapes hanging from the low ceiling, by the soft artificial light and the numerous framed documents on the paneled walls. He caught his breath and shut up, impressed that he had driven them to do something about him at last, to stop him, as if he were a runaway windup toy on which they had placed an overdue restraining hand. And what they had done was this relaxed elderly woman who smoked with a slender black cigarette holder, something he had never seen before.

He grew very fond of her and she allowed this fondness. Now, at fifteen, Paul didn't remember much of what they had done or said together except for the mazes. Dr. Trowbridge was very keen on maze games. She produced a new one almost every time Paul came. They bored him, but he felt it would sound impolite or ungrateful to tell her that, particularly as she appeared to enjoy them so. As time passed, he graduated from large wooden block mazes to small cardboard or plastic structures, to dittoed sheets, the most abstract. (Yes, she said, when he remarked on the dittos, she had other young patients. This bothered him, the idea of other children bending their heads with her over the same dittoed sheets, basking in her endless, soothing calm, especially since he never saw them in the small waiting room that hummed with white noise. But as they talked it over he came to accept a nonexclusive relationship.) He hadn't understood the purpose of mazes at first, and performed aimlessly, until Dr. Trowbridge explained that the purpose was to find the most direct way out. Even then they didn't make much sense—why not linger, he thought, on the intricate paths—but he tried to be cooperative. She taught him to work backwards from the goal. Dr. Trowbridge didn't take things as seriously as his parents, nor was she appalled by his lapses into violence. And as she listened and nodded in her quiet way, it began to seem that there was space in him to absorb still another shaming incident with a bit of compassion. This lack of seriousness in her puzzled him, though, for he knew what her purpose was. She was hired specifically to take him seriously, to find out what made him so difficult. She was a superior being who lived above the fray. At least that was what he inferred. Her office was hushed like a holy place. With her he was not difficult.

Then, one nasty day, she announced that he was getting too old for her. She was a child psychiatrist, she explained, and he at thirteen was no longer a child. He was ready to move on to a specialist in adolescence. Paul made a scene, of course; it was the least he could do to preserve his self-respect. He ripped the mobile from the ceiling, tangling and cutting his fingers in the wires, and shouted bitter accusations, which she sat through quietly as if she had expected them.

"I know how you feel," she said. "Separation anxiety." That phrase from the occult language was a further betrayal, and sent him further into rage. He was heading for the curtains, the blood pounding in his head, lunging to fling them down, when she said, "Please, Paul. It's so hard to get curtains. They have to come and measure, and bring samples of fabric. It takes weeks. Please." She smiled mildly, and he stopped.

By now he had forgiven her and thought about her with gentle nostalgia, since he was fairly well settled in with Dr. Crewes, whose office was just off Lake Shore Drive. Dr. Crewes was not like Dr. Trowbridge, either in spirit or in appearance. She was much younger, for one thing, maybe thirty or thirty-five, he guessed. Sometimes he thought she was smarter, too; she sounded smarter, in any case. She chain-smoked and fiddled with things on her desk and had a sharp, knifelike voice that sometimes echoed gratingly in his ears hours after he left her. She wasn't easygoing, but to compensate, there was a simmering excitement in talking to her. Lately a pleasant sexual buzz hovered around him when he sat opposite Dr. Crewes. They talked about it, naturally, and she said evenly that it was quite all right. It was to be expected. She smiled and showed two perfect rows of small sharp teeth. Dr. Crewes had a broad face, wide green eyes, and shoulder-length straight brown hair that she dashed nervously off her forehead. She never removed her very large round tinted glasses. Usually she wore pants suits with soft sweaters and odd loops of beads. Once, on a rainy day, she had worn blue jeans. Paul encountered her sometimes in his dreams wearing a succession of bizarre costumes, but he never touched her. Either he was afraid, or she drifted away when he reached out.

With the professional help of Drs. Trowbridge and Crewes, Paul had inched his way through youth as through a mined field. He had reached his second year of high school, a better than average student, though there had been months now and then of neglecting his studies and becoming obsessed by games—first backgammon, then chess, most recently horse racing. He won $150 at the track last summer, which he never told his parents about, but he told Dr. Crewes. She seemed proud of his skill in calculating odds, and made clever, provocative analogies between games of chance and real-life situations. Paul told her everything. Even the things he deliberately planned not to tell—in bouts of resistance—she somehow got out of him, or else once they passed by undiscussed, they came to seem insignificant.

Now, Monday, he had made a special appointment with her, apart from his scheduled Thursdays and Saturdays, to discuss the calamity. His parents, after nearly two decades of marriage, were, incredibly, intolerably, separating. Immediately. His father had told him only last night. There had been a vicious scene, during which his mother retreated to the bedroom while he and his father shouted at each other. She was the one being left. His father was going to live with a woman about ten years older than Paul. The very thought of her was intolerable.

His father was a psychoanalyst, his mother was a psychotherapist, and his father's girlfriend was a psychiatric social worker in training, who had first appeared as his student in a seminar. Paul did not have the naive illusion that the membership of all three parties in what his parents called "the helping professions" was any guarantee against emotional upheaval. No. He had matured that much since Dr. Trowbridge. The wretched triangle of experts did not strike him as bizarre, any more than the fact that each of them continued daily to counsel others in torment. He had more than once overheard his parents remark on how the prolonged work of clearing the treacherous paths of the self disposes one to instability. Just like coal miners get black lung, thought Paul.

Indeed, among their friends, largely pairs of analysts, therapists, and social workers, Paul had already witnessed suicide, alcoholism, recurrent infidelity, breakdowns, and violence. So the source of his feeling of utter shock was merely that he had always believed Richard and Nan perfectly matched.

This was what he sullenly told Dr. Crewes now, after which she asked in cool tones, "How does it make you feel?"

He replied by resting his head on her desk and weeping. The sounds of his sobs were ugly to him, great gasping noises like the screeching of gears in an immense and overloaded machine.

Dr. Crewes played with the button of a ballpoint pen lying on her desk while she waited. "It's terrible for you, I can see, especially after all the progress we've made."

"I can't understand it," Paul wept. He blew his nose and tried to control the trembling of his shoulders. "The worst thing is that I can't believe it. How could he go and do this to us, after all those years? How could he? I'd like to . . ." His bony boy's fingers locked and tugged and twisted like an interpreter's making signs for a deaf-mute. "I could tear him to pieces."

"You seem to be identifying strongly with your mother."

"Well, for Christ's sake," said Paul, "it's not a question of identifying. I mean, look what he's doing to me! Shit, I didn't do anything to him except get born, and now . . . I don't know, maybe it *is* me. Maybe he can't put up with me anymore."

"Ah," said Dr. Crewes. "You see, your guilt is coming out. What did I do to deserve this, and so forth. You did nothing. You have to separate that out. What exactly did he say to you?"

"After dinner last night he said he had to have a talk with me. So we sat down. He said he was leaving right away, and he couldn't really explain but it was no longer possible—that's what he said, no longer possible, get that—for him to go on living with my mother. Then he said he was in love. In love! At his age!"

"And what did you say?"

"Nothing. Not until he started on the piano. See, I was being very quiet. I couldn't say anything, I was so shocked. And at that point my mother was puttering around the dining room table, clearing the dishes away like she just worked there or something. I didn't want to give him the satisfaction of answering. But then he got started on the piano. Which was right there, too, staring us in the face. Well, you know about the piano."

The baby grand piano had been a joint acquisition. Paul and his father both played extremely well. They had shopped for it together two years ago to replace an old upright, when it became obvious that Paul's was no ordinary talent. Paul still remembered what a good time they had had in the showrooms, trying out all the models with snatches of sonatas and popular tunes. Finally they settled on a large black Steinway. Paul cared for it like an attentive parent, cleaning its keys and polishing its glossy surface. He was as fussy about his piano, his father used to joke, as Nan was about her expensive carpeting.

"So he says"—and here Paul mimicked his father's thin raspy voice and ponderous delivery—"'Paul, I know this will seem unfair to you, but I have to have the piano.' 'Over my dead body,' I said. Then he started yelling and running around the room, about how he's tired of giving and has to start taking for himself. And then . . ."

"Well?"

"Well, I sort of got hysterical and tore the place up." Paul grinned, a tentative flicker of light, then his mouth set sullenly again. He stared at the harsh Van Gogh print of sunflowers above Dr. Crewes' head, which often had a semihypnotic effect on him.

"You look proud of yourself."

"Well, then to calm me down, I guess, he said okay, he'd leave the piano. Then a minute later, no, he'd take it. Meanwhile my mother went off to their room. She said she was tired and going to sleep, and he could handle this scene since the whole thing was his idea anyway, and he should have given me more time to adjust to the change. Honestly, by the time it was all over I swear I didn't know if he was taking it or leaving it."

"What about your mother's going off to her room? How did you feel about that?"

"What? Hell, I don't know. I guess I thought she could have stuck up for me more. But she's got her problems too. Listen, I'd like to kill the both of them. What the fuck am I going to do?"

"You're filled with rage and guilt, Paul. As is to be expected. You have to understand that, and that's what we'll have to work on, whatever happens. We'll have to deal with your rage and guilt."

"Deal with! Deal with!" Paul leaped up, his thick gray sweater hanging loosely from his shoulders as he waved his arms violently in the air. He was a tall, sandy-haired boy with gaunt cheeks and a wide mouth. He had ice-blue eyes that in moments of excitement became flecked with pale-green flamelike shapes. "Is all of life one long process of dealing with things? Is that all there is to it? Hell!"

Dr. Crewes flashed her teeth in one of her courteous, enigmatic smiles. With a familiar final gesture, she reached for her appointment book. The fifty-minute hour was over.

"Thanks," said Paul. "I must say I expected more sympathy from you. I mean, simply as a human being. You've known me all these years."

"Yes," she said, "you're disappointed. I can see that. But if I gave you the sympathy you want, it wouldn't help the treatment. I understand how you feel—we'll have to deal with that too."

He set out to walk the mile home, though the cold winds off the lake were fierce. Night was falling. The sky was a dull gray. He had heavy schoolbooks to carry and his bus was right at the corner. But he felt like walking, masochistic or not. Thinking, out in the cold. He was disturbed at how he hadn't been able to get across to Dr. Crewes that his reaction was not yet loss or sadness but only shock. It was inconceivable that they were not happy with each other. He had thought of them, sometimes with mild sarcasm, as practicing experts in marital happiness.

They left for work together in the morning—his father would drop his mother off at the Carl Rogers Institute, loosely connected with the university—leaving Paul alone to clear the breakfast dishes. Often, calling goodbye from the kitchen as he heard the door click open, he had felt like the parent, sending the youngsters off to school with a sense of release. Then his father picked her up at five-thirty. Sometimes they stopped to shop on the way home. They cooked dinner together—Nan was a meticulous and inventive cook—while talking over their cases. The last year or two, Paul had found the daily progress of these cases rather tedious, so he had taken to staying in his room until they called him to the table. But they seemed to enjoy it, that was the crucial point. Finally at dinner they would ask, "And how are things going with you, Paul? Everything under control at school?"

It was beginning to rain. Little pellets of ice hit his face and clung to his eyelashes. He trudged along Fifty-fifth Street, thinking. Once a week his father went out again in the evening to give a seminar to social work trainees. Paul turned a windy corner, winced with pain and cold as a fluttering twig blew at his cheek. As he blinked, he could see some faceless dark feline creature leering at his father, raising her hand often to impress him with pretentious answers, luring him away from home, where he belonged. He was not going to think about that part of it.

They had been happy—he had watched them for years at it, and if he couldn't trust what he saw anymore, then what could he rely on? In school they were learning about a dead philosopher called Berkeley, who said that nothing we see is really there. Of course Paul had thought it was pure nonsense, but maybe Berkeley was right. Maybe everything in the world was deceptive, his parents included.

Richard and Nan generally did not go out on week nights since they got up so early every morning. They read side by side, or else his mother made phone calls to her friends while his father did paper work at the small desk in the living room. Occasionally people dropped over, therapists who talked about their cases. Paul would greet them—they liked to scrutinize him; he had something of a reputation for his violent tendencies, and he rather enjoyed their veiled curiosity. He might listen to them talk for a while, then go to his room. They did not stay late. But weekends were another matter entirely, devoted to pleasure. Nan and Richard would wake early as usual, and as soon as the few chores were done, take off in their shorts and running shoes along the Midway—weather permitting, as they said. In the winter it was swimming in the university pool. They seemed to have a passion for rhythmic movement which Paul did not share. When he was twelve he had rebelled, declaring that he no longer wished to accompany their leisure-time rounds like a pet—their five-mile runs, their serious movies on social themes, their bargain-hunting expeditions, their drawn-out dinners in foreign restaurants, their eternal Sunday afternoons at friends' houses, drinking cocktails and eating through numberless bowls of salted nuts. His mother was hurt, but his father smoothed it over. "Typical of adolescence. He's finding his own style. It's natural that he should be bored with us. Let him alone." "All right, Paul," Nan said, in a voice straining not to sound resentful. "From now on you can make your own plans. You have your keys to come and go."

Of course they were happy, thought Paul, wiping the wetness from his face with his glove. It was unmistakable. Sometimes they seemed such a closed, snug unit that he felt like an intruder. They had spent years alone together before he was born, and he suspected that they had never grown used to the fact of his presence, or sensed quite what to do about it. One evening last fall he was studying in his room and didn't come out to greet them when they returned from work. When he finally emerged at seven o'clock they were busy in the kitchen, earnestly reconsidering one of his mother's drug addicts. "Why, Paul, my goodness, I forgot all about you," his mother said, and rushed over to kiss his cheek. "You must be starving. Here, have some crackers while we finish getting dinner ready."

The only times he didn't feel like an intruder, but like the very whirling axis of their lives, were the times he got into trouble and caused them trouble. When it was found in his freshman year at U

High that he had been cutting classes for weeks, when it came out a year later that he was the mysterious decimator of the school library, with a cache of unstamped books on the floor of his closet, when it was discovered that he was the founder and guiding genius of the widespread and lucrative football pool the school principal had been trying in vain to stamp out, then their evenings turned into long tearful family confrontations. What Nan and Richard said during these sessions was confusing: at first they threatened to stop paying for his analysis if he didn't give up his antisocial behavior. But at the end, at the reconciliation, they said he needed more intensive treatment, and that they would all go together to talk to Dr. Crewes. Those discussions caused him pain and anger and remorse, yet when they were over Paul felt a satisfactory sense of wholeness. He pulsed with energy and appetite; while his parents crept to bed weary and enervated, Paul would fix himself a triple-decker sandwich and a glass of milk, and eat voraciously. Then he rested, complacent in the knowledge that thoughts of him would keep them lying awake for hours.

Still, despite the trouble he used to cause them (he had been somewhat better lately—the result of good treatment, his father claimed as he puffed on his pipe), he knew they were happy. It was a quiet life, but they appeared to thrive on it. A quiet life indeed; a year ago he used to rage over it in his sessions with Dr. Crewes, caricaturing it with contempt as a suffocating, middle-class, middle-of-the-road, mediocre dead life. But Dr. Crewes had helped him deal with those feelings of rage and rebellion. When he was grown, Dr. Crewes said, he could lead whatever sort of life he chose. Meanwhile, in their home, he must have some respect for their preferences, which were in fact his parents' ways of dealing with their own needs and hostilities and fears. Paul was stunned by that profound insight. He glimpsed a baffling world where every attitude was a way of dealing with the attitude beneath it; as time passed, attitudes heaped up in stratified layers like geological formations. Social criticism had no place in the analyst's office. Gradually he gave up his scorn. To understand all is to forgive all, somebody once said. They seemed so happy and settled, it was uselessly cruel to keep battering at the walls of their comfort. They called each other dear and darling and did small favors for each other like making cups of tea or fetching newspapers, with glowing benign faces that seemed to portray an utter and wholesome rightness. They had found their center, he thought, borrowing Dr. Crewes' phrase. They were all center, no movable electrons.

Then this mad dash to the periphery, this flying apart, must be some form of illness, like a virus, that could attack and disjoint the entire system. But like a virus it could go away just as mysteriously as it had come. As he walked and mulled it over, stepping carefully on the slippery sheet of ice underfoot, Paul became fervently convinced it would go away. It was some sort of emotional disruption in his father, certainly, and it would have to be dealt with, but it was not anything that came from the center.

He entered his apartment building with relief, chilled to the bone. His lips were stiff and chapped. It must be below twenty degrees out there, and God knows what with the windchill factor. Perhaps he should have taken the bus. But at least he had thought things through a little. He had faith now that it would all work out eventually. Just a half hour ago he had imagined the session with Dr. Crewes was a waste of time, yet after going over the facts he felt much better. He recalled some of the things Dr. Crewes had said, and they seemed quite perceptive. Very often, in his long experience, the sessions did seem a waste of time, and then later he would realize how much had actually been accomplished. The sessions had a delayed effect, like some medications. It was all very intriguing. Maybe he would study medicine after all and go into psychiatry rather than music. With his background he had a head start.

He was almost smiling as he got off the elevator. He walked briskly, stuffing his damp gloves in his pockets and looking forward to a hot dinner. It might not work out right away, he mustn't expect miracles, but he couldn't be deceived by the happy tableau they had presented for so long. Berkeley was absurd, as he had thought at the beginning. What you see, you see because it is there. Meanwhile he ought to comfort his mother and explain things to her. Caution her about trying to rush things one way or the other. Nan was like that. Once a decision was made she immediately had to do tangible acts to certify it, as if it might slip through her fingers. He remembered how, when she and Richard decided last September to go to Barbados over Christmas, she had rushed out to buy new luggage. Paul unlocked the door and stepped into the hall. It was dark.

"Mom?"

"Yes. I'm in here, Paul."

He flicked the hall switch—a warm glow of light filled the tidy narrow space. Nan was curled up on the living room couch, doing nothing, not even reading the paper that lay spread out in her lap. She was tall and dark blond, rather like Dr. Crewes, but older and fairer in complexion. She had a pleasant, squarish face with thin lines of anxiety around the eyes and the small mouth. She could look quite attractive, Paul always imagined, if she wore clothes with some dash. But as though unaware of the passage of time, Nan wore the placid styles of her youth two decades ago, shirtwaist dresses, pleated skirts, and shoes with high thin heels. She wore pearls and clip-on earrings and used hair spray. Still, he thought uncomfortably, she was not the kind of woman to drive a man away. She was warm and capable and easy to be with. If he were his father, he would think he hadn't done so badly after all those years.

"Hi," he said. "Why are you sitting here in the dark?" He turned on another light, then followed her fixed stare across the large room.

Stunned, Paul saw why she wasn't speaking. There was a huge nude space in the corner near the window where the piano should have been. Three hollows in the rug where the legs had rested.

"Shit!" he screamed. He tore off his coat, threw it onto the floor with his books, and rushed to the space as if the piano could spring back, conjured by the pressure of his lanky body. "Shit! He can't do that!" And he let out a long howl. He could feel the blood rushing and pounding in his chest, his face growing unbearably hot. This was how it always happened, starting with the rush of blood. There were no words for this storming bloody torrent. He thrashed around looking for objects to attack and hurl.

"Paul," his mother said quietly. She didn't sound restraining, only tired. "Paul, don't, please don't go into that. I'm too worn out. I couldn't stand it."

He stood quivering like a besieged animal.

"Thank you. Come here and sit down by me." She patted the cushion next to her. "Can you?"

He obeyed, sat down next to her on the couch, and sobbed loudly again.

"Paul, I am so sorry. Really I am. I am so sorry for what this is doing to you."

"What about you? What are you going to do about it?"

"I don't know," she said in a high voice. She ran both hands through her fine hair, pulling it all back from her face so that for an instant she looked austere. "I've been thinking that I'll go back into treatment. I could go back to Dr. Steinberg. He was always very supportive." She pressed the fingertips of both hands together, forming a little spired temple. "To find out what I've done, why this is happening. I'm totally in the dark. Oh, I know I've made a lot of mistakes, that I have certain ways. . . . I'm sure some things must have driven him crazy. But still—"

"I meant," he cried, "what are you going to do about the piano?"

"Oh, the piano. I don't know. What can I do? He did it while we were both out. I came home a little while ago and found it gone. He took all his clothes too." She spoke calmly, as if from a vacant space inside.

"I have to get the piano back. Where is it?"

"In his apartment, I guess."

"What apartment?"

"Didn't he tell you? He's got an apartment with this Cheryl, on Dorchester. He arranged it all last month, before we knew."

Paul hung his head over his knees. "He can't get away with this," he mumbled.

"Would you like some dinner?"

"I don't know. I don't feel like eating anymore."

"I'll make something anyway. You've got to try."

It was odd seeing her in the tiny kitchen by herself. They had always done their fancy dishes together. Paul watched from the living room: Nan moved in slow motion, opening cabinets with faltering hands and a vague air, very slowly taking cans and boxes off the shelves and staring at their labels for long moments as if she had never seen them before. Then she opened the refrigerator door and stood looking inside it for a long time. Paul stared at her back; her shoulders began to shake as though she had opened the door onto a pathetic scene.

"Oh, forget it, you don't have to cook."

She finally removed something wrapped in aluminum foil and let go of the door. "No, it's all right. I've got to get used to it. This is some chicken Kiev left from yesterday. He made it, actually. You see—" and she tossed her head archly—"he leaves something of himself with us."

"How long have you known?" he asked her while they ate.

"A week. I wanted him to tell you before, to give you some time, but he said no. He insisted. A clean swift break was what he wanted. It's been absolute hell, knowing all week and not being able to tell you. He's not himself, Paul, this cruelty, this coldness. That bothers me more than anything else. It's like a sickness. I think he's psychotic. I really do. I think he's sick. It has to do with his mother. He needs help."

The food was sticking in his throat. Everything he ate felt dry and scratchy as straw. He kept taking gulps of milk to wash it down, but he could still feel the lumps lying heavily in his chest. "I'm going over there tomorrow to get the piano back. You'll give me the address."

His mother pushed her plate away and got up. "I'm going to call him." She brushed a few crumbs off her blouse and caught them in the palm of her hand. Paul realized how wan and weary she looked. Her face was shiny, her lipstick faded, and her skirt wrinkled as though it had been crushed underfoot. "I can't just let it fall apart like this. It's too hasty. It doesn't make any sense. Maybe I can talk to him about it." Nan went to the phone.

"Wait. What if she answers?"

"Her?" His mother smiled wryly. "I don't care a thing about her. As far as I'm concerned, she doesn't exist. I've met her, you know, around the university. We once discussed Karen Horney. Isn't that funny? She's nothing at all. Just young."

"So why . . .?"

Nan tilted her head and gave him a peculiar look that he couldn't decipher, almost a grin, as she raised the receiver. She took a folded piece of paper from her pocket. "His number. How do you like that? I've got to consult a scrap of paper to telephone your father."

Evidently the girl didn't answer, since his mother began talking right away. "Richard, it's me. Look, Richard . . ." Her voice was shaking, cajoling and vulnerable. Paul felt flushed; he began clearing the table noisily to drown out her words, while his ears strained to hear above the clatter. Nan waved her hand at him to be quiet.

"Richard, look, I'm not calling to pester you or whine, believe me. I want what's best for you. I mean, whatever you think is right for your particular needs. But I think, I've been thinking, this has all been too fast—I mean, I can't absorb it. Can't we get together and talk about it, just so it isn't so abrupt? Maybe," she added timidly, "even see someone about it, together?"

A very short silence. His mother sat down quickly, perched on a hard chair. Paul scraped the leavings of the two plates into the garbage can.

"All right. But, Richard, can I tell you one thing? Before you get all involved in your—your new life, as you call it, Richard, think about what you're doing. It isn't so simple. You have a . . . a problem, this is an emotional crisis. Try to see it that way, Richard. I think you need help. Maybe you should go back to see Dr. Jonas alone, have a consultation."

Another silence. Her lips twitched. "You've never talked like that. That's what makes me think—"

Then, after a dead pause, "All right, if that's how you've decided it's going to be, I'll call a lawyer in the morning." She hung up.

Paul was holding a pot half-filled with reheated rice. He walked slowly into the living room. "But you didn't mention the piano!"

"He's really finished. He said . . . incredible things."

"The piano!" he shrieked.

"The piano," she repeated, as if it were an unfamiliar word. "Oh, the piano. I'm sorry."

He dumped the rice on the carpet, at her feet, and slammed the pot down after it. Then he grabbed his coat. As he went out the door he glimpsed Nan sinking slowly to her knees and scooping up handfuls of rice.

He skipped school the next day and walked all the way to the Point and back. There had been a thaw after yesterday's rain, so that the gutters were running with slush. At about seven he went to his father's place. It was a sleek new apartment building, steel and glass. The doorman stopped him to ask his name and destination, and Paul laughed curtly as he replied. When he got up to the sixth floor his father was at the apartment door, waiting.

"Paul."

"I came for the piano."

"Paul, you can't carry it away."

"Aren't you going to let me in? I'm kind of cold."

His father stepped aside. The girl was sitting cross-legged on the floor, leaning against a pile of crammed cartons. They were apparently in the middle of their dinner, which was Kentucky Fried Chicken. A large paper bucket bearing the face of the jovial colonel lay on its side, spewing out chicken parts and discarded bones. They were drinking wine out of paper cups, Bolla Soave, the same kind his father and Nan drank at home. The girl was pretty much what Paul had expected. It was reassuring yet eerie to see his banal predictions verified. She had short straight black hair that fell in bangs to her green-shadowed eyelids, and she wore a long red and green flowered gypsy dress with a round neck. Silver earrings dangled nearly to her shoulders. Her bare feet, sticking out from under the dress, were very small and delicate. But she was plumper than Paul had envisioned. She had enormous breasts. Paul imagined his father's head nuzzling the huge breasts while the girl lay naked on the bare wood floor, her legs raised and parted. She wiped the chicken grease off her lips and hands and stood up.

"Cheryl, my son Paul."

Cheryl came towards him smiling, extending a hand.

Paul turned away from her. "I want to talk to you."

"Cheryl, would you mind?" It was a disgrace—he was apologetic.

Cheryl went into another room and closed the door behind her. Paul hadn't heard the sound of her voice.

The apartment was cluttered yet looked bare and unlived in—it could be adapted to any pattern of life his father and this Cheryl fell into. Odd pieces of furniture, cartons, shopping bags, a broom and dustpan, were placed haphazardly, like litter. Looking around, Paul recognized with a slight shock two bridge chairs, a brass magazine rack, a straw wastebasket.

"Where is it?"

Richard finally shut the front door. "Where is what?"

"You know, the piano."

"Oh, in the living room. This way."

It stood alone in a large room that was empty except for a cream-colored shag rug on the floor and two more bridge chairs from home.

"Didn't she bring any bridge chairs of her own?"

Richard cleared his throat and patted his graying hair. "Look, believe me, I know this confrontation is very difficult for you."

"Oh, never mind that crap. I really didn't think you'd do it. I didn't realize what a bastard you were underneath."

Richard paled. "Well," he said coldly, "take it. No one's stopping you."

"Don't worry. I'll have a mover here tomorrow. I'm taking the day off from school."

"Paul." His father motioned to one of the old bridge chairs. "Let's start again. Sit down. Please." Richard sat. His stomach, as he settled in the small chair, sagged with flab, despite all his running. He was so pathetic that finally Paul sat down too.

Richard's thinning hair was tousled. Paul wondered if she had rumpled it in a moment of affection. In his white shirt, dark trousers, and silver-rimmed glasses, his father resembled the benevolent village druggist Paul had often seen advertising toothpaste on television.

"I think I'm going to laugh," said Paul. "You and her." He motioned with a flip of his hand towards the door where Cheryl had disappeared. He expected, hoped, his father would respond angrily again, but Richard only nodded, as if it were the most natural coupling in the world.

"Are you feeling all right, Paul? Have you talked it over with Dr. Crewes? Don't hold anything back. Tell her what it's doing to you. It's best to get it out, you know that. You think I'm a bastard, fine, tell her. Say anything. She'll help you deal with it." His mother was right. Richard spoke in a tinny mechanical way, as if his real self were elsewhere. Once again Paul was forced to think he must be sick.

With pity he went over to Richard and put a hand on his shoulder. "What is it that's making you do this to us?" he asked kindly.

It was past eleven when Paul left for home. They had had a long and, he felt, meaningful talk. They both cried, Paul copiously, Richard joining in as one might to be sociable. At around nine Cheryl had padded into the room tentatively, but Paul shook his head, no, so Richard motioned her away. About an hour later they moved into the other room, where at Richard's suggestion Paul ate some cold Kentucky Fried Chicken. Then Cheryl, who must have entered the living room by another route, began playing a Scarlatti sonata on the piano. Richard closed the door.

"She's very good," he said. "She never could afford a piano of her own before. It makes her very happy."

Paul felt much better when he left. He understood, at least partially, why his father had done this shocking thing. According to Richard, the root cause was that he had smothered his rage at Nan's compulsiveness and rigidity for many long years. Now it had finally erupted, as it had to someday, in this form. Also, according to Richard, he was not sick but healthy for the first time in his life. His pathology, he outlined carefully in simplified terms that Paul could understand, had been in submitting to Nan's rigid controls. Now, with maybe twenty or more years ahead of him, he was going to start a new life and integrate his personality. It would be, he said, a voyage of self-discovery. He swallowed some wine as he talked of self-discovery, and in his eagerness to explain, a few drops dribbled along his chin. He had had trouble with women, he said, ever since boyhood—his mother got him off on the wrong track, as mothers tend to do (they both smiled knowingly), and as a result his whole marital relationship with Nan had been an unconscious working out of unresolved hostility towards his mother. He sucked deeply on his pipe amid pained reminiscences of his mother. This revelation surprised Paul slightly. His grandmother was a kindly, frail old woman with an unexpected and remarkable sense of humor; true, he thought, she did have a tendency to shower them with food and gifts on the rare occasions when they visited, but he had never realized, until Richard told him, just how controlling she was. As for Nan, Paul knew of course that Nan kept the house neat and worried excessively about getting places on time, but he had never dreamed of the tortuous ramifications these failings might have had in Richard's mind.

"We'll see each other often, Paul," Richard said as he was leaving. "We'll have an even better relationship, now we can be more open with each other."

Paul was relieved to find Nan wasn't waiting up for him. He felt funny—no, he could recognize and accurately name the sensation now, thanks to Dr. Crewes—ambivalent about telling Nan of his visit. He was filled with elation at the true communication he and Richard had achieved, and what he craved more than anything else was to share that elation with someone close. Yet that person couldn't be Nan since, in some complicated way, it had been achieved at her expense. He had to hide it from her, to protect her from more pain. Paul couldn't be angry with Nan for her pathology—with his background in treatment he knew better than that;

he could only be sad at how it had wrecked the family. With the dim light of the hall behind him he looked in on her from her bedroom door. She was wearing a faded blue flannel nightgown and sleeping discreetly on her side of the big bed, her thumb touching her lips. He pitied her.

He didn't get up at the usual time the next morning. When Nan finally came to awaken him he said he had a bad cold and wouldn't be going to school. He was planning to surprise her with the piano.

"I'm sorry you're sick. It's all that walking in the rain. Can I get you some aspirins? A cup of tea?"

"No, I don't have any fever."

"You were out late again last night. With friends?"

"Yes."

"Well," she sighed, gazing sleepily around the room, "I'd better run. I've got my battered wives group coming first thing in the morning, then I'm taking a couple of hours off, first to see the lawyer, and then I'm seeing Dr. Steinberg for a consultation. I've got to get this thing straightened out in my head so I can start dealing with it realistically. I'm just not able to function this way. Patients talk to me at work and I drift off, I just can't concentrate."

"Well, maybe he can help you."

"You don't have an appointment with Dr. Crewes today, do you?"

"No, tomorrow."

"Okay, take care of yourself. I'll phone later to see how you are. You're sure it's nothing more than a cold? Does your throat hurt?"

"No, I'm sure. So long."

As soon as she was gone he leaped out of bed and telephoned the moving company around the corner. He had worked there last summer, so they knew him well. They would do it on short notice if he offered to help.

When all the arrangements were made he had a sudden doubt— maybe he had better call his father. In the elation of last night he had forgotten to remind Richard to leave his key with the superintendent. Cheryl might not be in, and even if she was, he didn't feel up to dealing with her yet.

Richard was with a patient, the secretary said.

"This is his son. It's urgent."

"What is it, Paul?" Richard's voice came across anxiously. "Are you all right? Is Mother?"

"Yes, yes, we're fine. It's about the piano. I wanted to get you early. Could you have your super let the movers in? I'm not sure what time. Sometime between one and five, they said."

"But, Paul, I don't remember saying anything about the piano."

"But—I told you I was coming today. Don't you remember? And then we talked, and—"

"Paul, I'm sorry, I'm with a patient and I can't talk. There's been a misunderstanding. Can I call you back in half an hour?"

"The piano!" Paul screamed, frantically winding the cord of the phone around his arm and stamping his foot. "You've got to give back the piano!"

"Paul, please calm yourself. I can't talk now. Paul?"

"You shit, you fucker, you motherfucking lying bastard, I'm going to kill you—"

"Paul, if you don't stop I'll call Dr. Crewes and have her come over and give you something." In a quieter, muffled tone, "Excuse me, Mrs. Reed, I'm sorry for this interruption—an emergency. Paul, are you there? We must talk this over calmly, don't do anything violent. Paul?"

Paul tore the cord out of the wall and hurled the phone to the floor.

In half an hour he was at the door of his father's new apartment, breathing hard. He knocked quietly, so as not to alarm her. Paul had it all planned. This time he hadn't broken his mother's dishes or uprooted her plants. He had controlled himself with effort, hoarded it for the explosion. It was a new experience for him, dressing swiftly with deft hands, plotting and savoring his vengeance. His excitement was so strong, seething and boiling in his thighs, that it felt almost like physical pleasure. It was uncanny—as he left the building he had an erection.

"Who is it?" A high young voice. She pronounced the phrase with a rising and falling melody.

"Paul. Richard's son."

"Oh." The door opened. In jeans, a navy-blue turtleneck sweater, and high boots she looked completely different, swinging and competent and held together. She wasn't as plump, either, as she had appeared last night in her long dress. She wore horn-rimmed glasses that made her face serious and purposeful. Her skin was bright with morning. "Hello, Paul. I was just on my way out. Your father's gone to his office already. Would you like to call him?"

"I didn't come for him."

"Oh, me?" She was bewildered for an instant, then masked it quickly with politeness. "Why, sure. Come in. Have you had breakfast?"

He shoved past her. It was difficult to keep his arms from flying at the cartons and ripping them apart, but he wanted to carry this out perfectly, according to plan. He had a goal. He went to the living room. The bridge chairs were still close together, facing each other for intimate talk, as he and Richard had left them last night.

"Do you want to hear me play something?"

"Well . . . sure. Go ahead," she said.

He plunged into a flamboyant, racing Beethoven Rondo. His fingers recoiled instantly, for she had gotten the keys dirty with her chicken grease. But he kept on playing.

"You're terrific. Listen, please come over and play it whenever—"

"You like Scarlatti, right? Bach? That's your sort of thing?" He didn't need an answer. Her music was right on the rack. Grinding his teeth together till they ached, he tore the first thin book through. She reached out to stop him, shrieking with disbelief, but he waved her off with a long arm, hitting her on the shoulder so that she stumbled a few steps away. Then he did the other books, one by one, systematically. She looked on in silence.

Then she said, "Those can be replaced, you know."

He shredded every page of her music till the room was scattered with scraps, black notes strewn on the bare floor like trampled insects.

"Look, I understand your rage. It's separation anxiety, very common, very normal. Can't we talk about it?"

Paul laughed. "Do you want to deal with it too?"

He came towards her.

"Paul, you're upset, you need help. What—"

She was at the wall, one shoulder tensed and huddled against it. Her hands flew to her chest in a crossed, protective gesture. He liked that sight of her in dread, liked it so much that he paused, relishing it like the taste of something tart on his tongue.

"Paul, please, I didn't do anything to you. Listen, my parents were divorced too, I know how you—"

He hit her across her open mouth and stepped back. At last he felt some small relief from his seething. He was overheated, and took off his heavy jacket.

"Don't. Don't do anything! Please!" It was a little girl's voice now.

He laughed again. It made him feel years older to think she was afraid of that. "Stand up straight and look at me."

She obeyed.

"I'm not going to do that. You think I'd do that? You're crazy. You think I want to be where he's been, in that filthy hole?"

He hit her across the face four or five times until he felt satisfied. She tried to fight back, but she was so much smaller and weaker that he could restrain both her wrists with one hand. She kicked at him, aiming for the groin, but he kicked back, flicking her feet away as he might throw off an overeager dog. Her glasses lay smashed on the floor. Then he dragged her through the rooms until he found one with a double-bed mattress on the floor. He pushed her down on it.

"There. That's all. Aren't you relieved? And don't forget to tell him, when he comes back, that I want the piano."

He had planned to do more, to hit her harder and longer and all over, but he had lost the will. It was not the pleasure he had anticipated. He was stretched out on the couch when his mother came home.

"Paul, are you feeling any better? I called twice but you didn't answer. Were you asleep?" She set down her packages and came over to feel his forehead. "You feel cool. You don't look too well, though. Listen," she went on, "I brought home some Kentucky Fried Chicken for us. I know it's kind of tacky, but I just couldn't face cooking. Dr. Steinberg said I shouldn't try to do everything, just take things slowly, one at a time. Not push myself. I know you could use a decent meal, but— Paul? Are you there?"

"It's okay. Actually I adore Kentucky Fried Chicken."

"I'll make you some tea with it." She started towards the kitchen. At the threshold the telephone lay in parts at her feet. "Oh, no . . . This is your work, I take it?"

"Elves."

"Oh, Paul. Paul, honestly, I'm not in any state to deal with this now. I swear I don't know what to say. I didn't need this. I didn't need this at all," she muttered.

"They'll come to replace it if you call your business office. You can use the extension meanwhile."

"But why?"

"He's not returning the piano. His little pussycat plays it too. She's very talented."

"Oh, God. The rotten bastard. It doesn't excuse this mess, though. Pick it up, for heaven's sake. And will you call the phone company in the morning? You have to learn to take the consequences of your actions."

"Sure," said Paul. "No sweat."

She served the chicken and mashed potatoes on their bone china plates, and opened a bottle of Bolla Soave for herself, pouring it into a wine goblet. Nan had her hair pulled back in a bun, which made her seem older. He saw her as she would be in twenty years, her parched remains. They ate silently for a while, and then abruptly Nan put down her fork and began to speak, her eyes fixed on a point beyond Paul.

"I had a good session with Dr. Steinberg today. He's very supportive. God knows I can use some support in this. He says there are whole areas of pathology that I've repressed completely, that I must bring out in the open if I want to be in touch with reality. I'll have a lot to do. But first, he says, I have to deal with the real feelings of loss and jealousy and fear and all that, that I'm feeling. But I haven't seemed to be feeling them, have I?"

Paul shrugged. "How do I know what you're feeling?"

"That's the trouble. Neither do I."

She drank, gulped, and began to sob loudly over her goblet of wine. "Oh, God, why did this have to happen! We were happy, weren't we? We seemed all right, didn't we? I don't know anything anymore. I can't even remember, it's all gone. I know I'm compulsive in some ways, but I never thought—" She pounded her fist on the table. "Why is he so hateful to me? I'd like to kill him. And I'm terrified. Terrified."

"Is that what you're supposed to do when you deal with your feelings?" Paul inquired as he continued to eat. "It didn't sound quite right."

She groaned and shuddered, hiding her face. "You're right, you're right. I'm totally out of touch. I can't even convince myself."

"I'm sorry. I didn't mean it. I shouldn't have said that."

Nan wiped her eyes with her linen napkin. "I have a patient whose husband beats her," she said dully. "She comes in and talks about it. And I think, while I listen, that's better than this—this screen between us. I haven't known him for years. It's been like a play."

He led her to the couch and sat next to her. She seemed genuinely present for the first time in days—it made him want to talk, to seize the opportunity. "Mom? Do you know what I did today?"

Immediately he regretted his words. Nan raised her head with a start; the familiar shadow of dread crossed her face, and her eyes closed.

"What?"

"Oh, nothing. I mean, I just slept the whole day. I guess I was that wrung out."

"Oh, Paul, it must be hell for you, and neither of us is doing you much good. You've got to rely on Dr. Crewes. She'll help you, she knows you, and she can be objective about the situation. That's what you need. You're seeing her tomorrow, aren't you? You'll be well enough to go out tomorrow."

The next morning the phone, the extension in the master bedroom, rang before eight, as Paul was dressing. This was nothing unusual; the phone had been ringing steadily ever since his father left—friends calling daily for reports on his mother's emotional condition. Several called quite early so as to be undistracted, before leaving for tightly scheduled days at the office. Paul ignored it and began getting his books together. In two days he had completely forgotten what was happening in school, that world having flicked off like a light bulb. He even had to check his program card to remind himself which class to report to first. He was trying to fix his thoughts on the day ahead when, passing by his parents' bedroom on his way out, he saw Nan sitting on the edge of the bed with the phone at her ear, listening, not whispering rapidly as she usually did. As she listened, tears ran down her face, which she wiped carelessly with the belt of her coarse woolen bathrobe. Paul stopped in the doorway to watch.

"Yes, yes, of course I will. I know." Her voice was gentle, lower and more intimate than he had ever heard it. He was embarrassed, as if he were surprising her naked. Her whole body seemed to have softened and relaxed; her face was somber but live with emotion. "It's all right," she was saying. "You know I do. I can. I'll do anything." She hadn't yet combed her hair, and it hung in soft pale clumps over her forehead and cheeks and neck. Her words came out husky with sleep and tears. She held her unbelted robe loosely around her body with one arm, while she stretched her long bare legs in front of her, as though feeling their weight and mass after long disuse. "No, no, I'm not crying. I'll be right there. Don't do anything. I have to finish dressing." Paul reddened and turned away.

"That was him," she came to tell Paul, tying the robe quickly. She looked haggard now. He noticed how much weight she had lost over the week. "He wants me to come to his office right away. He had a fight with her last night, and he realized he can't stay with her. Paul, I'm worried. But relieved, in a way. He says he suddenly sees that this is all some kind of pathological outburst, that he's having a sort of breakdown. He's canceled all his patients. I'd better get over there."

"And you think . . . something may work out?"

"I don't know. But he turned to me—that's a good sign. He sounded more like himself, except weak. Like he was . . . in need. Oh, Paul, I hope we can . . . God knows I'll do anything."

She rushed off to dress.

Paul didn't go to school after all, but instead walked the streaming slushy Hyde Park streets most of the day. That afternoon he told Dr. Crewes that he had beaten up Cheryl.

"Did you want to rape her too?"

"Oh, no, I don't think I'm ready for rape yet. I'm only fifteen, you know. Don't rush things."

"You can be funny if you want to, but you know it's just avoidance, Paul. Resistance."

"Okay, okay. No, I didn't want to rape her. I'm not even sure how to go about raping someone, but I think if I wanted to I could have done it. You know I don't have the proper inner restraints. That's my problem, right, what we're supposed to be dealing with?"

"Maybe you were afraid you couldn't measure up to your father?"

"Huh?"

"And now you're worried that you may not be punished for it. Your father hasn't called or come around to express his disapproval, has he? So you may in effect be rewarded for what you did, if your parents do get back together. You would then see this violence as having a positive effect. Which would be very confusing."

He tried in vain to follow her path of reasoning. "I never thought of that."

"There are a lot of things you haven't thought of. Now, what do you feel about your parents seeing each other today?"

"Good. I mean, anything but this hell. It can't get worse, can it?

They were happy, you know. Oh, sure, pathologies, repressions, all that shit, but they were okay."

"Do you really think so, or do you just want very much to believe it?"

"Well . . . it's funny you should say that. See, we were reading this eighteenth-century philosopher in school and—"

"Wait a minute. Let's not get into philosophy. Let that rest a minute. What were you really feeling when you hit that young woman?"

"It was terrific. Like, sexy. Like jerking off."

"You see, even your imagery—"

"Oh, I'm teasing you." He laughed. "You're playing right into my hands. What's wrong with you today, Claudie? Is something bothering you?" Her name was Claudia. He used it sometimes with joking bravado, and she didn't seem to mind, in fact he suspected that she liked it. But she hated his diminutive version; it worked every time.

Dr. Crewes started to put a cigarette between her lips but it slipped out of her grasp and rolled along the waxed floor. Paul retrieved it for her. "It seems to me," she said, holding the burning match, "that your one 'success,' as it were, in overpowering a woman has made you very . . . skittish, so to speak, and your attitude—towards me, for example—is colored by it."

"Okay, you know you turn me on. I've told you that before. What does it have to do with anything? Listen—my family is living through this—this nightmare. Are you going to help me or aren't you?"

Dr. Crewes puffed and blew smoke at the ceiling with apparent concentration. "I'm trying to, Paul. All right, let's get back to the violence. After your phone conversation with your father about the piano, did any alternatives occur to you, any possible responses other than going to his apartment and attacking his mistress?"

"Mistress! Jesus, I thought that was only in books." He reflected, and answered thoughtfully, "The way I saw it, it was going to be the piano or her that got it. Something had to get it. But I realized that if I broke up the piano I'd be sorry later. Self-defeating. You see, I thought it out logically. So it had to be her. Now, considering everything we've been dealing with all these years, I think that was progress. Don't you?"

She stubbed out the cigarette with sharp taps of annoyance.

Paul arrived home before his mother that afternoon, feeling almost lighthearted. Certainly he had been flippant during the session, but maybe that was a good sign. There was reason to hope. He was impatient to hear how things had gone between them. He was also starving, he had realized on the way home, and so he stopped to buy a real dinner: two large steaks, a box of spaghetti and a can of clam sauce, a head of lettuce and two ripe tomatoes. He had the water boiling for the spaghetti and was trimming the steaks when his mother entered. Paul rushed to the door, the carving knife still in his hand.

"Well, how was he? What happened?"

Nan squeezed his hand with her chilly gloved fingers. "Oh, Paul. Oh, so much happened. Let me get my coat off. Would you make me a strong Scotch? I'm worn out."

She collapsed in the nearest chair, Richard's leather recliner.

"Well, tell me, for Christ's sake."

"First of all, he's sending back the piano tomorrow. I wanted you to know that right off. He realized how horrid and selfish he's been about that."

"Great, but I mean what really happened?"

"I thought you'd be so excited about the piano. He told me, by the way, how much it meant to you. That is, precisely how far you would go. . . ." She frowned for an instant. She was looking more like herself, Paul noticed. "But we won't go into that now. No more guilt and recriminations. I guess we've all been overwrought and irrational. Still, Paul, really! . . . Well, anyway, he's sick, as I thought. He's a man who's sick and needs help badly. While I was there I made an appointment for him with Dr. Jonas for tomorrow morning."

"But what happened, about you and him?"

"Shh. Don't yell. And don't wave the knife around like that, you'll hurt yourself. This whole Cheryl episode was the working out of a psychosis. I'm mixed in, his mother, the works. Classic."

Groaning with impatience, Paul went to the kitchen and got out the Scotch and ice cubes.

"Anyway," she went on, "we talked and cried, and he was different. Like he used to be, not with that cold surface. Oh, Paul." Her face eased for a moment. "I wasn't wrong all those years, was I? I mean, we loved each other, didn't we?"

"I thought so. Here's your Scotch."

"Thanks." Nan took a short swift drink, tossing her head back expertly. "Ah, that's good. He was heartbroken at what he's made us all go through. He said he was even afraid to call, he was afraid I wouldn't want to see him. Of course I'd see him, no matter what. He's totally bewildered and mixed up. But I think he's past the worst."

"How about you?"

"I don't know. I'm glad, I'm hopeful. Anxious, too. I'll know better how I feel after I talk to Dr. Steinberg tomorrow, and hear what happens with Dad and Dr. Jonas. Meanwhile we'll just have to wait. How did it go with Dr. Crewes today?"

"The usual. I'm cooking steaks. We'll celebrate."

"Oh, Paul, that's sweet of you. For the first time in a week I feel like eating."

"Will he be home for dinner?" he asked hesitantly.

"Oh, no, not yet. We're not ready to face that yet. We're both still too—too sore. It's better to wait a few days till we figure out what to do. Maybe he'll come Saturday. But don't count on it. Don't count on anything."

"Oh. I guess I had this silly idea that it would all straighten out overnight."

She came over and stroked his head. "No. It's not that simple. There's still a lot of struggle and pain ahead. We'll have to change the whole structure of our relationship. Everything out in the open." Nan drank some more, her eyes bright with zeal. "I'm going to change. It won't be easy, but—"

"All right, all right. Let me get back to the kitchen."

He went to bed peaceful, with only a few nagging doubts that mutated into strange dreams in which a pack of women chased him up and down a beach, half threatening, half in play. He raced up and down the concrete path bordering the shore of the lake, darting into a grove of trees to elude them, enjoying the game, but afraid too. Then he found that if they got too close all he had to do was wave his erect penis at them and they retreated in a tight cluster, backing off with round gazing eyes. He awoke suddenly on sticky damp sheets. Claudia would love this one, he thought, as he rolled over to a dry part of the bed.

He rushed directly home the next day, Friday, to see if it had arrived. School hadn't been too painful. Refreshing, almost. He had forgotten the minor comfort of having a warm, predictable place to go each day. Of course there were problems, as he had expected. For one thing, Paul was informed that he was failing American History because he had handed in no work for two weeks. A failure would mean being dropped from the basketball team, unless he had a very good excuse. Also, the teachers were waiting for the spring term's program choices: if he really wanted medicine later on, maybe he should take chemistry now and drop music. This was a decision he wanted to talk over with Richard and Nan. He hoped desperately that Richard would come to dinner tomorrow. They would all sit in the living room and discuss things calmly and peacefully, as they used to. He would have to tell them how he hadn't been in school—they would find out sooner or later. His home room teacher, naturally, was demanding an explanation of his absence all week. Nan and Richard would ask where he had been. On the streets. But then again they might be too preoccupied even to ask.

He paused before opening the door, trembling. Then he rushed in. The piano was home, back in place, where it should be. Tears of relief came to his eyes at the sight of it. So it was all right to have trusted them, this time. He touched the keys hesitantly, awkwardly, as if he hadn't touched them for weeks, then wiped them off with a damp rag. He took out his Beethoven, his Joplin, his folk song books, and rearranged them on the rack where they belonged.

Then he played till Nan returned, running through nearly every piece he knew, one after the other. It was the beginning of good times again. For they had been good—he hadn't appreciated his life before. Even Nan's and Richard's old, dull, suffocating ways would be welcome now, anything after this week.

"Oh, I see it's back," Nan called from the hall. "I'm glad." She came over and kissed Paul. "At least one thing is in place again." She was almost in place again too, Paul saw. That brisk, self-assured everyday coping, Nan's distinctive note, was returning. He watched as she stepped into the kitchen, where she washed her hands and immediately began to slice onions for her special chili with avocado and sour cream. She seemed to know exactly what to do; it was a relief. Still, it was odd how he missed the wan, weepy Nan, strung out on the taut threads of her agony, or that other strange, sensual Nan, with the nighttime voice and undone hair.

"I called him today," she chattered from the kitchen, "and asked how it went with Jonas, and he said all right. That was all he said about it. I think we should relax for a couple of days and let things take their course. Oh, he will be here for dinner tomorrow night after all. Sort of a phased re-entry." She slid the onions into a frying pan and a hot sizzle arose, like the sizzle of Nan's energy returning. "He asked about you. Also, I saw Dr. Steinberg again this morning."

"Oh. What did he have to say?"

"Well, for one thing, he said to act spontaneously, out of feeling, not from a predetermined script, you know, with built-in expectations. Why don't you play something till it's ready, Paul?"

He chose ragtime, an ironic beat. His father would be home tomorrow night; that was all that mattered. The rest of it was puzzling. He clung to the one stable fact: Richard would come tomorrow; they would talk calmly about his problems in school; things would be normal again.

Paul went out early the next morning while Nan was still asleep, leaving a note saying he would be at the library. He had phoned to cancel his eleven o'clock Saturday morning appointment with Dr. Crewes, explaining to her tape machine that he had urgent schoolwork to make up. Restless with energy, lying sleepless in bed as a gray light dawned, he had formulated a practical plan. He could work all day, getting as much of the history done as possible, and hand it in Monday along with a note from one of his parents pleading family difficulties, some crisis or other. They would know what to say. With luck he would catch the teacher in a sympathetic mood; then he could remain on the basketball team.

He sat over his books for hours, surprised that he was able to concentrate. Throughout, the prospect that Richard would be there at night sustained him like a snug life jacket. By five o'clock he was weary and pleased with himself. When he got in from the bitter cold, he saw Nan's coat thrown carelessly over a chair, her open pocketbook hanging by its strap from a doorknob. A half-empty coffee cup rested on the carpet near the couch. That was unlike her. Paul hoped she wasn't sick. Nothing could go wrong tonight. He had been through enough—it had to end now. His back and chest broke out in a cold sweat. He had done all that homework; he had controlled himself; now he needed to talk to them. As he turned the lights on he felt a twinge of pain and remembered one more detail that demanded attention: the school nurse had told him last Friday that he might need glasses; the glare of the fluorescent bulbs hurt his eyes. This week they had been aching more than ever, especially today in the library. Paul had felt the pain but not registered it as a discrete fact, it had been so merged in the larger pain.

There was no answer when he called out, so he knocked on Nan's bedroom door, then opened it. She was lying fully dressed on the bed, one arm shielding her eyes.

"Mom, are you sleeping?"

"Paul?" She raised her head. "No. I didn't hear you come in. What time is it?"

"Twenty after five. Are you sick?"

"No. I'm not sick."

He had never heard that voice before. It was low, not sensual but vacant, and sounded like it came from the marrow of her bones. He rushed over. "What's the matter with you?"

"He called this morning. He's decided after seeing Dr. Jonas, the high priest, that what he needs is a complete separation, even though he's not going back to his girlfriend." Her face was totally motionless except for her lips, which barely moved as she spoke.

Paul sat down on the bed. He hardly grasped the sense of her words, so stunned was he by this new, hollow voice coming out of her. It must be Nan, he thought wildly, yet it was not Nan. In panic, he hunched his shoulders and made a supreme effort to sit still and speak quietly.

"He's not coming back?"

"No. I told you. He's—uh, let me see, what does he have now? Oh, it's a midlife crisis, the doctor said. It's so hard to keep up with the diagnoses."

"Are you being funny?"

"Yes, I think so. Isn't it funny?" She didn't laugh or smile, though. "He wants control over his own life, he wants—um, let's see, what else—he wants to change his patterns of response." She spoke in a dull, singsong manner, almost demented, almost like a chant. "There is allegedly a whole phase of early development he never went through. And of course he needs to get in touch with his true feelings. That, by all means. Who could quarrel with that?"

"Mom, should I call a doctor for you? I mean, a regular doctor?"

"No. I'm quite well. I am in touch with my feelings at last. I have no feelings."

"Please!" he shrieked, his voice cracking high like a much younger boy's. "Stop it!"

"Sorry," she said in the same flat way. "That wasn't true. The truth is—what is the truth? Can you believe, I think I love him. But how can I love that bastard? It's an obscenity."

He got up. His veins were throbbing with blood again. It was himself he would hurl this time, knock himself out cold to lose consciousness. Bang his head on the wall till it broke open and spilled like a coconut oozing milk. The roots of his hair prickled; he felt a falling, thudding drop in his intestines.

She half sat up, leaning on her elbows, and gave him a stabbing, menacing look. "If you do that," she said slowly in her hollow tone, "if you throw anything or touch anything, I swear I will tear you to shreds." Her fingers bent stiffly and curled up.

She was hypnotic. He wished he could go to her and cry on her breast, but she had become too awesome for that, a terrible, mythical creature.

"Thank you," she said, relapsing into herself, and lay back again.

Paul went to his room, sat on the bed, and shook. Everything shook, inside and out. He watched the shaking hands with a removed fascination. Soon he heard a key in the lock and he jumped to his feet. The door opened and closed, then a shuffling sound, then the bumping of wooden hangers in the front closet.

"Paul? Are you home?"

He tried to answer but nothing came out of his throat, which had locked shut. He walked to the living room.

"Hello, Paul. I wanted to see you," his father said. His suit was creased. His striped shirt was wrinkled, too. He lit a cigarette.

"I . . ." Paul tried to say, but only a crackling sound came. Tears filled his eyes. He feared that he was going to collapse into his father's arms and cry like a child. He didn't want to do that, but he felt it was going to happen anyway. Then he heard the soft padding sounds of his mother's slippered feet and he waited, gripped with curiosity to see who she would be this time. Nan was simply herself, worn, gray-faced, smoothing her dress and brushing the hair out of her eyes.

"Richard? I wasn't expecting you."

"Hello, Nan. I thought I was coming for dinner. Or do I have the wrong night?"

"Dinner?" she whispered.

"Dinner. What's the matter? Are you sick or something?"

Nan leaned on the kitchen doorframe. "Richard, I assumed after you called this morning that you weren't coming."

Paul rolled his aching eyes from one to the other. It was like a play, just as she had said.

"Oh, did I say that? I don't remember. I wanted to see Paul.
Nan, we can still see each other, after all—"

"Richard, you're insane." It was that voice again.

"Now let's not get started like that. Can't we even meet without
accusations? Always the same old story. God, how did I ever put
up with it for so long," he grumbled bitterly, turning away and
walking to the window with his hands thrust in his pockets.

Nan straightened up. "All right. Dinner." Her voice was
charged now with an eerie brightness. "What's for dinner? Anyone
have any ideas? What can we serve on short notice for our distinguished guest?"

"I'll get dinner," said Paul.

They stared at him in surprise, as if they had forgotten he was
there.

"I'll get dinner," he repeated in a loud, hoarse voice. Paul shoved
past Nan into the kitchen. His hands were shaking again. He
yanked open a drawer and took out the carving knife. Clutching its
handle tightly to steady the trembling, he held it out straight in
front of him and returned to the doorway. He looked from one to
the other. They were standing in the same places, Nan slumped
against the doorframe and Richard farther away, at the window,
hands in his pockets. They didn't know yet. Nan was not looking
at him but at Richard.

His father noticed him first. "Paul?" he said quietly, and started
towards him. Then Nan saw too and gasped. Her hand jerked up
to her mouth.

"Don't come near me," said Paul. Nan stepped aside, but Richard moved closer to grab his wrist. Paul flicked the knife upward so
it grazed the sleeve of Richard's jacket.

"I'm going to solve all your problems for you," Paul said.

"Paul, no, put it down, please," said Nan. He ignored her. Richard was affecting nonchalance now, standing nearby in a relaxed
pose, waiting for Paul to lose his nerve and drop the knife.

Paul imagined the thrust, how hard and deep he would have to
push, the resistance of the flesh and then the crowning surge of
warm blood. It would be the greatest release of his life, a great

flow, a torrent. He stepped toward Nan, who cringed, then he stepped back. He moved toward Richard, who inched back cautiously. To Nan again. Then Richard. Then Nan. They were holding their breath, terrified of him. Whose blood? The question darted through his head, in and out of turns and dark corridors, a maze with no exit, and then suddenly balked, up against a flat wall of flaming red, he swiveled the knife and sliced inside his own wrist. A path opened, a thin red line, then an ooze, a stream, dripping from his trembling arm onto the green carpet. He dropped the knife. They were upon him, Nan whimpering and rocking to and fro, Richard embracing him and sobbing. Nan ran for a dish towel and bound it tightly around his wrist.

"Quick, let's get him into the car," she cried. "Get his coat."

Richard stood sobbing in choking gulps. "Oh my God. Oh my God."

Nan threw a coat over Paul's shoulders and pushed them both towards the door. She was swift and efficient.

"I did this," moaned Richard. "This is my doing."

She had a moment, at the elevator, to place a hand on his shoulder and lean against him. "Oh, Richard," she said gently in a soft wail, "you can't leave now. Oh, you can't. You see how much he needs you."

Richard nodded again and again, wiping his eyes with his fist.

The towel was sopping with blood, but luckily Nan had remembered to bring along extras. She changed the bandage and dropped the dripping red towel in a trash can outside the front door.

"Poor child," she murmured. "Oh, my poor baby."

"I'll do anything for him now," said Richard. He had stopped crying and was slamming the car door shut and starting the engine. "He'll need more intensive treatment. I'll have a consultation with Dr. Crewes. Can you stand to have me—"

"We'll work everything out, everything. Just so long as he's all right," said Nan from the back seat, where she sat cradling Paul's head in her lap.

THE MIDDLE CLASSES

They say memory enhances places, but my childhood block of small brick row houses grows smaller every year, till there is barely room for me to stand upright in my own recollections. The broad avenue on our corner, gateway to the rest of the world, an avenue so broad that for a long time I was not permitted to cross it alone, has narrowed to a strait, and its row of tiny shops—dry cleaners, candy store, beauty parlor, grocery store—has dwindled to a row of cells. On my little block itself the hedges, once staunch walls guarding the approach to every house, are shrunken, their sharp dark leaves stunted. The hydrangea bush—what we called a snowball bush—in front of the house next to mine has shrunk; its snowballs have melted down. And the ledges from each front walk to each driveway, against whose once-great stone walls we played King, a kind of inverse handball, and from whose tops we jumped with delectable agonies of fear—ah, those ledges have sunk, those leaps are nothing. Small.

In actuality, of course, my Brooklyn neighborhood has not shrunk but it has changed. Among the people I grew up with, that is understood as a euphemism meaning black people have moved in. They moved in family by family, and one by one the old white families moved out, outwards, that is, in an outward direction (Long Island, Rockaway, Queens), the direction of water—it seems not to have occurred to them that soon there would be nowhere to go unless back into the surf where we all began—except for two of the old white families who bravely remained and sent reports in the outward directions that living with the black people was fine, they were nice people, good neighbors, and so these two white families came to be regarded by the departed as sacrificial heroes of sorts; everyone admired them but no one would have wished to emulate them.

The changes the black families brought to the uniform block were mostly in the way of adornment. Colorful shutters affixed to the front casement windows, flagstones on the walkways leading to the porch steps, flowers on the bordering patches of grass, and quantities of ornamental wrought iron; a few of the brick porch walls have even been replaced by wrought-iron ones. (Those adjacent porches with their low dividing walls linked our lives. We girls visited back and forth climbing from porch to porch to porch, peeking into living room windows as we darted by.) But for all these proprietary changes, my block looks not so very different, in essence. It has remained middle class.

Black people appeared on the block when I lived there too, but they were maids, and very few at that. Those few came once a week, except for the three families where the mothers were schoolteachers; their maids came every day and were like one of the family, or so the families boasted, overlooking the fact that the maids had families of their own. One other exception: the family next door to mine who had the snowball bush also had a live-in maid who did appear to live like one of the family. It was easy to forget that she cleaned and cooked while the family took their ease, because when her labors were done she ate with them and then sat on the porch and contributed her opinions to the neighborhood gossip. They had gotten her from the South when she was seventeen, they said with pride, and when her grandmother came up to visit her the grandmother slept and ate and gossiped with the family too, but whether she too was expected to clean and cook I do not know.

It was less a city block than a village, where of a hot summer evening the men sat out on the front porches in shirtsleeves smoking cigars and reading newspapers under yellow lanterns (there were seven New York City newspapers) while the wives brought out bowls of cherries and trays of watermelon slices and gossiped porch to porch, and we girls listened huddled together on the steps, hoping the parents would forget us and not send us to bed, and where one lambent starry summer evening the singular fighting couple on the block had one of their famous battles in the master bedroom—shrieks and blows and crashing furniture; in what was to become known in local legend as the balcony scene, Mrs. Hochman leaned out of the open second-floor casement window in a flowing white nightgown like a mythological bird and shouted to the assembled throng, "Neighbors, neighbors, help me, I'm trapped up here with a madman" (she was an elocution teacher), and my mother rose to her feet to go and help but my father, a tax lawyer, restrained her and said, "Leave them alone, they're both crazy. Tomorrow they'll be out on the street holding hands as usual." And soon, indeed, the fighting stopped, and I wondered, What is love, what is marriage? What is reality in the rest of the world?

The daughters of families of our station in life took piano lessons and I took the piano lessons seriously. Besides books, music was the only experience capable of levitating me away from Brooklyn without the risk of crossing bridges or tunneling my way out. When I was about eleven I said I wanted a new and good piano teacher, for the lady on Eastern Parkway to whose antimacassared apartment I went for my lessons was pixilated: she trilled a greeting when she opened the door and wore pastel-colored satin ribbons in her curly gray hair and served tea and excellent shortbread cookies, but of teaching she did very little. So my mother got me Mr. Simmons.

He was a black man of around thirty-five or forty recommended by a business acquaintance of my father's with a son allegedly possessed of musical genius, the development of which was being entrusted to Mr. Simmons. If he was good enough for that boy, the logic ran, then he was good enough for me. I was alleged to be unusually gifted too, but not quite that gifted. I thought it very advanced of my parents to hire a black piano teacher for their nearly nubile daughter; somewhere in the vast landscape of what I had yet to learn, I must have glimpsed the springs of fear. I was proud of my parents, though I never said so. I had known they were not bigoted but rather instinctively decent; I had known that when and if called upon they would instinctively practice what was then urged as "tolerance," but I hadn't known to what degree. As children do, I underestimated them, partly because I was just discovering that they were the middle class.

Mr. Simmons was a dark-skinned man of moderate height and moderate build, clean-shaven but with an extremely rough beard that might have been a trial to him, given his overall neatness. A schoolteacher, married, the father of two young children, he dressed in the style of the day, suit and tie, with impeccable conventionality. His manners were also impeccably conventional. Nice but dull was how I classified him on first acquaintance, and I assumed from his demeanor that moderation in all things was his hallmark. I was mistaken: he was a blatant romantic. His teaching style was a somber intensity streaked by delicious flashes of joviality. He had a broad smile, big teeth, a thunderous laugh, and a willing capacity to be amused, especially by me. To be found amusing was an inspiration. I saved my most sophisticated attitudes and phraseology for Mr. Simmons. Elsewhere, I felt, they were as pearls cast before swine. He was not dull after all, if he could appreciate me. And yet unlike my past teachers he could proclaim "Awful!" with as much intrepidity as "Beautiful!" "No, no, no, *this* is how it should sound," in a pained voice, shunting me off the piano bench and launching out at the passage. I was easily offended and found his bluntness immodest at first. Gradually, through Mr. Simmons, I learned that false modesty is useless and that true devotion to skill is impersonal.

Early in our acquaintance he told me that during the summers when school was out his great pleasure was to play the piano eight hours in a row, stripped to the waist and sweating. It was January when he said this, and he grinned with a kind of patient longing. I recognized it as an image of passion and dedication, and forever after, in my eyes, he was surrounded by a steady, luminous aura of fervor. I wished I were one of his children, for the glory of living in his house and seeing that image in the flesh and basking in the luxuriant music. He would be playing Brahms, naturally; he had told me even earlier on that Brahms was his favorite composer. "Ah, Brahms," he would sigh, leaning back in his chair near the piano bench and tilting his head in a dreamy way. I did not share his love for Brahms but Brahms definitely fit in with the entire picture—the hot day, the long hours, the bare chest, and the sweat.

Mr. Simmons had enormous beautiful pianist's hands—they made me ashamed of my own, small and stubby. Tragicomically, he would lift one of my hands from the keyboard and stare at it ruefully. "Ah, if only these were bigger!" A joke, but he meant it. He played well but a bit too romantically for my tastes. Of course he grasped my tastes thoroughly and would sometimes exaggerate his playing to tease me, and exaggerate also the way he swayed back and forth at the piano, crooning along with the melody, bending picturesquely over a delicate phrase, clattering at a turbulent passage, his whole upper body tense and filled with the music. "You think that's too schmaltzy, don't you?" laughing his thunderous laugh. The way he pronounced "schmaltzy," our word, not his, I found very droll. To admonish me when I was lazy he would say, "*Play* the notes, *play* the notes," and for a long time I had no idea what he meant. Listening to him play, I came to understand. He meant play them rather than simply touch them. Press them down and make contact. Give them their full value. Give them yourself.

It seemed quite natural that Mr. Simmons and I should come to be such appreciative friends—we were part of a vague, nameless elite—but I was surprised and even slightly irked that my parents appreciated him so. With the other two piano teachers who had come to the house my mother had been unfailingly polite, offering coffee and cake but no real access. About one of them, the wild-eyebrowed musician with the flowing scarves and black coat and beret and the mock-European accent, who claimed to derive from Columbia University as though it were a birthplace, she commented that he might call himself an artist but in addition he was a slob who could eat a whole cake and leave crumbs all over the fringed tapestry covering her piano. But with Mr. Simmons she behaved the way she did with her friends; I should say, with her friends' husbands, or her husband's friends, since at that time women like my mother did not have men friends of their own, at least in Brooklyn. When Mr. Simmons arrived at about three forty-five every Wednesday, she offered him coffee—he was coming straight from teaching, and a man's labor must always be respected—and invited him to sit down on the couch. There she joined him and inquired how his wife and children were, which he told her in some detail. That was truly dull. I didn't care to hear anecdotes illustrating the virtues and charms of his children, who were younger than I. Then, with an interest that didn't seem at all feigned, he asked my mother reciprocally how her family was. They exchanged such trivia on my time, till suddenly he would look at his watch, pull himself up, and with a swift, broad smile, say, "Well then, shall we get started?" At last.

But my father! Sometimes my father would come home early on Wednesdays, just as the lesson was ending. He would greet Mr. Simmons like an old friend; they would clap each other on the shoulder and shake hands in that hearty way men do and which I found ridiculous. And my father would take off his hat and coat and put down his *New York Times* and insist that Mr. Simmons

have a drink or at least a cup of coffee, and they would talk enthu-
siastically about—of all things—business and politics. Boring, boring! How could he? Fathers were supposed to be interested in
those boring things, but not Mr. Simmons. After a while Mr. Simmons would put on his hat and coat, which were remarkably like
the hat and coat my father had recently taken off, pick up his *New
York Times*, and head for his home and family.

And my father would say, "What a nice fellow that Mr. Simmons is! What a really fine person!" For six years he said it, as if he
had newly discovered it, or was newly astonished that it could be
so. "It's so strange," he might add, shaking his head in a puzzled
way. "Even though he's a colored man I can talk to him just like a
friend. I mean, I don't feel any difference. It's a very strange
thing." When I tried, with my advanced notions, to relieve my
father of the sense of strangeness, he said, "I know, I know all
that"; yet he persisted in finding it a very strange thing. Sometimes
he boasted about Mr. Simmons to his friends with wonder in his
voice: "I talk to him just as if he were a friend of mine. A very
intelligent man. A really fine person." To the very end, he mar-
veled; I would groan and laugh every time I heard it coming.

Mr. Simmons told things to my father in my presence, important and serious things that I knew he would not tell to me alone.
This man-to-man selectivity of his pained me. He told my father
that he was deeply injured by the racial prejudice existing in this
country; that it hurt his life and the lives of his wife and children;
and that he resented it greatly. All these phrases he spoke in his
calm, conventional way, wearing his suit and tie and sipping coffee. And my father nodded his head and agreed that it was terribly
unfair. Mr. Simmons hinted that his career as a classical pianist
had been thwarted by his color, and again my father shook his
head with regret. Mr. Simmons told my father that he had a
brother who could not abide the racial prejudice in this country
and so he lived in France. "Is that so?" said my mother in dismay,
hovering nearby, slicing cake. To her, that anyone might have to
leave this country, to which her parents had fled for asylum, was
unwelcome, almost incredible, news. But yes, it was so, and when

he spoke about his brother Mr. Simmons' resonant low voice was
sad and angry, and I, sitting on the sidelines, felt a flash of what I
had felt when the neighbor woman being beaten shrieked out of
the window on that hot summer night—ah, here is reality at last.
For I believed that reality must be cruel and harsh and densely
complex. It would never have occurred to me that reality could
also be my mother serving Mr. Simmons home-baked layer cake or
my father asking him if he had to go so soon, couldn't he stay and
have a bite to eat, and my mother saying, "Let the man go home to
his own family, for heaven's sake, he's just done a full day's work."
I also felt afraid at the anger in Mr. Simmons' voice; I thought he
might be angry at me. I thought that if I were he I would at least
have been angry at my parents and possibly even refused their
coffee and cake, but Mr. Simmons didn't.

When I was nearing graduation from junior high school my
mother suggested that I go to the High School of Music and Art in
Manhattan. I said no, I wanted to stay with my friends and didn't
want to travel for over an hour each way on the subway. I imagined I would be isolated up there. I imagined that the High School
of Music and Art, by virtue of being in Manhattan, would be far
too sophisticated, even for me. In a word, I was afraid. My mother
wasn't the type to press the issue but she must have enlisted Mr.
Simmons to press it for her. I told him the same thing, about traveling for over an hour each way on the subway. Then, in a very
grave manner, he asked if I had ever seriously considered a musical
career. I said instantly, "Oh, no, that sounds like a man's sort of
career." I added that I wouldn't want to go traveling all over the
country giving concerts. He told me the names of some women
pianists, and when that didn't sway me, he said he was surprised
that an intelligent girl could give such a foolish answer without
even thinking it over. I was insulted and behaved coolly towards
him for a few weeks. He behaved with the same equanimity as
ever and waited for my mood to pass. Every year or so after that
he would ask the same question in the same grave manner, and I
would give the same answer. Once I overheard him telling my

mother, "And she says it's a man's career!" "Ridiculous," said my mother disgustedly. "Ridiculous," Mr. Simmons agreed.

Towards the end of my senior year in high school (the local high school, inferior in every way to the High School of Music and Art in Manhattan), my parents announced that they would like to buy me a new piano as a graduation present. A baby grand, and I could pick it out myself. We went to a few piano showrooms in Brooklyn so I could acquaint myself with the varieties of piano. I spent hours pondering the differences between Baldwin and Steinway, the two pianos most used by professional musicians, for in the matter of a piano—unlike a high school—I had to have the best. Steinways were sharp-edged, Baldwins more mellow; Steinways classic and traditional, Baldwins romantically timeless; Steinways austere, Baldwins responsive to the touch. On the other hand, Steinways were crisp compared to Baldwins' pliancy; Steinways were sturdy and dependable, while Baldwins sounded a disquieting tone of mutability. I liked making classifications. At last I decided that a Baldwin was the piano for me—rich, lush, and mysterious, not at all like my playing, but now that I think of it, rather like Mr. Simmons'.

I had progressed some since the days when I refused to consider going to the High School of Music and Art in Manhattan. If it was to be a Baldwin I insisted that it come from the source, the Baldwin showroom in midtown Manhattan. My mother suggested that maybe Mr. Simmons might be asked to come along, to offer us expert advice on so massive an investment. I thought that was a fine idea, only my parents were superfluous; the two of us, Mr. Simmons and I, could manage alone. My parents showed a slight, hedging reluctance. Perhaps it was not quite fair, my mother suggested, to ask Mr. Simmons to give up a Saturday afternoon for this favor. It did not take an expert logician to point out her inconsistency. I was vexed by their reluctance and would not even condescend to think about it. I knew it could have nothing to do with trusting him: over the years they had come to regard him as an exemplar of moral probity. Evidently the combination of his being so reliable and decent, so charming, and so black set him off in a class by himself.

I asked the favor of Mr. Simmons and he agreed, although in his tone too was a slight, hedging reluctance; I couldn't deny it. But again, I could ignore it. I had a fantasy of Mr. Simmons and myself ambling through the Baldwin showroom, communing in a rarefied manner about the nuances of difference between one Baldwin and another, and I wanted to make this fantasy come true.

The Saturday afternoon arrived. I was excited. I had walked along the streets of Manhattan before, alone and with my friends. But the thought of walking down Fifty-seventh Street with an older man, clearly not a relative, chatting like close friends for all the sophisticated world to see, made my spirits as buoyant and iridescent as a bubble. Mr. Simmons came to pick me up in his car. I had the thrill of sliding into the front seat companionably, chatting like close friends with an older man. I wondered whether he would come around and open the door for me when we arrived. That was done in those days, for ladies. I was almost seventeen. But he only stood waiting while I climbed out and slammed it shut, as he must have done with his own children, as my father did with me.

We walked down broad Fifty-seventh Street, where the glamour was so pervasive I could smell it: cool fur and leather and smoky perfume. People looked at us with interest. How wondrous that was! I was ready to fly with elation. It didn't matter that Mr. Simmons had known me since I was eleven and seen me lose my temper like an infant and heard my mother order me about; surely he must see me as the delightful adult creature I had suddenly become, and surely he must be delighted to be escorting me down Fifty-seventh Street. I would have liked to take his arm to complete the picture for all the sophisticated world to see, but some things were still beyond me. I felt ready to fly but in fact I could barely keep up with Mr. Simmons' long and hurried stride. He was talking as companionably as ever, but he seemed ill at ease.

Lots of people looked at us. Even though it was early April he had
his overcoat buttoned and his hat brim turned down.

We reached the Baldwin showroom. Gorgeous, burnished
pianos glistened in the display windows. We passed through the
portals; it was like entering a palace. Inside it was thickly carpeted.
We were shown upstairs. To Paradise! Not small! Immensely high
ceilings and so much space, a vista of lustrous pianos floating on a
rich sea of green carpet. Here in this grand room full of grand
pianos Mr. Simmons knew what he was about. He began to relax
and smile, and he talked knowledgeably with the salesman, who
was politely helpful, evidently a sophisticated person.

"Well, go ahead," Mr. Simmons urged me. "Try them out."

"You mean play them?" I looked around at the huge space. The
only people in it were two idle salesmen and far off at the other
end a small family of customers, father, mother, and little boy.

"Of course." He laughed. "How else will you know which one
you like?"

I finally sat down at one and played a few timid scales and ar-
peggios. I crept from one piano to another, doing the same, trying
to discern subtle differences between them.

"Play," Mr. Simmons commanded.

At the sternness in his voice I cast away timidity. I played
Chopin's "Revolutionary Etude," which I had played the year before at a recital Mr. Simmons held for his students in Carl Fischer
Hall—nowadays called Cami Hall—on Fifty-seventh Street, not
far from the Baldwin showroom. (I had been the star student. The
other boy, the musical genius, had gone off to college or otherwise
vanished. I had even done a Mozart sonata for four hands with Mr.
Simmons himself.) Sustained by his command, I moved daunt-
lessly from Baldwin to Baldwin, playing passages from the "Revolutionary Etude." Mr. Simmons flashed his broad smile and I
smiled back.

"Now you play," I said.

I thought he might have to be coaxed, but I was forgetting that
Mr. Simmons was never one to withhold, or to hide his light. Besides, he was a professional, though I didn't understand yet what

that meant. He looked around as if to select the worthiest piano, then sat down, spread his great hands, and played something by Brahms. As always, he *played* the notes. He pressed them down and made contact. He gave them their full value. He gave them himself. The salesmen gathered round. The small family drew near to listen. And I imagined that I could hear, transmogrified into musical notes, everything I knew of him—his thwarted career, his schoolteaching, his impeccable manners, his fervor, and his wit; his pride in his wife and children; his faraway brother; his anger, his melancholy, and his acceptance; and I also imagined him stripped to the waist and sweating. When it was over he kept his hands and body poised in position, briefly, as performers do, as if to prolong the echo, to keep the spell in force till the last drawn-out attenuation of the instant. The hushed little audience didn't clap, they stood looking awed. My Mr. Simmons! I think I felt at that moment almost as if he were my protégé, almost as if I owned him.

We didn't say much on the way home. I had had my experience, grand as in fantasy, which experiences rarely are, and I was sublimely content. As we walked down my block nobody looked at us with any special interest. Everyone knew me and by this time everyone knew Mr. Simmons too. An unremarkable couple. At home, after we reported on the choice of a piano, Mr. Simmons left without even having a cup of coffee. He was tired, he said, and wanted to get home to his family.

Later my mother asked me again how our expedition had been.

"Fine. I told you already. We picked out a really great piano. Oh, and he played. He was fantastic, everyone stopped to listen."

My mother said nothing. She was slicing tomatoes for a salad.

"I bet they never heard any customer just sit down and play like that."

Again no response. She merely puttered over her salad, but with a look that was familiar to me: a concentrated, patient waiting for the proper words and the proper tone to offer themselves to her. I enjoyed feeling I was always a step ahead.

"I know what you're thinking," I said nastily.

"You do?" She raised her eyes to mine. "I'd be surprised."

"Yes. I bet you're thinking we looked as if he was going to abduct me or something."

The glance she gave in response was more injured than disapproving. She set water to boil and tore open a net bag of potatoes.

"Well, listen, I'll tell you something. The world has changed since your day." I was growing more and more agitated, while she just peeled potatoes. Her muteness had a maddening way of making my words seem frivolous. She knew what she knew. "The world has changed! Not everyone is as provincial as they are here in Brooklyn!" I spit out that last word. I was nearly shouting now. "Since when can't two people walk down the street in broad daylight? We're both free—" I stopped suddenly. I was going to say free, white, and over twenty-one, an expression I had found loathsome when I heard my father use it.

"Calm down," my mother said gently. "All I'm thinking is I hope it didn't embarrass him. It's him I was thinking about, not you."

I stalked from the room, my face aflame.

I went to college in Manhattan and lived in a women's residence near school. For several months I took the subway into Brooklyn every Wednesday so I could have a piano lesson with Mr. Simmons, it being tacitly understood that I was too gifted simply to give up "my music," as it was called; I slept at home on my old block, then went back up to school on Thursday morning. This became arduous. I became involved with other, newer things. I went home for a lesson every other Wednesday, and soon no Wednesdays at all. But I assured Mr. Simmons I would keep renting the small practice room at school and work on my own. I did for a while, but the practice room was very small and very cold, and the piano, a Steinway, didn't sound as lush as my new Baldwin back home; there was an emptiness to my efforts without the spur of a teacher; and then there were so many other things claiming my time. I had met and made friends with kindred spirits from the High School of Music and Art, and realized that had I listened to my mother I might have known them three years sooner. The next year I got married, impulsively if not inexplicably; to tell why, though, would take another story.

Naturally my parents invited Mr. and Mrs. Simmons to the wedding. They were the only black people there, among some hundred and fifty guests. I had long been curious to meet Mrs. Simmons but regrettably I could not get to know her that afternoon since I had to be a bride. Flitting about, I could see that she was the kind of woman my mother and her friends would call "lovely." And did, later. She was pretty, she was dressed stylishly, she was what they would call "well-spoken." She spoke the appropriately gracious words for a young bride and one of her husband's long-time students. In contrast to Mr. Simmons' straightforward earnestness, she seemed less immediately engaged, more of a clever observer, and though she smiled readily I could not imagine her having a thunderous laugh. But she fit very well with Mr. Simmons, and they both fit with all the other middle-aged and middle-class couples present, except of course for their color.

Mrs. Simmons did not know a soul at the wedding and Mr. Simmons knew only the parents of the boy genius and a few of our close neighbors. My mother graciously took them around, introducing them to friends and family, lots of friends and lots of family, so they would not feel isolated. I thought she overdid it—she seemed to have them in tow, or on display, for a good while. I longed to take her aside and whisper, "Enough already, Ma. Leave them alone." But there was no chance for that. And I knew how she would have responded. She would have responded silently, with a look that meant, "You can talk, but I know what is right to do," which I could not deny. And in truth she was quite proud of knowing a man as talented as Mr. Simmons. And had she not introduced them they certainly would have felt isolated, while this way they were amicably received. (Any bigots present successfully concealed their bigotry.) My mother was only trying to behave well, with grace, and relatively, she succeeded. There was no way of behaving with absolute grace. You had to choose among the various modes of constraint.

For all I know, though, the Simmonses went home and re-marked to each other about what lovely, fine people my parents and their friends were, and how strange it was that they could spend a pleasant afternoon talking just as they would to friends, even though they were all white. How very strange, Mr. Simmons might have said, shaking his head in a puzzled way, taking off his tie and settling down behind his newspaper. It is a soothing way to imagine them, but probably false.

I had always hoped to resume my piano lessons someday, but never did. And so after the wedding Mr. Simmons disappeared from my life. Why should it still astonish me, like a scrape from a hidden thorn? There were no clear terms on which he could be in my life, without the piano lessons. Could I have invited the Sim-monses to our fifth-floor walk-up apartment in a dilapidated part of Manhattan for a couples evening? Or asked him to meet me some-where alone for a cup of coffee? At what time of day? Could my parents, maybe, have invited the Simmonses over on a Sunday afternoon with their now teen-aged children and with my husband and me? Or for one of their Saturday night parties of mah-jongg for the women and gin rummy for the men and bagels and lox for all? Could Mr. Simmons, too, have made some such gesture? Pos-sibly. For I refuse to see this as a case of *noblesse oblige:* we were all the middle classes.

But given the place and the time and the dense circumambient air, such invitations would have required people of large social imagination, and none of us, including Mr. and Mrs. Simmons, had that. We had only enough vision for piano lessons and cups of coffee and brief warm conversations about families, business, pol-itics, and race relations, and maybe I should be content with that, and accept that because we were small, we lost each other, and never really had each other, either. Nonetheless, so many years later, I don't accept it. I find I miss him and I brood and wonder about him: where is he and does he still, on summer days, play the piano for eight hours at a stretch, stripped to the waist and sweat-ing?

SOUND IS SECOND SIGHT

A farmer of austere habits lived some ways from town in a ramshackle farmhouse, and he looked as forlorn and ramshackle as his house with its weatherbeaten wooden slats and cracked shingles. Tall, taciturn, dressed in drab, loose-fitting clothes, he would gaze down at the ground as he walked. He carried a gnarled walking stick and let his mud-colored hair droop around his face, and so he appeared older than he was. Actually he was not old at all, nor crabbed as some believed, merely a solitary. Out of habit he kept his distance, and the people of the town thought it best to keep their distance as well.

His only companion was a greyhound dog, slender, blond, and frolicsome after the manner of her kind. She was fiercely devoted to the farmer and, unlike the townspeople, not frightened off by his gnarled walking stick or his silence or his gaunt, shielded face. Outdoors, in the fields or in town, the farmer and his dog were silent and undemonstrative, yet they had the air of creatures very much attuned and in comfort together. The townspeople were puzzled by the dog. Not a farm dog by any means. Not a dog that could be useful. Her very prettiness and uselessness seemed out of place in that stony countryside, and when she strutted down the main street she drew hostile glances. Rumors sprang up that the dog, for all her prettiness, had sinister powers; possibly even the farmer did. Her origins were mysterious: all anyone knew was that after vanishing for several days the farmer had returned with the dog perched in the front seat of his truck, sniffing in her disdainful way.

In fact he had found her in a nearby and larger market town. The dogcatcher had seemed hesitant to sell her: a well-meaning fellow, he hinted that the dog had brought bad luck to former owners, best leave her to her fate. But the farmer had a sudden craving for the pretty creature, whom he had spied standing in a corner of the yard apart from the pack of other animals; she reminded him of himself, isolated, the butt of nasty tall tales, perhaps even ill-treated when young, as he had been. She had an unearthly howl, the dogcatcher also warned, wild enough to rouse the dead. But she made no sound at all in her corner of the cluttered yard, so the farmer paid no heed and bought her.

Evenings, alone in the house, they romped together in front of the fire, the farmer bellowing and laughing, the dog yelping and snapping playfully. She barked seldom. Her bark was indeed loud and piercing, almost a howl, and it was as if she held it in out of deference to human ears. Despite his carelessness about the outside of the house, the farmer kept the inside pleasant and tidy: the wood floors, with their wide planks, were swept clean, the logs piled near the fireplace had a sweet smoky smell, and the soft cushions on the floor were inviting. Besides all that, the dog got good food to eat; she made a contented, obedient housemate.

And then one day after spending almost a week away at the nearby market town, the farmer and his dog came home with a bright-eyed wife, who also excited curiosity among the townspeople, and a few of the more outspoken wondered slyly whether he had found her in the same mysterious way as he had found the dog. She was small and rounded, with rosy cheeks, milky skin, and black curls. She smiled indulgently at the confusion of the dog, who bristled when she stroked her blond fur. She laughed at the farmer's long shield of hair and brushed it off his really rather handsome face with a tender gesture. Nor was she much bothered by the ramshackle appearance of the house, for she saw that the inside was cheerful and tidy. The vegetable garden behind the house was her delight: under the farmer's care, tomatoes and beans and peas were flourishing in such abundance she could hardly pick them fast enough. The people of the town, who could find nothing to fault her with since she was unfailingly courteous and proper, were astonished that so sprightly a creature could be happy living with the taciturn farmer, yet she appeared quite happy. When the three of them walked down the main street, it was the farmer and his wife, now, who were silent and undemonstrative, yet seemed very much attuned and in comfort together. The dog fretted along-side. Occasionally she gave out her lacerating howl, which made passersby start, and startled even the farmer, who hastened to quiet her. The dog was not neglected—the farmer still stroked her and spoke kindly to her and took her along daily to the fields, but in the nature of things it was not the same.

Evenings, in the broken-down house, the farmer and his wife lay on rugs in front of the fire, while the dog fussed in a cold corner, ignoring their beckonings. The farmer had never been so happy in his life. He had grown up lonely and lived lonely, and, given the awkward shyness that no one till now had found appealing, had never expected to be other than lonely till the day he died. He was no less astonished than the townspeople that this pretty, loving wife welcomed his company and settled so easily into his house. It was a gift he could not fathom, dared not even question, and while it did not change his appearance—he still dressed in drab, non-descript clothing—or the appearance of his house—still forlorn and ramshackle—he felt himself a changed man. For this his heart was full of gratitude to his wife, and in his innocence, he envi-sioned living with her serenely to the end of his days.

What the farmer loved most about his wife was not her prettiness or her sweet nature, but her voice. It was like music; it could sing out low like a cello or high like a flute, and flit through the whole range in between. When she called to him in the fields, midday, her pure long-lasting note cut a path through the air. When she rushed to greet him or tell him news of the garden her voice was full, impelled by energy. And when she lay with him before the fire its timbre was more than deep—dense, as if the sound itself might be grasped and held, caressed. To the farmer her voice expressed all moods and possibilities; living with her after living silent for so long with the dog was like embracing another dimension, having a sixth sense.

The dog clearly did not love the sound of the wife's voice, although it was never anything but gentle and cajoling, in a futile effort to win her trust. The dog still bristled at her touch and took food grudgingly from her hands. If the farmer whistled her over while his wife was nearby, she hung back and needed to be coaxed. And when the two were alone, the dog would snap at her skirts, or snarl, or set up a howling the wife could not stop. In the garden she stepped across the wife's path to trip her up. In the kitchen she knocked over a tureen of soup—the wife had to jump aside so as not to be scalded. She reproached the dog softly, in dismay more than anger. The wife did not mention these incidents to the farmer—they seemed, after all, so petty. She was a tolerant soul who took what came along. She too had been lonely and ill-treated as a child, and also, because of her prettiness, suspected of evils she did not commit, so she found herself fortunate in her new life; her thoughts were rooted in its daily pleasures. She was hardly one to brood over the fussing of a dog: surely the creature would come round in time.

This happy period in the farmer's life lasted for three years, and then the wife took sick with a mysterious illness, not painful but enervating. It had never been seen before in that region, and there seemed nothing anyone could do to save her. The farmer fed her with his own hands and pleaded with her to rally, if only for his sake, but she shook her head gravely, like one already past the threshold. In despair he wanted to take the very strength from his own body and feed it to her. But she was doomed. Stunned with grief, he buried her some distance from the house. After a time, though his grief remained acute, there mingled with it a feeling that, just as he had grown up lonely and lived lonely, so he was to remain lonely till the day he died, and that the time with his wife was a fleeting interlude given to him unfathomably. He sought solace in the company of his dog, who became frolicsome and good-tempered as in the early days. When they walked together in the town they once again had the air of creatures very much attuned and in comfort together. As for the townspeople, after paying their condolences they kept their distance as before.

One moonlit summer night as he lay awake with the windows wide open, the farmer heard his wife's voice calling his name far out across the fields. He rushed to the window and called back into the night. Over and over her voice called, now closer, now farther off, as if it were drifting about, seeking him in the dark but powerless to find the way. Then the dog went to the window and began to bark. As the shrill howling persisted, the voice came closer and closer until at last it was there in the room, that voice he used to feel was almost palpable. The farmer was overjoyed. All night long his wife's voice talked with him and kept him company, while the dog crouched silent in a corner. They talked, as always, of small daily things—the farm and the town, the vegetable garden—and of love. The range and timbre of the wondrous voice were unaltered by death. As day broke she left.

She came often after that. Each time, the farmer passed the whole night with her, talking of daily things and feeling joyful, if baffled, at this great gift given back to him, at least in part. Whenever her voice sounded from far off, the dog would go to the open window to help her find her way. For only that horrible howling, puncturing the night like an arrow, could guide her; the farmer's own, human, voice was of no avail.

For a long time the farmer lived thus, enjoying the mild companionship of the dog by day and the beloved voice of his dead wife by night. But the dog was growing old. During their walks through the fields he noticed that she trudged ever more slowly, breathing with effort. Yet fiercely devoted, she strove to keep up with him, would not desert his path. One day the farmer sensed she was no longer behind him; he went back a short distance and found her collapsed on the ground. He carried her back to the house, settled her on a rug in front of the fire, and gave her water from his cupped hand till she closed her eyes and died. He buried her under a tree near the barn.

Now the farmer suffered an excruciating loneliness. In daylight he walked alone and in the dark he knew the agony of hearing his wife's voice calling out there, unable to find him without the howling to guide her. Many nights the voice called, raw with pleading, while the farmer shouted out the window to no avail. As the voice despaired and faded he would shut the window with bitter tears in his throat. The voice stopped seeking him. He pondered whether it was worse to have no gifts at all, or to have gifts given and so cruelly withdrawn.

Then one night as he lay sleepless, there came the awful voice of the dog, howling far across the fields. The farmer rushed to the window. The dog's voice came steadily closer, finding its way with ease. Although he could neither stroke her nor play with her, and although she kept silent once in the room, the farmer took comfort and rested more calmly, feeling her presence. He reflected, though, how strange it was to have as companion a voice that had best not make itself heard, for very ugliness.

On a moonlit night when the dog had come, the farmer was sitting at the window when he heard his wife's voice again, calling over the fields. He leaped to his feet and called back as loudly as he could. Suddenly from right beside him came the lacerating howl of the dog, slicing into the still night. He longed to hug her in gratitude, but there was nothing to the touch. Just as before, the dog's voice howled until the wife's voice found its way into the room. The farmer was trembling with emotion; he longed to embrace her, but again he had to content himself with what he was given.

His wife's voice was joyous too; but scarcely had she begun to speak of this recovery of each other than her voice was overpowered by the dog's insistent howl. Sternly, the farmer commanded the animal to be silent, but for the first time she refused to obey him. The wife's voice grew higher, urgent: she was calling for help. Her words became screams, then pure shrieks of sound swooping through the air; meanwhile the howling reached an unearthly pitch, filling up the room, exulting in its rough, wild fury kept at bay so long. The farmer veered about in a frenzy of helplessness, arms outstretched and flailing for something to touch. The wife's terrified shrieks got short and staccato, like the plucking of a taut string against the prolonged howls tearing into the dark. Madly, the farmer raced about, hands plunging and stabbing at the empty night. Till at last there was one drawn-out, descending note wailed in unison with the dog's rapid panting, and then both voices sank and subsided, and there was nothing.

When the townspeople came to investigate they found the farmer gone, the house abandoned. The bedroom was all in disorder, as if a rampaging wind had whipped things up and left them to fall where they might. From near the window, reported some, came now and then a hoarse, panting noise, like a beast out of breath.

MRS. SAUNDERS
WRITES TO THE WORLD

Mrs. Saunders placed her white plastic bag of garbage in one of the cans behind the row of garden apartments and looked about for a familiar face, but finding nothing except two unknown toddlers with a babysitter in the playground a short distance off, she shrugged, gazed briefly into the wan early spring sun, and climbed the stairs back to her own door. She was looking for someone because she had a passion to hear her name spoken. But once inside, as she sponged her clean kitchen counter with concentrated elliptical strokes, she had to acknowledge that hearing "Mrs. Saunders" would not be good enough anymore. She needed—she had begun to long, in fact, with a longing she found frightening in its intensity—to hear her real name.

She squeezed the sponge agonizingly over the sink, producing a few meager drops. No one called her anything but Mrs. Saunders now. Her name was Fran. Frances. She whispered it in the direction of the rubber plant on the windowsill. Fran, Franny, Frances.

Anyone seeing her, she thought, might suspect she was going crazy. Yet they said it was good to talk to your plants. She could always explain that she was whispering to them for their health and growth. Fran, Franny, Frances, she breathed again. Then she added a few wordless breaths, purely for the plants' sake, and felt somewhat less odd.

There was no one left to call her Fran. Her husband had called her Franny, but he was long dead. Her children, scattered across the country, called her Ma when they came at wide intervals to visit, or when she paid her yearly visit to each of the three. Except for Walter, she reminded herself, as she was fussy over accuracy, except for Walter, whom she saw only about once every year and a half, since he lived far away in Oregon and since his wife was what they called unstable and couldn't stand visitors too often or for too long a period.

Her old friends were gone or far off, and the new ones stuck to "Mrs. Saunders." The young people who moved in and out of these garden apartments thought of themselves as free and easy, she mused, but in fact they had their strange formalities, like always calling her Mrs. Saunders, even though they might run in two or three times a week to borrow groceries or ask her to babysit or see if she needed a lift to the supermarket. She pursed her lips in annoyance, regarded her impeccable living room, then pulled out the pack of cigarettes hidden in a drawer in the end table beside her chair. Mrs. Saunders didn't like these young girls who ran in and out to see her smoking; it wasn't seemly. She lit one and inhaled deeply, feeling a small measure of relief.

It wasn't that they were cold or unfriendly. Just that they didn't seem to realize she had a name like anyone else and might wish to hear it spoken aloud once in a while by someone other than herself in her darkened bedroom at night, or at full volume in the shower, mornings. And though she knew she could say to her new neighbors, "Call me Fran," as simply as that, somehow whenever the notion came to her the words got stuck in her throat. Then she lost the drift of the conversation and worried that the young people might think her strange, asking them to repeat things they had probably said perfectly clearly the first time. And if there was one thing she definitely did not want, she thought, stubbing the cigarette out firmly, it was to be regarded as senile. She had a long way to go before that.

Suddenly the air in the neat room seemed intolerably stuffy. Cigarette smoke hung in a cloud around her. Mrs. Saunders felt weak and terribly unhappy. She rose heavily and stepped out onto her small balcony for a breath of air. Jill was lounging on the next balcony with a friend.

"Oh, hi, Mrs. Saunders. How are you? Isn't it a gorgeous day?" Tall, blond, and narrow-shouldered, Jill drew in a lungful of smoke and pushed it out with pleasure.

"Hello, Jill dear. How's everything?"

"Struggling along." Jill stretched out her long jean-clad legs till her feet rested on the railing. "Mrs. Saunders, this is my friend, Wendy. Wendy, Mrs. Saunders. Mrs. Saunders has been so terrific to us," she said to Wendy. "And she never complains about the kids screeching on the other side of the wall."

"Hi," said Wendy.

"Nice to meet you, Wendy," said Mrs. Saunders. "I don't mind the children, Jill, really I don't. After all, I had children of my own. I know what it's like."

"That's right. Three, aren't there?"

"Yes," Mrs. Saunders said. "Walter, Louise, and Edith. Walter was named after his father."

"We named Jeff after his father too," Wendy remarked.

"Mrs. Saunders sometimes babysits for Luke and Kevin," Jill explained to Wendy. "They adore her. Sometimes they even tell us to go out so she can come and stay with them. I don't know what it is you do with them, Mrs. Saunders."

She smiled, and would have liked to linger with the two young women, but suddenly she had to go in, because a furious sob rose in her throat, choking her. She threw herself down on the bed and wept uncontrollably into the plumped-up pillows. Everyone in the world had a name except her. And it would never change. Nobody here, at this stage in her life, was going to come along and start calling her Fran. Franny, surely never again. She remembered the days—they were never far from her mind—when her husband was sick and dying in the bedroom upstairs in the old house, and fifteen, maybe twenty times a day she would hear his rasping, evaporating voice calling, "Franny, Franny." She would drop everything each time to see what it was he wanted, and although she had loved him deeply, there were moments when she felt if she heard that rasping voice wailing out her name once more she would scream in exasperation; her fists would clench with the power and the passion to choke him. And yet now, wasn't life horribly cruel, she would give half her remaining days to hear her name wailed once more by him. Or by anyone else, for that matter. She gave in utterly to her despair and cried for a long time. She felt she might die gasping for breath if she didn't hear her own name.

At last she made an effort to pull herself together. She fixed the crumpled pillows so that they looked untouched, then went into the bathroom, washed her face and put on powder and lipstick, released her gray hair from its bun and brushed it out. It looked nice, she thought, long and still thick, thank God, falling down her back in a glossy, smooth sheet. Feeling young and girlish for a moment, she fancied herself going about with it loose and swinging, like Jill and Wendy and the other young girls. Jauntily she tossed her head to right and left a few times and reveled in the swing of her hair. As a matter of fact it was better hair than Jill's, she thought, thicker, with more body. Except it was gray. She gave a secretive smile to the mirror and pinned her hair up in the bun again. She would go into town and browse around Woolworth's to cheer herself up.

Mrs. Saunders got a ride in with Jill, who drove past the shopping center every noon on her way to get Luke and Kevin at nursery school. In Woolworth's she bought a new bathmat, a bottle of shampoo and some cream rinse for her hair, a butane cigarette lighter, and last, surprising herself, two boxes of colored chalk. She couldn't have explained why she bought the chalk, but since it only amounted to fifty-six cents she decided it didn't need justification. The colors looked so pretty, peeking out from the open circle in the center of the box—lime, lavender, rose, yellow, beige, and powder blue. It was spring, and they seemed to go with the spring. It occurred to her as she took them from the display case that the pale yellow was exactly the color of her kitchen cabinets; she might use it to cover a patch of white that had appeared on one drawer after she scrubbed too hard with Ajax. Or she might give Luke and Kevin each a box, and buy them slates as well, to practice their letters and numbers. They were nice little boys, and she often gave them small presents or candy when she babysat.

Feeling nonetheless as though she had done a slightly eccentric thing, Mrs. Saunders meandered through the shopping center, wondering if there might be some sensible, inexpensive thing she needed. Then she remembered that the shoes she had on were nearly worn out. Certainly she was entitled to some lightweight, comfortable new shoes for spring. With the assistance of a civil young man, she quickly was able to find just the right pair. The salesman was filling out the slip. "Name, please?" he said. And then something astonishing happened. Hearing so unexpectedly the word that had been obsessing her gave Mrs. Saunders a great jolt, and, as she would look back on it later, seemed to loosen and shake out of its accustomed place a piece of her that rebelled against the suffocation she had been feeling for more years than she cared to remember.

She knew exactly the answer that was required, so that she could find reassurance afterwards in recalling that she had been neither mad nor senile. As the clerk waited with his pencil poised, the thing that was jolted loose darted swiftly through her body, producing vast exhilaration, and rose out from her throat to her lips.

"Frances."

She expected him to look at her strangely—it was strange, she granted that—and say, "Frances what?" And then, at long last she would hear it. It would be, she imagined, something like making love years ago with Walter, when in the dark all at once her body streamed and compressed to one place and exploded with relief and wonder. She felt a tinge of that same excitement now, as she waited. And it did not concern her that the manner of her gratification would be so pathetic and contrived, falling mechanically from the lips of a stranger. All that mattered was that the name be spoken.

"Last name, please." He did not even look up.

Mrs. Saunders gave it, and gave her address, and thought she would faint with disappointment. She slunk from the store and stood weakly against a brick wall outside. Was there to be no easing of this pain? Dazed, she stared hopelessly at her surroundings, which were sleek, buzzing with shoppers, and unappealing. She slumped and turned her face to the wall.

On the brick before her, in small letters, were scratched the words "Tony" and "Annette." An arrow went through them. Mrs. Saunders gazed for a long time, aware that she would be late meeting Jill, but not caring, for once. She broke the staple on the Woolworth's bag, slipped her hand in, and drew out a piece of chalk. It turned out to be powder blue. Shielding her actions with her coat, she printed in two-inch-high letters on the brick wall outside the shoe store, FRANNY. Then she moved off briskly to the parking lot.

At home, after fixing herself a light lunch, which she ate excitedly and in haste, and washing the few dishes, she went back down to the garbage area behind the buildings. In lavender on the concrete wall just behind the row of cans, she wrote FRANNY. A few feet off she wrote again, FRANNY, and added WALTER, with an arrow through the names. But surveying her work, she took a tissue from her pocket and with some difficulty rubbed out WALTER and the arrow. Walter was dead. She was not senile yet. She was not yet one of those old people who live in a world of illusions.

Then she went to the children's playground, deserted at naptime, and wrote FRANNY in small letters on the wooden rail of the slide, on the wooden pillars of the newfangled jungle gym, and on the concrete border of the sandbox, in yellow, lavender, and blue, respectively. Choosing a quite private corner behind some benches, she crouched down and wrote the six letters of her name, using a different color for each letter. She regarded her work with a fierce, proud elation, and decided then and there that she would not, after all, give the chalk to Luke and Kevin. She was not sure, in fact, that she would ever give them anything else again.

The next week was a busy and productive one for Mrs. Saunders. She carried on her usual round of activities—shopping, cooking, cleaning her apartment daily, and writing to Walter, Louise, and Edith; evenings she babysat or watched television, and once attended a tenants' meeting on the subject of limited space for guest parking, though she possessed neither a car nor guests; she went to the bank to cash her social security check, as well as to a movie and to the dentist for some minor repair work on her bridge. But in addition to all this she went to the shopping center three times with Jill at noon, where, using caution, she managed to adorn several sidewalks and walls with her name.

She was not at all disturbed when Jill asked, "Anything special that you're coming in so often for, Mrs. Saunders? If it's anything I could do for you . . ."

"Oh, no, Jill dear." She laughed. "I'd be glad if you could do this for me, believe me. It's my bridge." She pointed to her teeth. "I've got to keep coming, he says, for a while longer, or else leave it with him for a few weeks, and then what would I do? I'd scare the children."

"Oh, no. Never that, Mrs. Saunders. Is it very painful?" Jill swerved around neatly into a parking space.

"Not at all. Just a nuisance. I hope you don't mind—"

"Don't be ridiculous, Mrs. Saunders. What are friends for?"

That day she was more busy than ever, for she had not only to add new FRANNYs but to check on the old. There had been a rainstorm over the weekend, which obliterated her name from the parking lot and the sidewalks. Also, a few small shopkeepers, specifically the butcher and the baker, evidently cleaned their outside walls weekly. She told Jill not to pick her up, for she might very likely be delayed, and as it turned out, she was. The constant problem of not being noticed was time-consuming, especially in the parking lot with its endless flow of cars in and out. Finished at last, she was amazed to find it was past two-thirty. Mrs. Saunders was filled with the happy exhaustion of one who has accomplished a decent and useful day's work. Looking about and wishing there were a comfortable place to rest for a while, she noticed that the window she was leaning against belonged to a paint store. Curious, she studied the cans and color charts. The colors were beautiful: vivid reds, blues, golds, and violets, infinitely more beautiful than her pastels. She had never cared much for pastels anyway. With a sly, physical excitement floating through her, Mrs. Saunders straightened up and entered.

She knew something about spray paint. Sukie, Walter's wife, had sprayed the kitchen chairs with royal blue down in the cellar last time Mrs. Saunders visited, nearly two years ago. She remembered it well, for Sukie, her hair, nose, and mouth covered with scarves, had called out somewhat harshly as Mrs. Saunders came down the steps, "For God's sake, stay away from it. It'll choke you. And would you mind opening some windows upstairs so when I'm done I can breathe?" Sukie was not a welcoming kind of girl. Mrs. Saunders sighed, then set her face into a smile for the paint salesman.

As she left the store contentedly with a shopping bag on her arm, she heard the insistent beep of a car horn. It was Jill. "Mrs. Saunders, hop in," she called. "I had a conference with Kevin's teacher," Jill explained, "and then the mothers' meeting to plan the party for the end of school, and after I dropped the kids at Wendy's I thought maybe I could still catch you."

Jill looked immensely pleased with her good deed, Mrs. Saunders thought, just as Louise and Edith used to look when they fixed dinner on her birthday, then sat beaming with achievement and waiting for praise, which she always gave in abundance.

"Isn't that sweet of you, Jill." But she was not as pleased as she tried to appear, for she had been looking forward to the calm bus ride and to privately planning when and where to use her new purchases. "You're awfully good to me."

"Oh, it's nothing, really. Buying paint?"

"Yes, I've decided to do the kitchen and bathroom."

"But they'll do that for you. Every two years. If you're due you just call the landlord and say so."

"But they don't use the colors I like and I thought it might be nice to try. . . ."

"It's true, they do make you pay a lot extra for colors," Jill said thoughtfully.

Mrs. Saunders studied the instructions on the cans carefully, and went over in her mind all the advice the salesman had given her. Late that evening after the family noises in the building had subsided, she took the can of red paint down to the laundry room in the basement. She also took four quarters and a small load of wash—the paint can was buried under the wash—in case she should meet anyone. She teased herself about this excessive precaution at midnight, but as it happened she did meet one of the young mothers, Nancy, pulling overalls and polo shirts out of the dryer.

"Oh, Mrs. Saunders! I was frightened for a minute. I didn't expect anyone down here so late. So you're another night owl, like me."

"Hello, Nancy. I meant to get around to this earlier, but it slipped my mind." She took the items out of her basket slowly, one by one, wishing Nancy would hurry.

"Since I took this part-time job I spend all my evenings doing housework. Sometimes I wonder if it's worth it." At last Nancy had the machine emptied. "Do you mind staying all alone? I could wait." She hesitated in the doorway, clutching her basket to her chest, pale and plainly exhausted.

"Oh no, Nancy dear. I don't mind at all, and anyhow, you look like you need some rest. Go on and get to sleep. I'll be fine."

She inserted her quarters and started the machine as Nancy disappeared. The clothes were mostly clean; she had grabbed any old thing to make a respectable-looking load. The extra washing wouldn't hurt them. With a tingling all over her skin and an irrepressible smile, she unsealed the can. Spraying was much easier than she had expected. The *F*, which she put on the wall behind the washer, took barely any time and effort. Paint dripped thickly from its upper left corner, though, indicating she had pressed too hard and too long. It was simple to adjust the pressure, and by the second *N* she felt quite confident, as if she had done this often before. She took a few steps back to look it over. It was beautiful— bold, thick, and bright against the cream-colored wall. So beautiful that she did another directly across the room. Then on the inside of the open door, rarely seen, she tried it vertically; aside from some long amateurish drips, she was delighted at the effect. She proceeded to the boiler room, where she sprayed FRANNY on the boiler and on the wall, then decided she had done enough for one night. Waiting for the laundry cycle to end, she was surrounded by the red, lustrous reverberations of her name, vibrating across the room at each other; she felt warmed and strengthened by the firm, familiar walls of her own self. While the room filled and teemed with visual echoes of FRANNY, Mrs. Saunders became supremely at peace.

She climbed the stairs slowly, adrift in this happy glow. She would collect her things from the dryer late tomorrow morning. Lots of young mothers and children would have been in and out by then. Nancy was the only one who could suspect, but surely Nancy didn't come down with a load every day; besides, she was so tired and harassed she probably wouldn't remember clearly. Mrs. Saunders entered her apartment smiling securely with her secret.

Yet new difficulties arose over the next few days. The deserted laundry room at night was child's play compared to the more public, open, and populated areas of the development. Mrs. Saunders finally bought a large tote bag in Woolworth's so she could carry the paint with her and take advantage of random moments of solitude. There were frequent lulls when the children's playground was empty, but since it was in full view of the balconies and rear windows, only once, at four-thirty on a Wednesday morning, did she feel safe, working quickly and efficiently to complete her name five times. The parking lot needed to be done in the early hours too, as well as the front walk and the wall space near the mailboxes. It was astonishing, she came to realize, how little you could

rely on being unobserved in a suburban garden apartment development, unless you stayed behind your own closed door.

Nevertheless, she did manage to get her name sprayed in half a
dozen places, and she took to walking around the grounds on
sunny afternoons to experience the fairly delirious sensation of her
identity, secretly yet miraculously out in the open, sending humming rays towards her as she moved along. Wherever she went she
encountered herself. Never in all her life had she had such a potent
sense of occupying and making an imprint on the world around
her. The reds and blues and golds seemed even to quiver and
heighten in tone as she approached, as if in recognition and tribute,
but this she knew was an optical illusion. Still, if only they could
speak. Then her joy and fulfillment would be complete. After her
walks she sat in her apartment and smoked and saw behind her
closed eyes parades of brilliantly colored FRANNYs move along in
the darkness, and felt entranced as with the warmth of a soothing
physical embrace. Only once did she have a moment of unease,
when she met Jill on her way back in early one morning.

"Mrs. Saunders, did anything happen? What's the red stuff on
your fingers?"

"Just nail polish, dear. I spilled some."

Jill glanced at her unpolished nails and opened her mouth to
speak, but apparently changed her mind.

"Fixing a run in a stocking," Mrs. Saunders added as she carried
her shopping bag inside. She sensed potential danger in that meeting, yet also enjoyed a thrill of defiance and a deep, faint flicker of
expectation.

Then one evening Harris, Jill's husband, knocked on Mrs. Saunders' door to tell her there would be a tenants' meeting tomorrow
night in the community room.

"You must have noticed," he said, "the way this place has been
deteriorating lately. I mean, when we first moved in four years ago
it was brand-new and they took care of it. Now look! First of all
there's this graffiti business. You must've seen it, haven't you?
Every kid and his brother have got their names outside—it's as bad
as the city. Of course that Franny character takes the cake, but the

others are running her a close second. Then the garbage isn't removed as often as it used to be, the mailboxes are getting broken, there's been a light out for weeks in the hall. . . . I could go on and on."

She was afraid he would, too, standing there leaning on her doorframe, large and comfortably settled. Harris was an elementary-school teacher; Mrs. Saunders guessed he was in the habit of making long speeches. She smiled and wondered if she ought to ask him in, but she had left a cigarette burning in the ashtray. In fact she had not noticed the signs of negligence that Harris mentioned, but now that she heard, she was grateful for them. She felt a trifle weak in the knees; the news of the meeting was a shock. If he didn't stop talking soon she would ask him in just so she could sit down, cigarette or no cigarette.

"Anyhow," Harris continued, "I won't keep you, but I hope you'll come. The more participation, the better. There's power in numbers."

"Yes, I'll be there, Harris. You're absolutely right."

"Thanks, Mrs. Saunders. Good night." She was starting to close the door when he abruptly turned back. "And by the way, thanks for the recipe for angel food cake you gave Jill. It was great."

"Oh, I'm glad, Harris. You're quite welcome. Good night, now."

Of course she would go. Her absence would be noted, for she always attended the meetings, even those on less crucial topics. Beneath her surface nervousness the next day, Mrs. Saunders was aware of an abiding calm. Buoyed up by her name glowing almost everywhere she turned, she felt strong and impregnable as she took her seat in the community room.

"Who the hell is Franny anyway?" asked a man from the neighboring unit. "She started it all. Anyone here got a kid named Franny?" One woman had a Frances, but, she said, giggling, her Frances was only nine months old. Mrs. Saunders felt a throb of alarm in her chest. But she soon relaxed: the nameplates on her door and mailbox read "Saunders" only, and her meager mail, even the letters from Walter, Louise, and Edith, she had recently noticed, was all addressed to Mrs. F. Saunders or Mrs. Walter Saunders. And of course, since these neighbors had never troubled to ask. . . . She suppressed a grin. You make your own bed, she thought, watching them, and you lie in it.

The talk shifted to the broken mailboxes, the uncollected garbage, the inadequacy of guest parking, and the poor TV reception, yet every few moments it returned to the graffiti, obviously the most chafing symptom of decay. To Mrs. Saunders the progress of the meeting was haphazard, without direction or goal. As in the past, people seemed more eager to air their grievances than to seek a practical solution. But she conceded that her experience of community action was limited; perhaps this was the way things got done. In any case, their collective obtuseness appeared a more than adequate safeguard, and she remained silent. She always remained silent at tenants' meetings—no one would expect anything different of her. She longed for a cigarette, and inhaled deeply the smoke of others' drifting around her.

At last—she didn't know how it happened for she had ceased to pay attention—a committee was formed to draft a petition to the management listing the tenants' complaints and demanding repairs and greater surveillance of the grounds. The meeting was breaking up. They could relax, she thought wryly, as she milled about with her neighbors, moving to the door. She had done enough painting for now anyway. She smiled with cunning and some contempt at their innocence of the vandal in their midst. Certainly, if it upset them so much she would stop. They did have rights, it was quite true.

She walked up with Jill. Harris was still downstairs with the other members of the small committee which he was, predictably, chairing.

"Well, it was a good meeting," Jill said. "I only hope something comes out of it."

"Yes," said Mrs. Saunders vaguely, fumbling for her key in the huge, heavy tote bag.

"By the way, Mrs. Saunders . . ." Jill hesitated at her door and nervously began brushing the wispy hair from her face. "I've been meaning to ask, what's your first name again?"

In her embarrassment Jill was blinking childishly and didn't know where to look. Mrs. Saunders felt sorry for her. In the instant before she replied—and Mrs. Saunders didn't break the rhythm of question and answer by more than a second's delay— she grasped fully that she was sealing her own isolation as surely as if she had bricked up from inside the only window in a cell.

"Faith," she said.

The longing she still woke with in the dead of night, despite all her work, would never now be eased. But when, in that instant before responding, her longing warred with the rooted habits and needs of a respectable lifetime, she found the longing no match for the life. And that brief battle and its outcome, she accepted, were also, irrevocably, who Franny was.

The profound irony of this turn of events seemed to loosen some old, stiff knot in the joints of her body. Feeling the distance and wisdom of years rising in her like sap released, she looked at Jill full in the face with a vast, unaccustomed compassion. The poor girl could not hide the relief that spread over her, like the passing of a beam of light.

"Isn't it funny, two years and I never knew," she stammered. "All that talk about names made me curious, I guess." Finally Jill turned the key in her lock and smiled over her shoulder. "Okay, good night, Mrs. Saunders. See you tomorrow night, right? The boys are looking forward to it."

THE WRATH-BEARING TREE

"Six-two-four Avenue D?" the old man asks me. He clutches at my wrist with knobby fingers. "Six-two-four Avenue D?"

"I'm very sorry. I can't help you."

"Come on, don't pay any attention," my father mutters impatiently, pulling at my other arm. We proceed. Beyond my back the old man whimpers to a woman by his side, "No one wants to help me."

"That's the way it is with these young people. They won't give you the time of day."

Anger and guilt rise in me simultaneously like twin geysers. I hastily prepare two lines of defense, one to assuage the guilt, the other to justify the anger. Number one, he's already asked me three times today. Number two, I have enough troubles of my own.

I am taking my father for a stroll down the hospital corridor, our arms linked at the elbow like a happy couple on a date. An intrusive third wheel is the IV tube dangling from its chrome stand, a coatrack come to life. My father is here in order to die. Even now, terminally ill, he walks very fast, he runs.

The old man, the one searching for 624 Avenue D, is the spectacle of the floor. Ambulatory, he spends long hours in the waiting room, where he occasionally urinates on the floor. Also, from time to time he exposes himself, spreading wide the folds of his white cotton gown with a quick flapping like a gull's wings. This is disconcerting to new visitors, but my sister and I merely smile now, humoring him. We have found that a brief, friendly acknowledgment will satisfy him for the day. Between ourselves we call him the flasher, and giggle. "How's the flasher today?" "Not bad. He looked a little pale, though." Having seen his private parts so often, I feel on intimate terms with him, like family. He is not really annoying except when he gets on one of his 624 Avenue D jags, lasting for two or three days, after which he returns to simple urinating and self-exposure.

My father, thank God, would never expose himself. The humiliation. As a child I once accidentally glimpsed a patch of his pubic hair; he looked as though he might faint with shock when he saw me in the room. My father, thank God, is in full possession of his mental faculties. Just yesterday he gave a philosophical disquisition, shortly after taking a painkiller. "There are times," he said, "when the mere absence of pain is a positive pleasure." He paused, and swallowed with difficulty. We could see his throat muscles straining. "That is," he went on, "under certain extreme conditions a negative quality can become a positive one." My heart swelled with love and pride. Isn't he smart, my father? He cannot resist saying things twice, though, that is, paraphrasing himself, a trait I have inherited. I think it comes from a conviction of intellectual superiority, that is, an expectation of inferior intelligence in one's listeners.

"Six-two-four Avenue D?" The old man looms up, having padded in on soundless feet, before my sister and me in the waiting room.

"I think it's the other way," I say gently. "Try that way." He shuffles towards the door. My sister and I are chain-smoking and giggling, making up nasty surmises about the patients and their visitors.

"That one will probably put arsenic in her grandma's tea the day she gets home." She points to a young girl with long gold earrings and tattered jeans, who is speaking sternly about proper diet to an old woman in a wheelchair.

I nod and glance across the room at a fat, blue-haired woman wearing a flowered, wrinkled cotton housedress. "Couldn't she find anything better to visit the hospital in? He might drop dead just looking at her."

We giggle some more. "How did the Scottish woman's kidney operation go?"

"All right. They took it out. She'll need dialysis."

"At least she's okay." We lower our eyes gravely. We like the Scottish woman. There is a long silence.

"Norman died last night," she says at last.

"Oh, really. Well . . ." This is not a surprise. Norman was yellow-green for two weeks and wheeled about morosely, telling his visitors he was not long for this world. He convinced everyone and turned out to be right. "That's too bad. He was nice."

"Yes, he was," she agrees.

Suddenly we are convulsed with laughter. Just outside the waiting room the old man has flashed for an elegant slender woman in a gray silk suit and bouffant hairdo, and carrying a Gucci bag. It greeted her the instant she stepped off the elevator. The astonishment on her face is exquisite and will sustain our spirits for hours.

It occurs to me that my sister and I have not been so close since my childhood, when I used to hold the book for her as she memorized poems. I was eight when she began college. Her freshman English teacher made the class memorize reams of poetry; thanks to him my head is filled with long, luminous passages. I sat on her bed holding the book while she pranced around the room reciting with dramatic gestures:

> *And this was the reason that, long ago,*
> *In this kingdom by the sea,*

> *A wind blew out of a cloud, chilling*
> *My beautiful Annabel Lee;*
> *So that her highborn kinsmen came*
> *And bore her away from me,*
> *To shut her up in a sepulchre*
> *In this kingdom by the sea.*

What are kinsmen, I wanted to know. And what is a sepulchre? I thought it terribly mean of her highborn kinsmen to drag Annabel Lee away, even if she did have a cold.

"'That is no country for old men,'" she intoned solemnly, "'The young/In one another's arms, birds in the trees . . .'" When she came to "sick with desire/And fastened to a dying animal," she grew melodramatic, clutching her heart and pretending to swoon. I was an appreciative audience. "'Already with thee! tender is the night.'" She would flutter her wings like a bird, and if I giggled hard enough she would be inspired, at "Now more than ever seems it rich to die," to stretch out flat on the bedroom floor.

Eliot was her favorite. But even here, though reverent, she could not resist camping. "'I an old man,/A dull head among windy spaces.'" She let her jaw drop and lolled her head about like an imbecile. She sobered quickly, though, delivering the philosophical section with an awesome dignity reaching its peak at "These tears are shaken from the wrath-bearing tree."

"What does that mean?" I interrupted.

She could not tell me. She herself was only seventeen. But she said it beautifully, standing still in the center of the room, hand resting on her collarbone, head slightly cast down, long smooth hair falling over her shoulders: "'These tears are shaken from the wrath-bearing tree.'"

Evenings, after I held the book and corrected her for about an hour, she would get dressed to go out on dates. Indeed, my memories of my sister at that period show her doing only those two things—memorizing poetry and getting dressed for dates. She let me watch her. She kept perfume in a crystal decanter whose top squeaked agonizingly when it was opened or closed. The squeak made me writhe on the bed

in spasms of shivers. She squeaked it over and over, to torment me,
while I squealed, "Stop, please, stop!" She laughed. "Come here,"
she said. "I'll give you a dab." I went. But before she gave me a dab
she squeaked the top again. When she left home three years later to
get married I inherited her large bedroom. She left the perfume
decanter for me, and often, feeling lonely, I squeaked it for the thrill
of the shivers and for the memories.

Now she is in her forties, the mother of two grown sons. "Do
you still remember all the poetry?" I ask.

She smiles. She has an odd smile, withholding, shy, clever, and
she says, "'Shall I compare thee to a summer's day? Thou art more
lovely and more temperate.'" When she gets to "Nor shall Death
brag thou wand'rest in his shade," she stops, her voice choking.
We light up more cigarettes. "Six-two-four Avenue D?" he asks us.
"Oh, for Christ's sake," she says, stubs out the cigarette angrily,
and stomps off to the ladies' room.

I sit at my father's bed, waiting for the night nurse to come. The
man in the next bed and his wife are trying to make conversation
with my father about an earthquake in China. My father, who in
good health was gregarious and an avid follower of current events,
has his lips sealed in wrath.

"Maybe he's not quite with it, huh?" the man's wife says.

I rise staunchly to his defense. "Oh, he's with it, all right."

She pulls the curtains around her husband's bed, as she does
every evening for fifteen minutes. I envision them engaged in silent, deft manual sex.

"You don't have to stay here, you know," my father says.

"Why not? Don't you want me to stay?"

"Of course."

"So I'll stay then." This is the closest I have come to telling him
I love him. Not very close. I long to tell him I love him and am
sorry for his suffering, but am afraid he would consider that in bad
taste. My father does not consider love or sorrow in bad taste,
only, I imagine, talking about them. That he is dying is an evident
obscenity that cannot be spoken. I do not want to say anything at
this critical moment that he would consider in bad taste, or that

might imperil his final judgment of me. My mouth waters with the sour bad taste of unspoken words. Reality, in fact, is in bad taste.

"Six-two-four Avenue D? Six-two-four Avenue D?" The flasher is at the bedside. I point towards the door and he moves off.

"What the hell does he want, anyway?" my father asks.

"Six-two-four Avenue D."

He shrugs and grins. I do the same, like a mirror. We understand each other.

The next day my mother and I stand at his stretcher in the corridor of the hospital basement after X-rays, waiting fifteen furious, endless minutes for an orderly to wheel him upstairs to his bed. He moans in pain on the hard pallet and wants my mother to wheel the stretcher upstairs herself. She says that is against hospital rules. Propping himself up on his elbows to glare at her, he shouts hoarsely: "Law and order! Law and order! That is the whole trouble with some people. Rules are made by petty minds, for petty minds to obey. Throughout history, the great achievements were made by those who broke the rules. Look at Galileo! Look at Lenin! Look at Lindbergh! Daring!" This speech has been too much for him. He falls back on the stretcher, his mouth wide open, panting. I grab the back of the stretcher with one hand, the IV pole with the other, and we dash on a madly veering course through the labyrinth of the basement towards the forbidden staff elevator. Our eyes meet in an ecstasy of glee and swift careening motion. I remember how he drove me anywhere I asked at seventy miles an hour, his arm out the window, fingers resting on the roof of the car, an arm sunburned from elbow to wrist. Oh Daddy, for you I am Galileo, I am Lenin, I am Lindbergh! Daring! We reach his bedside unstopped by any guardians of the law. He grips my hand in thanks, my life is fulfilled.

Actually, my mother is not at all a fanatical law-and-order person. Only right now she thinks, hopes, yearns to believe that if she obeys all the rules in life God will look down on her with favor and let my father live. I know that he cannot live, so I can afford to be lawless.

I carry his urine in a blue plastic jug given to me by an orderly like a sacred trust, to present to the proper nurse. I cannot find the right nurse, they all look alike. I have never looked at them, only stepped on the toe of one, in protest. As I search, a new patient approaches me, a small woman with straight white hair drifting about her cheeks in a girlish bob. "Have you seen my children?" She has a sweet face and a gentle, pleasing voice. "No? You haven't seen them? Two little children, a boy and a girl, curly hair?"

I shake my head again. "I'm awfully sorry, I haven't."

The next day I see them. They visit with her in the waiting room, large, weary, middle-aged, and kind. They treat her ever so kindly in the waiting room, and she treats them with aloof politeness. An hour after they leave she stops me in the corridor. "Have you seen my children? A boy and a girl, curly hair?"

The day before the operation, cousins whom I cannot bear arrive to pay their respects. I wish the flasher would come in and perform for them but he stubbornly stays away. I even consider going to fetch him, but that would be exploitation. My sister is doing her duty entertaining the guests. Let her. She is the big sister.

"Take me out for a drink," I whisper to my nephew, her older son.

He is a smart boy, though only twenty-three. He understands that his mother and I are losing our father and must be treated like children. He rises promptly like a great blond hairy tree, six foot two, and steers me to the elevator.

"I bet I can drink you under the table," I say.

I order Johnnie Walker Red, he orders Johnnie Walker Black. I wonder what is the difference between the red and the black, but not wishing to appear so ignorant in front of a younger man, I don't ask. From the way he drinks I realize he is an adult, and feel almost resentful that he grew up secretly, behind my back. I imagine now that women look at him with lust. I try, merely for distraction, to look at him with lust but cannot manage it.

During the third double Scotch my nephew says, "Have you met the woman who's looking for her children?"

"Yes."

"You know, I thought if we could introduce her to Six-two-four Avenue D maybe we could make a match."

I choke with laughter, sputtering Scotch all over the table. What a brilliant sally, a pinnacle of wit. I wish I had thought of it. Yet inside I am thinking, That is really in bad taste. Such bad taste. Young people.

He drinks four, I drink only three. I feel old, middle-aged. What do the other drinkers think about us? I don't look old enough to be his mother, nor young enough to be his girlfriend. They think he is a young man doing a middle-aged woman a favor, which he is. I wonder if I am boring him with my gloom. The hours I spent holding the book for his mother long before he was born or even dreamed of come back to me.

> *"Terence, this is stupid stuff:*
> *You eat your victuals fast enough;*
> *There can't be much amiss, 'tis clear,*
> *To see the rate you drink your beer.*
> *But oh, good Lord, the verse you make,*
> *It gives a chap the belly-ache."*

That is unfair. He is a good boy and I love him dearly. I put my hand on his. "Thanks for getting me out of there." What I really want to say is this:

> *'Tis true, the stuff I bring for sale*
> *Is not so brisk a brew as ale:*
>
> .   .   .   .   .
>
> *But take it: if the smack is sour,*
> *The better for the embittered hour;*
> *It should be good to heart and head*
> *When your soul is in my soul's stead;*
> *And I will friend you, if I may,*
> *In the dark and cloudy day.*

But I don't think he cares for poetry. I doubt if his mother ever told him how I held the book for her; she is not given to discussing the past, says she remembers very little.

The day of the crucial operation we crowd into the room to see my father wheeled out on the stretcher. There are too many of us for comfort, but what can we do? Everyone has a right to be there, everyone wants to say goodbye. Once again, his lips are sealed in wrath. You don't care about anyone but yourself, dying. Selfish. Brain. Heartless. I shout all this at him from behind closed, withering lips. What about us? What about me? Not one word for me? His eyes open. He looks around at us one by one, enumerating the members of his tribe. He is groggy from the shot, but he says mildly, "If you're all here, then who's home taking care of the little girls?"

Those are my little girls he's talking about. He has forgotten nothing and no one, keeps us arrayed in his eye like a family portrait, precious and indestructible. My heart leaps up, to a grief that cuts like a knife.

"Six-two-four Avenue D? Six-two-four Avenue D?" He edges up and appeals to the crowd of us around the stretcher. We ignore him. Go find the old woman with the children.

The odd thing is, I think, when it is over and we bid goodbye to the waiting room, that all along I knew exactly where 624 Avenue D was. It was near my high school. I had a friend who lived in 628, in a row of attached two-family houses on a modest, decent street. Had I met the flasher anywhere else but the terminal waiting room, I would gladly have given him directions to find his way home. There, I was powerless. I wish I could explain that to him.

PLAISIR D'AMOUR

Their names came to her in a dream, Brauer and Elemi. They were a couple, close to thirty. In the dream they walked holding hands along the southern edge of Central Park, stopping to admire the restless buggy horses pawing the pavement. Then they had breakfast in the Plaza Hotel: a waiter who bowed discreetly from the waist served them eggs Benedict and ambrosial coffee. Afterwards they walked in the park, where the smell of cut grass rose keen and fragrant. As if by telepathy, they stopped walking at the same moment and sat down on a bench to talk. Vera's first thought on awakening was that the dream had been so realistic; nothing happened in it that could not happen in real life.

She reached for an old plaid bathrobe—originally John's, but it had lost its aura of identity by now and felt anonymous. Vera, who was slim, had to fold over the excess fabric and belt it securely. In the kitchen she found her daughter, Jean, just sixteen, already finishing breakfast, peering through thick glasses at *Madame*

Bovary. The pot of coffee was waiting on the stove. Jean made it
nearly every morning, using a filter, and it was excellent. When
Vera praised it, as usual, Jean slowly closed the book, her eyes
fixed on the vanishing page till the two halves snapped shut. All
the years of inculcating good manners have worked, thought Vera.

"Thanks. Did you sleep all right? You didn't take any of those
pills, did you?"

She was touched by her daughter's concern. Vera only occasionally took the sleeping pills prescribed when she left the hospital five
months ago, but Jean was righteously wary of drugs. She also had
strong feelings against cigarettes, abortion, and war. "No, I haven't
taken them in over a week. I slept fine. I had a funny dream,
though."

"Oh, really? What?"

"This man and woman with very odd names who eat at the
Plaza and walk in Central Park."

Jean leaned forward smiling, her face resting in her palms, some
strands of loose blond hair falling over her hands. "What were their
names?" She was looking at her mother with almost the same eager
attention she showed to her friends. Unprecedented and flattering
though this was, Vera became aware that she did not wish to re-
veal the names of Brauer and Elemi.

"Oh, I forget. Except for the names it was a very ordinary
dream, only I can't seem to shake it. Do you know that feeling?"

Her interest extinguished, Jean carried her plate and mug to the
sink. Watching her, Vera received an abrupt flash of illumination:
the name Brauer had something to do with the German word *Frau*,
and "elemi" was a word she had often written in crossword
puzzles. It meant a soft resin used in making varnish. Also, it was
an auditory inversion of "Emily," the name of a beautiful girl she
had known at college and since lost track of. She sensed at once
that these connections were true and ingenious, but finally irrele-
vant.

Jean cast her mother a curious glance from the doorway. "You're
going to work today, aren't you?"

"Oh, yes. It doesn't matter if I'm late. Howard is away this week and nobody else cares." She had worked in the advertising agency for seven years. When she needed to take six weeks off because of illness after her husband's death, they had been very understanding. She noticed, though, that on her return, Howard, the boss, had watched her closely for signs of instability, of which there were none. Vera was recovered; it would not happen again.

"I won't be back till around seven," Jean called from the hall. "I have the Dramatics Society." Then she dashed back to the kitchen. "Do you think we'll get a letter from Freddy today?"

"I hope so." Vera smiled at her. "Any day now." Jean's older brother, away for his first year in college, had mentioned possibly bringing a friend home over Easter, someone Jeanie might like, Freddy wrote, since he refused to do the vivisection experiment in zoology. Although boys were Jean's preoccupation, few met her ethical standards.

As the door finally clattered shut Vera realized that she had not even recalled Freddy's existence this morning before Jean spoke of him. That had something to do with the dream about Brauer and Elemi, which hovered about her still like a pleasant, warm fog. All other mornings now, when she woke she mentally ticked off the names of her two children, like a miser whose hoard has been plundered counting over with melancholy the few coins remaining. She had begun it in the hospital, spurred by a chance remark of one of the nurses: "But you're not all alone, Mrs. Leonard. Think of your children. You have a lot to live for." Vera had smiled wanly as the nurse, round, Oriental, efficient, smoothed unruly wrinkles in the sheets with a firm hand. Trite as her counsel was, it had helped, Vera had to admit.

Naming over her connections was not the only new habit to have taken hold since the painful weeks of her illness. With John gone, so many of her rooted personal customs had altered. (An "un-timely" death, the minister had called it, and despite her suffering Vera almost grinned involuntarily: as a writer of copy she under-stood the lure of the ready-made phrase.) She no longer woke out-rageously early on weekdays to start dinner simmering in the slow cooker; she could fix something simple for herself and Jean after work. She no longer tore the crossword puzzle out of the paper, or worried about underwear hanging in the bathroom for days or library books kept past their due date. She shopped in bits on the way home from work instead of massively on Saturdays. Magazines could be tossed out when she finished reading them, instead of accumulating in unsightly piles for John eventually to glance at. There was no need now to struggle with clothes packed tight in a narrow closet, or to feel hesitant about taking taxis home on rainy days, or talking at length to her older brother, long-distance. All winter Vera had slept in flannel granny nightgowns, heedless of appearance, and let ashtrays overflow while she smoked in bed to her heart's content. In fact, as she often noticed guiltily, daily life was freer and easier without him. Yet she was lonely at night, and though she had tried she could not change the twenty-year habit of sleeping on one side of the bed, the right. If ever again she found herself in bed with a man, she thought in her more lighthearted moments, he had better approach her from the left or not at all.

On the bus going to work Vera let her eyes close and lapsed into a waking daze. She saw Brauer and Elemi again, this time following an Hispanic building superintendent up the stairs to see a vacant apartment. It was spacious, with five good-sized rooms and large windows overlooking Central Park. The walls were dingy, but the super promised they would be freshly painted for the new tenants. Brauer and Elemi were holding hands as before, their faces glowing with joy. When they looked at each other they knew immediately, without words, that they would take it. Brauer spoke to the super and gave him some money. Outside they stopped at the corner to buy frankfurters and orange drinks at a stand. Walking across the park, they passed the pond where miniature sailboats glided in the brilliant sunlight, then discovered a trio of students—violin, cello, and clarinet—playing ethereal chamber music under a grove of trees. Brauer tossed some coins into the violin case and they walked on, holding hands, to the Frick museum, where they sat down in the indoor sculpture garden. Vera was so enchanted that when she opened her eyes—some part of her mind attuned to the duration of the ride—she had to hurry through the crowd to get off at her stop. Again she was struck by the realism of the dream. She would have been less surprised had the dreams been re-creations of her own experience: there had been a phase, just after John's "untimely" death, when she brooded over episodes from their past. But she and John had not done any of the things that Brauer and Elemi did.

There were meetings with clients all morning, then a festive staff lunch for one of the young copywriters, whose wife had had a baby. Through it all Vera was suffused with a calm, happy glow which made her think of Eastern philosophies of acceptance, feeling beyond desire, the flow of being. These were things her son, Freddy, home from college at Christmas, had talked about. Later, in the company library, Will Pratt, one of the head accountants, approached her, slapping her warmly on the back so that she quivered. "Hey, Vera, you're certainly looking great today. I meant to tell you at lunch. What's up?"

"What do you mean? Nothing is up."

"Oh, come on. You don't get that glow just from martinis at lunch. You must be seeing somebody." He was gazing at her earnestly, with kindness beneath the brash grin, the nervous, swift dark eyes. She had known Will for years—he had been a help during the months of John's dying, letting her cry in his office, bringing her cups of coffee, even fixing her slipshod account sheets without complaint—so she shouldn't be alarmed by his bantering now. Nonetheless it made her eyelids twitch.

"No, really. No one."

"No one? Then you're a naturally beautiful woman. Lucky. Have a drink with me after work." Will had been divorced for some time and prided himself on his bachelorhood. She might have gone out with him now, as a friend—he asked her often—had he not also asked her often when John was alive and well.

"Thanks, Will, but I'm sorry. I've got to get home for Jean."

"Oh, Jean is no baby. What is it, Vera? Aren't we friends? Can't friends have a drink?" He came closer, frowning. She could feel his warm breath on her cheek, not unpleasant. When she kept silent his voice grew sharp and tight. "You've turned me down three

times in a month. What the hell is suddenly wrong with me anyway, I'd like to know?"

Vera stepped back in fright, holding a large slick magazine before her as a shield. "Nothing is wrong with you, Will. Of course
we're friends. It's just that evenings, you know, I'm tired. And I
worry about Jean—she's lonely too. I'm sorry." Not yet, she was
screaming inside her head. Not yet. Not ever.

Will was lighting a cigarette, his hands cupped around the match
so a small glow was visible between his thick fingers, like a distant
bonfire. He didn't answer.

Vera took another step back. A clasp had become unfastened;
she felt the slow sliding of her hair down the back of her neck. In a
moment it would be hanging loose. "Why don't we have lunch
tomorrow, Will? Or Monday?" Lunch seemed less perilous than
drinks after work.

"I'm generally tied up with business at lunch." Will moved to
the door. "But I'll give you a buzz next week, maybe. Take care."

Vera breathed deeply, as though she had barely escaped anni-
hilation by a massive natural phenomenon, an avalanche. Her hair
tumbled to her shoulders and the clasp fell to the floor, but Will
was gone by then.

On the bus that evening she closed her eyes as if in prayer and
whispered, Brauer, Elemi. And they came. They were lying in
bed under neatly arranged blankets, side by side, Brauer on the
right and Elemi on his left. Vera waited, but they did not stir.
They lay flat on their backs, holding hands, smiling and at peace.
The peace that passeth understanding, Vera murmured, and wondered what she meant by that.

They came often in the days and weeks that followed. Brauer
and Elemi did not make love, but they were certainly in love.
There was no mistaking their constant hand-holding, their long
searching glances, the soft sensual haze that floated about them.
They furnished their new apartment with colorful wall hangings,
lush ferns, and big floor pillows, and lay on the shag rug listening
to chamber music and jazz. Other evenings they danced the latest

dances in discotheques or went to Charlie Chaplin movies, where they shared bags of popcorn, laughed, and sometimes cried. They went ice-skating in Central Park, skimming along arm in arm through clusters of slower, more awkward skaters. Elemi, who was small and slight, wore a crimson velvet skating skirt with beige tights, a white turtleneck sweater, and a crimson beret. Tied to the laces of each skate were two red fur balls which bounced as she moved. She was a delicate sight. Vera, who did not skate, wondered if it was too late to learn. One day Brauer and Elemi rode into the country on their new mopeds—red for her, blue for him— and picnicked in a field under an elm tree. They tore chunks off a long French bread and drank red wine, then lay back to rest in the sun, with Brauer's head in Elemi's lap. She stroked his hair.

Vera was looking well, radiant, people told her, and she had stopped taking the sleeping pills altogether, which made Jean very happy. One of her women friends, less brash than Will, said Vera looked as though she were having a love affair. Vera shook her head and smiled, but inside she said, Yes, indeed I am.

Freddy brought Thomas, the boy who had refused to do the vivisection experiment, home for the Easter vacation. He was an amiable boy with a soft voice and long straight hair tied in a rubber band. Vera was glad to have him as a guest, and glad also to see Freddy thriving: his only complaints were about the dormitory food and the fact that he had no car. "I'd like at least to get a moped, Mom."

"Mopeds are about four hundred dollars."

"I'll get a part-time job and pay you back, I promise."

"I'll think about it." She hated to refuse him—he was a good boy, hardworking, not greedy, and she still remembered with emotion how he had hated to leave her so soon after his father's death. It had been poignant, his young grief mingled with his eagerness to start college. Naturally Vera had urged him to go. It was only after he left that she became ill. But deserving as he was, she had to be careful with money: there were still some hospital bills, Jeanie wanted contact lenses, and in a year and a half she too would be going off to college. Vera shuddered at the thought of her daughter gone. But she would have to release her, and when the time came would do so bravely and cheerfully.

Freddy was kinder to his sister since he had been away, and Jean, to impress Thomas, was agreeable and unselfish. Vera was thankful for the peace. If only John could see the children now. Enraged at their nasty quarrels, which had persisted for several years of shared adolescence, he often used to shout, "Don't you two have any feeling for each other besides hate?" She had tried to placate him with assurances that it would pass. Had he lived, she could feel vindicated.

In the evenings the four of them would linger at the table over coffee and have long, animated discussions. Freddy was not so much "into" Eastern philosophy anymore, he informed Vera. He was more into genetics, and he told of brilliant and daring experiments with DNA molecules. Thomas was into anarchy. After a while the young people would move to the living room and continue their talk sitting on the floor listening to records, while Vera finished cleaning up. They offered to help, but she said she didn't mind, it relaxed her. Besides, she didn't feel overburdened. Thomas liked to cook, and several evenings she found an excellent dinner all prepared: eggplant casserole, soybean ragout, salads with bean sprouts and alfalfa. When she inquired, he told her shyly that he was also into health foods. Vera was interested in those talks that continued in the living room, but she was hesitant about intruding, and so she went to her room. Often, sitting up in bed holding a forgotten book, she would lapse into visions of Brauer and Elemi traveling on foot through the jungles of South America. There were many dangers: disease, snakes, losing their way in the rough, unfamiliar terrain, but they were unafraid.

Once she saw a man in a television commercial who looked remarkably like Brauer, with broad shoulders, sandy, lank hair, generous eyes, and a stubborn mouth that lost its stubbornness as soon as he smiled. Hot from tennis, the man was reaching for a glass of iced tea. Vera jumped out of bed to flick off the set before he could say a word. She clapped her hands over her ears, for sometimes a few dying words escaped after it was switched off.

Jean was delighted to have Thomas around. Vera could tell by the brightness in her eyes and by her clothing, only the newest jeans and sweaters. But after the first four or five days the boys started to go out at night, leaving her at home. Jean sulked pathetically at the kitchen table, gnawing on a strand of hair.

Vera dried her soapy hands and sat down. "Listen, they're in college—they feel there's a great gap. In a year or two Thomas may think you're the most exciting person around."

"How can you be so idiotic as to think I care about that nerd," Jean replied coldly. "It's not him. It's me."

"What do you mean, it's you?"

"There is not one single boy in the entire junior or senior class who interests me at the moment, or who is interested in me. It makes life extremely tedious. But you wouldn't understand."

"I certainly do understand about being lonely," said Vera. "Things will change."

Jean leaped up and shrieked, "You always say that but they never do! No one will ever like me and I'll die a virgin! I'm ugly, who would ever want me!" She burst into tears and ran to her room, slamming the door. Vera followed. She sat near her on the bed and tried to take her hand, but Jean yanked it away.

"A virgin, how absurd. At sixteen! You have your whole life ahead of you. Lots of men—boys—will want you. Anyway, you're always telling me that women can have a full life without men, marriage is a trap, and so forth."

"I don't want to get married," Jean wailed. "I just want somebody to like me. I mean, look at this hair." She pulled at it wretchedly. "It's disgusting. Every girl in school has long blond hair. If they don't have it they bleach it. I'm so ordinary."

"You could cut it," Vera suggested. "Then you'd look different."

"Oh, you, you're impossible. You don't understand a thing. Would you please leave me alone in my room? I know you probably mean well, but I'd prefer to be alone."

"All right," said Vera, shrugging her shoulders. "But I don't think you're ordinary." She understood perfectly the dynamics of these scenes: in the morning Jean would once more brew her fine coffee, having forgotten everything. Vera had pity for her daughter, as well as tolerance for the sputtering fireworks of midadolescence. Still and all, it was terribly wearing, terribly debilitating. When she finished in the kitchen she sat down at the table, cradled her head in her arms, and closed her eyes. Brauer, Elemi, she murmured.

Suddenly, she didn't know how much time had passed, in the deep stillness of the apartment she thought she heard her name from far off. She didn't stir. The next moment someone was shaking her by the shoulder.

"Are you okay, Mrs. Leonard? I'm sorry to wake you."

Baffled, she looked up at the thin, freckled face. Ah, of course, it was Thomas, the boy staying with them for Easter. He was into anarchy and natural foods. "That's all right, Thomas. I'm fine."

Brauer and Elemi had been sailing to Europe, where they planned to go backpacking through France and Italy. They had just returned from a tour of the ship's kitchen and were deciding whether they wanted to play shuffleboard or simply laze in the sun. Meanwhile they stretched out on deck chairs and drank bouillon. The shock of the intrusion made the blood pound behind Vera's eyes.

"I didn't mean to disturb you, but it's so late. You'll get a stiff neck sleeping like that."

She rose and rubbed her eyes with a tight fist. "Where's Freddy?"

"Freddy—uh—he gave me an extra set of keys." He walked quickly away from her to the sink, turned on the water and filled a glass. "He was taking this girl home. She lived very far out. I don't know how long . . ."

Vera could see his Adam's apple bobbing up and down as he gulped the drink. "That's quite all right, Thomas." She smiled. "I don't mean to pry. Turn out the lights, will you, when you're finished. Good night."

Climbing into bed, she thought to herself, You'd better watch it, Vera, with your Brauer and Elemi.

When the holidays were over and Freddy and Thomas returned

to school, Jean acquired a boyfriend, a curly-haired, wildly energetic boy named Donald, who wore thick glasses too and was re-
putedly a mathematical genius. They spent long hours in her
bedroom discussing intellectual and moral issues with the door
open. Vera liked Donald, who often accosted her while waiting for
Jean and elaborated complex mathematical theories.

"Mrs. Leonard, did you know that if the fastest rocket ship de-
vised by man were to race the earth in one complete orbit around
the sun it would arrive two years later?"

"Is that so?"

She was lost in his fevered explanation of objects hurtling
through space at frenetic rates of speed—he paced rapidly as he
spoke, occasionally bumping into furniture—but impressed by his
mental stamina. When he left she felt as though a whirlwind had
passed through the apartment, and she sank down in a chair, murmuring, Brauer, Elemi.

For they were her constant companions. More alone now that
Jean had Donald, Vera took to strolling through Central Park. The
days were growing longer and balmy. It stayed light till after
seven. She would rush from the elevator after work, deliberately
not looking around in case Will might be there, and walk the four
blocks to the park, to find Brauer and Elemi waiting for her at their
favorite entrance, East Sixty-fourth Street, near the zoo. Of course
they didn't look at her directly or speak to her—they stayed
slightly off to her left—but they knew she was there and didn't
mind her walking near them. Sometimes they visited the animals.
Brauer would call to the elephants, imitating their heavy stamping
and the sullen arching of their trunks, while Elemi laughed and fed
them peanuts. Vera watched from a few yards off. Later, if she
stopped to buy an ice cream or a soft drink they paused and waited
for her. They talked incessantly in soft whispers; what they said
was not important, only the glow that enveloped them and that
they were generous enough to share.

One evening when Vera came in at dusk, Jean, who was flipping
hamburgers expertly, asked with an amused smile, "Come on, tell
me, Mom, are you seeing somebody?"

"Of course not," Vera said sharply. "What makes you say that?"

"Well, you're out a lot, you come home all sort of rosy, and, like, your mind is elsewhere. I think it's great. You don't have to keep it a secret from me. We're both women."

"Don't be silly." Vera quickly laid the plates on the table. "There's nothing of the kind. I walked home through the park, that's all."

Late one afternoon at work Will buzzed her on the intercom. "Vera." It sounded like a command.

"Yes?" She should have sounded more confident, she thought immediately. After all, his was the question, hers the answer.

"How about a drink tonight? It's warm, we can sit outside at The Blue Door. I haven't seen you in ages."

"Thanks, Will, it's a nice idea. But I'm sorry. I've—" She took a deep breath for courage. "I've got a date."

"You've got a date."

"I'm afraid so."

"I see." He hung up.

In a moment he was in her doorway, glaring. "I'd like to say a few words to you." He shut the door firmly behind him. His shirt-sleeves were rolled up above his elbows and his loosened tie hung diagonally across his chest. "It's not like I'm some stranger trying to pick you up on the street, you know. It's not like I'm out to make you and then laugh it off." He was trying with strain to keep his voice down. His thick hair hung crazily over his forehead, and as he spoke, enraged, he wagged a finger at her. She noticed the dark hairs on his hands and felt an odd flicker of desire. He was much larger than she. Vera was afraid. "You know who I am, Vera. Aren't I good enough to pass an hour with, goddammit? I was good enough last year, when you needed a shoulder to cry on. Sure, that was fine. That was all for you, all taking and no giving. But when I ask for something, your company for an hour, that's all, oh no, that's asking too much. And you won't come straight out and say you don't want to; no, you give these phony excuses. You know what you are?" He wagged the hairy finger close to her face and she blinked in terror. "You are one helluva selfish, stuck-up bitch."

She didn't know what she could possibly say in reply. But she didn't need to say anything, for as soon as he finished speaking he stalked out of her office and slammed the door loudly behind him. The sound seemed to invade her body and made her shrink in her chair. She folded her arms on her desk and laid her head down. I can't, she thought. She was sorry about Will, but it was impossible, she was too afraid.

The very first time, she remembered, John had whispered, "Are you afraid?" And when she nodded he stroked her cheek and said, "It will be all right. I'll take care of you." She had grown used to him, so that the fear had shrunk very small, to the size of a shriveled pea. But then he died. He promised to take care of her but he broke his promise. She could not do it again with another, who might not take care. Even with John, twenty years, the small fear remained, each time he touched her. Sometimes it was so small, a speck at the bottom of a canyon, that she could pretend it wasn't there. But it always was, and she came to understand that she needed it; she was grateful for it. It was the small fear that held her body together and kept her from flying completely wild and perhaps shattering. She was more afraid of what she might do, how she might be, without her small fear, her amulet, the pea under the mattress.

Vera raised her head. There was still some work to finish before she could leave. Would they wait? They were accustomed to her arriving promptly at five-fifteen. She hurried through her papers, especially careful with the account sheets, though, with Will so angry. It would be disastrous if she messed them up, and Will told Howard, and Howard began watching. There were still the hospital bills, Jean's contact lenses, Freddy's moped. . . . At last she was finished and dashed out, not even bothering to wash her face or fix her hair, which had fallen again and hung loose down her back. Let it. It didn't matter, with Brauer and Elemi.

It was nearly five forty-five when she reached the park entrance.

They were still there, thank heaven, sitting on a bench in the shade. Elemi preferred the shade. Vera stopped in relief, panting. She had run all the way. When Brauer and Elemi saw her they rose instantly, joining hands, and began their early evening stroll. Of course they had to wait, Vera realized as the slow walking calmed her senses. They are not real, they are mine. They can only do what I make them do. She laughed to herself, thinking of how foolish she had been to worry. They could not go off alone. They would always be there for her, and would do only what she wished and permitted, for they were her own invention.

Brauer was especially gentle towards Elemi this evening. He stroked her hand and picked out the softest, greenest patch of grass for her to sit on. When she twisted her ankle scrambling up a rock he rubbed it tenderly between his palms to ease the pain. Elemi tossed her head back, her long fair hair streaming out on the breeze, and looked up at Brauer with a gaze full of trust and gratitude. Tears came to Vera's eyes at the sight of them together.

Jean got her first real job, as a junior counselor at a summer camp in Maine. "What are you going to do on your vacation, Mom? Freddy will be working on the Cape, and you'll be all alone." They were drinking coffee together after dinner. Vera lit a cigarette and waved the smoke away from Jean, towards the open window.

"I don't know. Probably stay home and take it easy."

"You really ought to do something, Mom. You never go anywhere. You could visit Uncle Matt on Fire Island. They always ask you. Or take a trip. San Francisco? You've never been out West."

"Maybe. I'll see."

The apartment was lonesome with Jean gone, but once Vera was on vacation everything would be different. She had known for weeks what she wanted to do. The last evening after work, rather than leaving them on a park bench while she went dutifully home, she brought them right along with her: out the West Side entrance, down the street, into the lobby, up in the elevator. Brauer and

Elemi, as usual, were serene, undisturbed by the change. They had been so many places that new adventures did not intimidate them. Vera's hand trembled as she fit the key in the lock. She was overcome with shyness. Should she speak? Welcome them with some joking remark? She decided definitely not. That would be going too far.

"Well, here we are," she muttered to herself. She kicked off her shoes, turned on the air conditioner, fixed a gin and tonic, and flopped down in an armchair in an ecstasy of relaxation, solitude, and freedom.

Brauer and Elemi passed a quiet evening browsing through the books on the shelves, playing Mozart on the stereo, childishly exploring the bedrooms, Jean's, Freddy's, Vera's. As for Vera, it was the most beautiful evening she had spent in years, with nothing to be done, alone and yet not alone. She lay back in her chair listening to the music while they wandered about the apartment hand in hand, and she thought of all the things the three of them would do on her month off. They would go camping in Newfoundland, surfing on the beaches of Hawaii, ambling down the stone streets of Florence in the shadow of the great cathedral, strolling in tranquillity through the rock gardens of Kyoto. It was a summer of endless possibility.

At last Vera decided to go to bed: she was very tired. Brauer and Elemi could settle down anywhere they pleased—there was plenty of room. It was warm out and the air conditioner was not working well; she stripped off all her clothes and went to bed without a nightgown. She smoked a last cigarette as she did the daily crossword puzzle, then turned off the bedside lamp. The dark seemed to make the room warmer and almost fragrant, as if there were flowers not far off. Her body felt light and smooth under the cool sheet. She remembered John and ran her hand over the sheet on his side of the double bed. It was odd how little she dwelt on John. She had thought about him so much when she was sick in the hospital that now there seemed nothing left to think about. She didn't even miss him particularly anymore, though it had been better to sleep with him than alone. She had missed him so much during the months of his dying that now there was no missing left in her. She missed only the feeling of missing him.

Sometimes, from her great distance, she wondered if she had ever loved him. What was love? What did it feel like to love? Could real, flesh-and-blood people walk around forever holding hands, with stars in their eyes, like Brauer and Elemi? Of course not. They had to work, shop, prepare dinner, raise children. Her marriage, she judged, regarding it from her great distance, had been neither very unhappy nor very happy. It had been dull. Naturally there was a first flush of enchantment, but when that paled, it was dull, there was no use pretending otherwise. And even in that first flush of enchantment it had not been as beautiful as Brauer and Elemi. They had never gone places or done exciting things. Vera had had dreams but John was practical, and she was afraid to burden him further with her dreams. She was even a little embarrassed by them, next to his practical ways. Probably she had loved him, she decided. She had always behaved like a loving wife. Perhaps real love was dull.

She was just falling asleep when she sensed that Brauer and Elemi were in the room. Strange, she had not noticed them enter. Brauer had his hands on Elemi's shoulders. He pulled her towards him, clasped her tightly, and kissed her long on the mouth. Vera was surprised, and a trifle amused. Aha, she thought. So they are not such innocents. Elemi's arms closed around Brauer and she began caressing his back. Brauer bent and buried his face in her neck, roughly, and Elemi, her eyes closed, leaned her head back and gasped. Her fingers were taut and clutching at him. Vera's eyes began to pound. No, she thought in panic. Not yet. But they didn't stop. They sank down to the floor, where Brauer helped Elemi pull off her shirt, then put his lips to her breast. Elemi had her small white hand on the inside of his thigh. Vera shut her eyes tight but the vision remained. There was no way to get rid of them. Not yet, she tried to scream, but no sound would come. She felt herself grow inflamed, blood pounding and rushing to every surface. You want to see it, she whispered angrily. You know you want to see it. Yes, all along she had secretly wondered why, if

they were so in love, they never made love. They must have done
it behind her back, like naughty children. Why were they showing
her now? Why now, she wanted to scream at them. But of course
they would not hear. The pounding of her blood was unbearable.
Her eyes were hot and every inch of her skin ached as she
watched, for now they were intertwined in another long kiss, arms
and legs groping, seizing. Vera placed a hand beneath her heart to
calm herself, but the warm touch only made the throbbing worse.
If it kept on she would soon burst from her skin.

Furious at herself, she snarled, If you want to see it so badly
then take a good look. They were completely naked now. Vera
cried out in fright—Brauer was so strong and hard, Elemi so white
and frail. His fingers disappeared between her legs; Vera's spine
jerked in a spasm of terror. Elemi seemed nearly faint in her aban-
don. In the park so pretty and childlike, now she had her legs
spread apart, with her arms clinging around Brauer's neck and her
open lips reaching for his. Then he was on top of her. Vera stiff-
ened. Don't hurt Elemi, she whispered. Don't. Don't hurt. He
began to push. She could see Elemi's face very clearly, the tight
tendons of her arched neck, the trembling bluish-white of her eyelids, her mouth open as if in shock. Sweat glistened on Elemi's
forehead. Brauer kept pushing, merciless, rhythmic. Elemi's face
was so strained and twisted, Vera could not tell if it was misery or
joy. Her own body began moving up and down in rhythm with
Brauer's pushing and she could not stop it. No, not yet, she cried,
but she was powerless to stop herself or them. They had escaped
her. She had escaped herself.

On and on Brauer pushed—would he never stop? Vera ached to
know what Elemi was feeling, poor Elemi, straining with him,
pounding up and down on the floor so hard her frail body made a
soft thudding sound. Was that wild face twisted in misery or joy?
Somewhere within her she remembered that Elemi could feel only
what she wished her to feel, yet Vera was powerless, caught in
their unstoppable rhythm, for she could not choose between misery or joy. Brauer kept pushing, and Elemi's face kept the terrible

riddle, till Vera herself finally erupted from the inside out, shattering the air around her.

When it was finished she leaned back weakly and wiped her streaming brow with the back of her hand, amazed to have survived. Her body was utterly limp and exhausted, but when she focused her eyes she saw that they, the dream, strained on. Still he pushed without respite and still she thudded beneath him. They would never stop.

OVER THE HILL

I'm not sorry. I couldn't help it, the way she was acting with Pat. My mother, who is a draftsman (or draftsperson) in an architect's office, and Pat, who is an art teacher, somehow got the idea that they could make a lot of money on the side doing bartending at fancy parties. So they're taking a short course, one night a week. They both need the money. Pat is divorced also, and has two children to support.

Pat came over after supper with a shopping bag full of equipment, shakers and strainers and stirrers that she said she had picked up wholesale on the Bowery. "I felt like a bag lady," she said, "carrying this around all afternoon." My mother had stopped off at the liquor store on her way home from work. She lined up bottles on the table till our kitchen looked like a saloon. Then they put on their glasses and opened their notebooks, and practiced making these weird concoctions, Sloe Gin Fizzes, Sidecars, Sombreros, Margaritas, Harvey's Wallbangers, etc.

I was sitting and watching them, but not really paying attention at first. What I couldn't get out of my mind for some reason were those pregnant women I saw on the street yesterday. I swear, practically every woman on the street was pregnant—every age, race, religion, and creed. Some were already pushing strollers with babies. There was one blond girl in a long floaty Indian dress and hanging earrings. I thought she looked something like my mother might have looked years ago, and she was holding hands with this neat-looking guy with a red beard and a yellow checked shirt. I wondered if he was the one who made her pregnant. I even tried to imagine them, but as usual I was unsuccessful. If I ever get pregnant I plan to stay indoors the entire time, not only because of the way I would look, which is reason enough, but more because a pregnant person is living evidence that she actually did that with a man. Even though my mother claims everyone does it, everyone doesn't have to go around advertising it.

I went into my mother's room late last night when she came home from her date with James Wertheim, her new boyfriend who is a lawyer. I wasn't exactly waiting up, I was going over my social studies for the midterm. I am too old to have a babysitter—I am a babysitter myself—but I do like to know she is there when I go to sleep. I mentioned about seeing all the pregnant women and she said, "Oh yes, that's nothing unusual. They hibernate in winter, then they come out in spring." Obviously she didn't get my point, which is that it is unusual to see them all in one day. Anyhow, from pregnancy we drifted on to the subject of abortion. My mother's opinion was that under certain circumstances abortion might be a good idea. "Try to understand, Jodie. What if it happened to you? I don't mean right now." She laughed a sort of awkward laugh. "But when you were, oh, eighteen or nineteen and going to college or something, and unprepared for it." She stopped in the middle of getting undressed and sat down on her bed. It was kind of funny but nice, her sitting there in her bra and panty hose in the middle of the night, talking so earnestly about this topic.

I told her that in my opinion abortion is basically murder. I don't see how you can get around that. "Anyhow," I said, "it couldn't happen to me."

My mother crossed her legs in the lotus position and smiled. She is rather small and has a youthful figure for her age, as you would need to have to get in that position. (She is thirty-four, over the hill, despite her appearance.) "What do you mean, it couldn't happen to you?" she said. "It could happen to anyone."

I suppose she ought to know, since it happened to her in her senior year of college. Sometimes she says I am the most important person in the world to her. Usually it's after she's gotten disgusted with some man she thought was great but then didn't call her, or who turned out on closer inspection to be not so great. My father has pretty much dropped out of our family group. He used to write me from New Mexico but I haven't had a letter in several months, not even for my birthday last Monday, although I understand the mail is very slow these days.

"It couldn't happen to me," I repeated. "It just wouldn't."

She tossed her head back and laughed in this special way she has—she sort of shakes her hair, which is short and naturally curly, and her big hoop earrings shake too. (We had our ears pierced together just a year ago for my twelfth birthday—she was scared to death, I had to hold her hand.) Then she patted my head like I was a baby that had made an extremely amusing statement, and said I better get to sleep since I had two midterms the next day. She even wanted to come and tuck me in but I reminded her I was a little old for that.

Well, to return to tonight, there they are, she and Pat, having themselves a fine time fooling around with their shakers and glasses like kids playing tea party, the way my mother used to do with me.

"I can't drink all this garbage," my mother announced. "No one drinks this stuff anymore. I'm going to make myself a nice martini and sip along as we work."

"I'll sample," said Pat. "I've always had an experimenting nature."

"Why do you have to practice making all those drinks if no one drinks them anymore?" I asked.

"We have to do what the teacher says," my mother answers. She and Pat find this remark highly droll. They are old friends from high school and laugh at everything the other says as though they are a TV comedy team. It's true that Pat is a lot of fun to have around, as my mother says, but I get the impression she doesn't quite realize she is over the hill. She's very tall and has long auburn hair and wears fancy pants suits and silk shirts and scarves. She chain-smokes and laughs a lot and talks constantly, and she seems to bring out a silly streak in people around her. My mother is basically a more quiet type, and wears jeans with turtleneck sweaters and junk jewelry and clunky Frye boots. (She paid eighty-five dollars for those boots, incidentally, and bought me a fake pair for only thirty-two.)

"Now, do you serve this straight up or on the rocks?" Pat asks, holding up this shaker full of some yellowish stuff. Straight up means with no ice.

"Wait, I'll have to check my notes." In the midst of their giggling they had to keep putting on their glasses to check things in their notebooks. My mother wet the tip of her finger to turn the pages, which is another sign of age.

"On the rocks, it says. Wait, hold it, that's much too many rocks, Pat. Get some of those rocks out."

"I don't think there're too many."

"Come on," my mother says, "off with those rocks."

"I beg your pardon," Pat says, laughing. She is poking around at the ice cubes in the shaker with a long spoon, trying to get a few out. "You can't have too many rocks. I distinctly remember him saying that, Barbara."

"Like the Big Rock Candy Mountain," my mother says. "'Oh, the buzzing of the bees in the cigarette trees,'" she starts to sing.

"'Get a piece of the Rock,'" Pat sings.

"'Rock of ages, cleft for thee. Let me hide—'" But my mother has to stop singing, as they are both collapsing with laughter and Pat's rocks are melting all over the kitchen table. At this point I opened my math book and tried to do some homework, though there was not much room left. Besides being wet, the table was cluttered with pink and yellow and grayish concoctions in different-shaped glasses. I forgot to mention that they were both helping themselves to everything in sight. They said they had to, to see if they were coming out right.

"Do you have to be so noisy?" I said. "I'm trying to concentrate."

"Oh, Jodie is disapproving again. Do you feel left out, Jodie?" my mother said. "Wait, I'm going to make you something you can drink. Something spectacular, just for you."

"I don't like that stuff. It smells bitter."

"This won't be bitter." She put her glasses on again and flipped around in her notebook, then she poured a little bit of some really pretty green stuff over a shaker of ice, added cream and sugar and a few other things, put a big silver shaker on top, and began to shake it up.

"Remember, he said to shake very vigorously, Barbara," said Pat.

My mother shook harder. She looked like she was doing some kind of tribal dance, jiggling that thing up and down, and her whole body and her hoop earrings jiggling along with it.

"Watch out for your rocks, they could fall out," Pat said. "Did you remember to put in Frothee?"

"What's Frothee?" I asked.

"Frothee," my mother told me, still dancing around, "is this wonderful milky-white substance that spurts out of a little plastic container. On the table there, see? It's a magic fluid that makes everything it gets into creamy and yummy." Pat is again going into fits of laughter.

"I don't see what's so hilarious about Frothee," I said.

"Oh, you will," said Pat. "You will."

Finally my mother finished shaking and poured this beautiful thick light-green drink with a nice creamy top into a cocktail glass. "Here, try this. It's called a Grasshopper. But take small sips."

"Will it be bitter?"

She sipped it herself and smiled and twinkled her eyes at me over the rim of the glass. "Why don't you risk it?" she said.

It smelled light and minty, so I tried it. It was fantastic, like mint ice cream, not bitter at all. I must say, about my mother, that when she makes an effort she can really do things well.

"Is it good?"

"Not too bad." I drank some more. It felt smooth going down, like a malted with a little sting.

"Now, Jodie," said Pat, "for our next act I am going to demonstrate the wonders of Frothee, on the rocks." She studied something in her notebook for a couple of minutes, then filled her shaker with rocks, poured from a couple of bottles, and held up the little plastic container. "I squeeze the container gently," she said in this funny accent, like a foreign magician, "I squirt in three or four drops, and abracadabra! Whoosh!" She began to shake the mixture very vigorously. Since she is so tall the whole kitchen seemed to shake with her.

I didn't want to interrupt her performance to tell her that when she squeezed the white stuff out it reminded me of those spitters I had been passing all day. Spitters are mostly old men with baggy pants and dangling shoelaces, but on occasion you will see boys in tight jeans and leather jackets doing it (who will probably grow up to be old men with baggy pants and dangling shoelaces). What they do is, they sort of jerk their heads back and make this choppy gurgling noise in their throats like a car engine trying to start in cold weather, then flip their heads forward and shoot the stuff sideways out of the corner of their mouths, if they have any decency left aiming it off the curb. If you are watching closely you can see the gob shoot out and land in the street, where it makes a splatter and then lies there in a sunburst pattern till a car or bus comes along and rides over it. Naturally this is not the most pleasant thing to see, especially first thing in the morning on the way to two midterms, and I had the good fortune to run into quite a few, both going and coming. What bothers me most about the spitters is that they have no self-control whatsoever. It is also called expectorating. My mother and I have this routine that began last year when

we saw a funny sign about it in a bus terminal. Since then whenever we see a person doing it one of us whispers, Don't Expectorate if You Expect to Rate, and the other one answers, Don't
Expect to Rate if You Expectorate. I realize it is extremely corny
but for some reason it makes us crack up.

Anyhow, Pat was doing this flamenco-type dance as she shook
the drink, and my mother was clicking her fingers and providing
background music. It did come out very frothy, I must admit. I
think it was a Brandy Alexander. Needless to say, they went into
ecstasies over the way it looked. When they calmed down I asked
my mother if she would make me another Grasshopper, but she
said no, one was quite enough.

"But I don't feel anything."

"Absolutely not. You're still a child. Do you want to get
drunk?"

"You're the ones who are drunk. I really believe you two are
drunk."

"Oh, Jodie, come on. I haven't even had the equivalent of two
drinks. When have you ever seen me drunk? That child is so strict
with me," she said to Pat.

"Well, you're both acting so silly," I said.

"What is wrong with having a little fun?"

So I shut my mouth and went back to the math homework.

Pat took off her glasses and laid them on the table, then leaned
back in her chair and blew out a long puff of smoke at the ceiling.
She suddenly seemed very tired, and she waved her arm in a tired
way over the table full of half-empty glasses. "What are we going
to do with all of this? It's a pity to waste all our efforts."

"Listen," my mother said. "I have an idea. I can call James and
ask him if he wants to come over and drink some of it. Maybe he
can bring that friend of his I told you about, Sam Larkin? The
reporter. They live on the same block. You would like him, I
think."

"Oh, I don't know. I'm not dressed or anything."

"You look fine, Pat. It'll be fun."

"Well, I don't know."

"Every encounter is not a major thing. Look, you don't have to marry the man. I'm only suggesting that they come over for a drink. Informal, friendly, no big deal."

"Oh, all right," Pat said. "I'll have to use your hairbru h, though. I left mine home."

So my mother went to the living room to phone James, and they arranged that he would ask Sam and call back in a few minutes to let her know. While she and Pat sat around waiting for his call this jittery feeling crept into the air, like they were two kids waiting for their first date. One of them would make a remark and laugh a little, then it would die down and the creepy silence would come back. To pass the time they sipped from the drinks lined up on the table, first one then another, as if it didn't matter which.

"What is he like, anyway?" Pat asked.

"Who, James or Sam?"

"James."

I took my homework into the living room and shut the door, because if there is one thing I cannot stand, it is to hear grown women sounding like the high-school seniors who have taken over our pizzeria. They are both revolting, but at least the seniors are going through a normal phase for their age. I could still hear everything through the door, though. My mother told her how intelligent, good-natured, witty, etc., James was. Prince Charming himself, except for the horse. "Still, he's very reserved about some things," she said. "His privacy is important to him. I get the message that I shouldn't push anything. Not that I want to. I feel the same way myself."

"How about in the rocks department?" Pat asked, and she laughed.

"Pat, honestly, you must be looped."

"You're blushing, Barbara. Well, how about Sam? What is he like?"

Since my mother had only seen Sam twice there wasn't much to say, fortunately, as I was becoming sicker and sicker. After all, they are supposed to be mothers, though you'd never know it. First they spend the whole evening fooling around and drinking, with no self-control whatsoever, then they arrange this date, which will probably turn out to be a drunken orgy, music and laughing and everything, and I will have to go to my room to avoid it, then Sam will take Pat home and James will want to stay over and my mother will feel funny about it because of me, but in the end she'll let him, and I'll hear them whispering in her room, and in the morning he'll be gone before I get up and my mother will have that bright rosy but slightly guilty look, eyeing me like she's thinking, I dare you to say one word about it, and I'll go to school feeling all alone in the world and to top it off I will most likely meet a few dozen spitters along the way, not to mention pregnant women, since spring is almost in full bloom.

So when the phone rang about ten minutes later I dashed to get it first. My mother had taken Pat into the bedroom to give her the hairbrush and show her the new Frye boots.

It was James. He made his usual awkward attempt to be friendly, then said, "Can I speak to your mother, please?"

"Oh, she went out to meet some people. She just left."

"That's funny. I was supposed to call her back and come over with a friend."

"Yes, well, she got another call meanwhile and rushed right out. I think she was tired of waiting. Sorry."

There was a long pause. "I see. My friend's line was tied up before. Will you tell her I called, please?"

My mother appeared then. "Is that for me, Jodie? I'm expecting a call."

"Okay, 'bye," I said. "See you," and I hung up fast. "It was just Jennifer about the math homework." Jennifer calls every other night about the math homework.

"Oh." She looked like she was shrinking right before my eyes, very small and sad. "Well, listen, don't tie up the phone. James might call. He might be coming over."

They went into the kitchen again. It was very quiet. I could hear the glasses clinking on the table every now and then. Pat said, "Did you know Lisa had an abortion?"

"No! How awful."

"It wasn't so bad. She had broken up with him weeks before."

"Still," said my mother. "I'm glad I never had to. I don't know if I could."

"You've never . . ."

"No. Just lucky. Also careful."

Long silence.

"What do you suppose happened to them?" Pat asked.

"I don't know."

"Maybe the signals got crossed or something. Why don't you try again."

"Oh, all right. I don't like to but I will." She came into the living room and dialed. I watched her. Her shoulders slumped as she wound the cord round and round her wrist like a bracelet. I got a little scared, but it turned out to be a false alarm. "There's no answer," she told Pat back in the kitchen.

"Maybe he's on his way."

"I doubt it. He's not like that. He would have called first."

"Something must have happened."

"I'll wash out these shakers," my mother said. I heard water running for a few minutes, then silence again.

"I thought you and he were getting along so well," said Pat.

"So did I. You never know what they're thinking. They're so peculiar, all of them. Maybe he didn't like the idea of my asking him on the spur of the moment, or of asking Sam. Who the hell knows."

"There must have been a mix-up. Don't you think you ought to try once more?"

"Pat, I don't want to call again, all right? I'm going to make some coffee. I don't like those fancy drinks. I'm getting a headache."

"You're upset."

"No, it's nothing. I just thought it was different. . . . I'm sorry about Sam."

"Don't be silly. I never even met him. I'm sorry about . . ." Finally Pat said she'd help clean up. "We might as well throw all this in the sink, right?"

"Yes, go ahead. I'm certainly not going to drink it. Jodie," she called, "you should be going to bed, you have the dentist tomorrow." Then she said to Pat, "I wish I had never thought of calling, then this wouldn't have happened."

"Don't get so upset. He'll probably turn up tomorrow with some perfectly reasonable excuse."

"That's the whole trouble," my mother said. "They always have wonderful excuses."

They drank their coffee and finished cleaning up and Pat left. I kissed my mother good night and went to bed. She didn't look like she was in the mood for talking.

This incident is actually no big deal. I mean, James will call again sooner or later, I suppose, and then it will all come out. My mother will be furious, and when she's through yelling at me she'll calm down and explain for the twentieth time how she's not over the hill yet and wants some fun out of life, but don't I know I'm still the most important person to her. And I guess I will feel rotten. Still and all, a person has to make some effort to keep things under control and I'm glad I did, even if it was only for one night. Because with kids it's different, I mean, that is why they're kids, but if grownups don't act their age who is going to keep any kind of order in the world?

THE ACCOUNTING

Ron, my accountant, came over one morning to review our records of the six-month period just past. Usually I go to his office because I don't like a lot of people coming to the apartment, but I was recovering from mononucleosis—brought on by overwork, the doctor said—and was supposed to take it very easy.

Since it was Sunday, his day, Ron explained, he had brought along his five children from various marriages. They were four boys and a girl, which puzzled me. I had had the impression that his children were all boys. But the girl called him Daddy, so I must have been mistaken. He called her Erica or Angela; he introduced us in his customary offhand, mumbling manner, so that I couldn't quite make out whether he said Erica or Angela. Erica or Angela was wearing a dress, and that was puzzling too: all the girls I see out my window nowadays wear jeans or shorts. It was a white sundress with tiny blue and yellow flowers and a wide sash. A trifle short for this year, but at her age that hardly mattered.

Very delicate, very girlish. A throwback to an earlier day. I might have had a dress like that. The girl's long scrawny arms and legs stuck out plaintively from the pretty dress, and her light-brown hair needed washing and was not well combed. She looked like a girl without a mother, a girl dressed by a well-meaning amateur, although according to my accountant she did have a mother, a most attentive one. Three of the boys were dark, ruddy, and robust, wore red shirts, and smiled a lot. The fourth resembled his father: reedy and tall for his age, very pale, with straight rust-colored hair, full lips, and inquisitive, cunning green eyes. All the children seemed about five or six years old, though surely that was impossible. No, not impossible if they all had different mothers. Yes, impossible, if my accountant had been married to each of the mothers in succession, as he claimed. I would have liked to ponder this mystery for a while, being a writer of mysteries, wildly successful ones; it is precisely such anomalous little gems that shatter into stories when handled. But real life was trotting along with its demands: I led the hungry pack into the kitchen and gave them juice and cookies, and then we settled down, my accountant and I, spreading our papers on the dining room table rather than in my study down the hall, so we could keep an eye on the children. I poured him some coffee.

He put on his silver-rimmed bifocals and peered at me over the top. "They'll be very quiet," he said with his diffident smile. "They're good kids. I had no choice."

"I don't mind. I'm used to it."

That was automatic politeness. I am not used to small children around the house anymore. I have children myself, twin sons, but they are grown up, in college now, and quite able to take care of themselves. They have not been around the house for a very long time. My husband took them and left, years ago, when it became clear that I was choosing perfection of the work rather than of the life. True, I was a good provider, he said, but he needed more than that. Warmth, companionship.

From the dining room table I could see into the kitchen where the three ruddy robust boys were playing cards. Go fish or rummy—they each held seven cards. A little young for cards, weren't they? Well, my accountant was noted for his crafty intelligence. It shouldn't surprise me that his children were the same. The slender, pale boy who resembled his father was drawing an abstract, geometric design with crayons on a sheet of white paper, and the girl was breaking off pieces of her cookies and eating them in minuscule bites, staring straight ahead with a sly, ruminative expression. Her oily brown hair fell over her cheeks, and every now and then she wiped her fingers on it. I could give her a napkin, I thought, but we were in the middle of a technical point about foreign sales, and besides, she seemed like the kind of little girl who would not willingly accept a napkin, who preferred using her hair.

For about fifteen minutes he explained and advised while I nodded soberly and assented, but I was distracted by a rumbling noise, like heavy things being moved some ways off. All week long, outside in the hall and on the landings, men had been installing and painting new window frames. They must have to work on Sundays too, in these inflationary times. I used to work on Sundays myself before I got sick, not out of financial need but out of compulsion—a frenzy to make up for years when I hadn't worked at all. There was also a muted sound of footsteps, most likely on the roof—I live on the top floor. Lately men had been up there adjusting the television cables, and on warm spring mornings like this one, some of the younger tenants go up to sun themselves.

Suddenly a high and pathetic wail pierced the air. We dashed into the kitchen and found the little girl huddled in a corner between the refrigerator and a china closet, hugging her arms close to her body. Her face was screwed up in despair, and as she wailed she stamped one foot rhythmically on the floor.

"What is it? What is it, sweetheart?" my accountant cried, rushing over and taking her in his arms.

I sensed something specious about her wails. Having had children, I am a connoisseur of their cries. These had erupted too suddenly and at too high a peak; they had been aimed too carefully in our direction. The stamping foot wore a white anklet and a

black patent-leather Mary Jane. It looked odd, like some lone, detached thing pounding obsessively, like a heart in a researcher's jar.

"I want to go home," she wailed. "I don't like it here. There's
nothing good to eat." She rolled her eyes towards me accusingly.

"Didn't you like those cookies?" I asked.

"No. They were disgusting."

I looked over at the table. Her cookies were gone and in their
place was a perfect ring of golden crumbs. The other children,
oblivious of her wails, were still absorbed in their card game and
abstract drawing.

"But you ate them."

"I didn't realize they were disgusting till after I ate them." She
rolled her eyes again, with her head slightly tilted. A very knowing, almost decadent glance. For a moment those were the eyes of a
forty-five-year-old woman, cannily assessing her power.

"What a silly thing to say," said my accountant. "That makes no
sense at all, Erica." Or Angela. I could never quite make it out.

Her remark didn't seem so silly to me. I could remember feeling
the same way about several of my own experiences, though not
cookies. Her words and her mature glance interested me, and
while my accountant tried to soothe her and at the same time admonish her rudeness, I said, "I have apples. Maybe you'd like an
apple better. Also Doritos, but I happen to think they're disgusting. How about an apple?"

"I don't like apples. I happen to think they're disgusting too."
And then, after a brief struggle of the facial muscles, she finally
smiled unwillingly at her own absurdity. I smiled back. All three
of us began to laugh. But when she saw Ron and me exchange a
wry private look, the way grownups do at the caprices of children,
she stopped laughing and stamped her patent-leathered foot again.
In the distance, the rumbling, bustling noises got louder, and the
footsteps sounded closer.

"Now cut this out, Angela" (Erica?), Ron said, "and behave
yourself. There's not a thing wrong with you. This is all an act."

Slowly and deliberately the girl sank to the floor, sliding her
back against the refrigerator till her bottom hit the linoleum. She

hugged her knees to her chest, pulled her white flowered dress modestly around them, put her thumb in her mouth, and bent her head.

My accountant squatted down to her level. "Sulking is no fun," he said gently. "Wouldn't you rather read one of the books you brought along?"

The oily hair swung four times from side to side.

I was about to say something in defense of the cookies, Pepperidge Farm Capri, and really very good, when all at once there came muffled sniffs and sobs from behind us. The green-eyed boy who resembled my accountant was hunched over the kitchen table, weeping breathily.

"I can't believe this," Ron said. "They're usually so good. I can take them anywhere."

I shrugged. I tire easily these days and all I wanted was to get the accounting done with. Besides, I had a feeling that the girl, huddled on the floor, was peeking at me through her hair, waiting to see what I would do. The children might be in collusion, testing me in some way, but I had no idea how to behave to pass the test. There was nothing phony about the boy's sobs, though. My accountant must have felt that too: he sat down at the table, stroked the boy's head, and whispered something.

The three dark-haired robust boys continued to play cards, and I wondered what imminent scene they had in store. They might be triplets, yet my accountant had never mentioned having triplets, and it is the sort of thing one would mention, especially to someone who has had twins. They weren't identical—one's face was more round and merry, another had a faint cleft in his chin, and the arch of their eyebrows was not alike—but there seemed to be some visceral bond. When one smiled the others smiled too. They smiled in unison. They had the same mother, at the very least. Ten months apart? He had certainly kept her busy.

I went over to the weeping boy. "What's the matter? Can I do anything?" Not the cookies again? That would be too much.

The boy left his father's embrace and went to lean against the china closet near his sister, or half-sister, who didn't raise her head.

"I'm so unhappy. I have no one. My mother is away on vacation for three weeks and my father is on a business trip in Spain."

"Your father?" I turned to Ron. "Aren't you his father?"

"Yes, yes, of course," he said impatiently. "His mother just re-married, so he's a little confused."

"Well, don't you think you ought to straighten him out? After all . . ."

"He really knows, underneath. He's just saying that. Don't you know I'm your father?" he asked the boy.

"What's the difference who is, if everyone is gone?" With moist green eyes and skin the color of ivory, his face appealed to me, as if imploring me to agree. I didn't know what to say. I couldn't tell if that version of his life was real or not. And no one but me seemed disturbed by those rumbling noises.

"But I'm not gone," my accountant said. He sounded hurt, lov-ing, and exasperated all at once. He took the boy's hand in his. "I'm right here. Aren't I with you right now?"

Turning his back on his father, the boy blinked away tears and told me, "My father's name is Juan Diego Cesar Romero de Cas-tellan. He's Spanish. From Spain."

Again I glanced at Ron.

"It's true." His eyes clouded. "She married a Spaniard. He likes to pretend it's his kid. Can you imagine? The nerve of him!"

"It's a very long name," I said to the boy, and I smiled.

He smiled back. His anguish seemed to evaporate. The gleam that had left his father's eyes reappeared in his. Once more he looked cunning and inquisitive.

"A *hidalgo*," I added, and immediately amended it to "An *hidalgo*," not pronouncing the *h*.

"What is that?" the boy asked.

"Oh, a fine gentleman. A knight, maybe."

The boy grinned, and with a nervous, adult gesture, ran his fingers through his russet hair. His lips curved in irony and a shadow passed over his face, accentuating lines and deepening hol-lows, so that I had a fleeting intimation of those places on the face where furrows would appear years later. It was a glimpse of him as an adult, with glasses and a smooth coppery mustache and a faintly weary look, like his father.

"Do you realize," I said to him, "that a minute ago you were crying because you were so unhappy, and now you're laughing at a silly joke? So you see, things pass." I felt foolish as soon as the words were out. It wasn't at all a useful sort of thing to say to a five- or six-year-old boy. On the other hand it was a superfluous and pompous thing to say to that wry, adult face.

"Are you feeling better now?" his father asked. "I've told you that you'll be with me. You'll be staying with me the whole time she's gone. All right? So why don't you blow your nose and draw some more pictures."

We returned to the dining room, to the work we had barely begun, but after a few moments the rumbling, bustling noises and the sounds of footsteps became so loud that I excused myself and started down the hall to investigate.

Three men in single file were walking out of my bedroom and towards the front door of the apartment. They were short, dark, thin men dressed in white painters' clothes and white caps, and their shoes were spattered with paint. My face froze. Then I remembered the long fire escape outside my bedroom window, and I understood. They must have been painting the outsides of the window frames and had used my open window to get back in, the quickest, safest way. They appeared harmless and left without noticing me. It was odd that I hadn't been told of this arrangement in advance, but odd things do happen in apartment buildings these days. Superintendents are lax and take liberties with long-term tenants. I was just beginning to breathe again, accommodating this oddness and planning to mention it to the super in a diplomatic but firm tone, when two more people emerged from my bedroom and headed for the front door. Young women, one black and broad-boned, with a large Afro, and one white and slender, with blond hair in a straggly bun. Each one wore patched blue jeans and leather boots and carried a cork board about a yard square. The black woman had a Mexican-style striped poncho over her shoulders. A moment later more painters entered, followed by more young women in jeans carrying cork boards, cardboard boxes, and shopping bags. I watched as a bustling traffic moved in and out of my apartment, the painters silent—gliding, it seemed—with their paint cans and brushes, and the young women lively and chattering, with an air of purpose.

My instinct was to call Ron, but I didn't obey it. No, this was my place and I would handle it on my own. I strode down the hall and into the bedroom. A painter was climbing out the window onto the fire escape. The two young women with the Afro and the straggly bun were in there also, with several others. In the center of the large, bare room were things I had never seen before—green velvet cushions with fringes, and tall brass vases or urns that looked vaguely Oriental and might have been used in a religious rite; they held peacock feathers. The women were moving these objects here and there, stepping back to observe the design, moving them again.

I should have accosted them right then, but I went to see what was going on in the outside hall. I think I wanted to see how far this strangeness extended. I hoped I was not hallucinating because of the mononucleosis. I hoped the strangeness was not confined to my apartment. For the first time in a long while I wanted to feel common cause with my neighbors. Form a committee. Fight this latest infringement on tenants' rights. I did feel relief of a sort when I opened the door. Painters, the ordinary painters I had seen all week, were working on the window frames with serene up-and-down strokes. Over near the elevator was a small crowd of very real young women, black, white, and Oriental, wearing colorful shirts and dangling beads. They carried folding tables, cartons, and bags filled with all sorts of merchandise—pots, jewelry, ceramic tiles—and they were clearly headed for my door. I realized that the strangeness had nothing to do with simplicities like inside or outside my apartment. It would extend as far as I could see. And where I could not see—well, that was like the tree falling in the forest.

I shut the door quickly and returned to the bedroom. Two

young women brushed past me, and their touch, slightly electrical, shocked a response out of me.

"What's going on here? What do you think you're doing? This is my bedroom, not a public thoroughfare!" I said it to the large black woman with the Afro and the Mexican poncho, who had an air of authority.

"Yes, we know that." She was bent over, rummaging through a carton, and barely looked at me.

"Well, then pack that stuff up and get out!" I managed to sound properly outraged, but underneath I was afraid. They kept unpacking their things as if they hadn't heard.

Then the black woman stood up straight and turned in my direction. She had a square, smooth face with regal cheekbones, and seemed limitlessly self-assured. Eyeing me, she pulled off her poncho and carefully folded it into smaller and smaller triangles. At last she spoke, with the forced and finite patience one uses with a nuisance. "This is the Annual Upper Manhattan Crafts Fair, and we're getting our stuff organized."

"You'd better get it organized and out right this minute! I've never heard of anything like this. A fair! It's a felony!"

She turned back to her work to show that the conversation was over. A few women began setting up folding tables between the vases and the green velvet pillows.

A wave of exhaustion swept over me, a common aftereffect of mononucleosis. Even so, I thought of grabbing one of the heavy brass vases and brandishing it at their heads. I didn't. As intruders, they might be armed. Their multipocketed jeans, their loose ponchos and Mexican sweaters and colorful Pakistani shirts with endless folds could easily conceal weapons. Daggers. Even the dense recesses of their abundant hair.

I stepped back into the hall. "Ron!" I called. "Come here quick and help me!"

A moment or so later my accountant ambled down the hall.

"What's all this?" he asked in his judicious way. Ron is not easily shocked. He works with money, after all, which represents human desire in its crudest form. For some clients he has managed to yoke into balance enormous fluctuations of investment and reward, that is, of desire and gratification.

"I don't know. It's a madhouse!" I waved my arms and babbled. "They say it's some kind of crafts fair, God only knows. But look! In my apartment! I mean—how can this be? Just get them out, will you?"

As I spoke, painters glided back and forth with their brushes and cans. They ignored the young women, a dozen or so now, who were setting things up on the folding tables. My bedroom is an airy corner room, twenty-four by thirty. That they had chosen it for their fair was really a supreme irony, because I had striven so hard all these years to keep it empty, for my fantasies. My mystery stories, I mean. The room has almost no furniture. In my mind I would use it as a blank stage. I would furnish it, and it would become the setting for any scenes I imagined.

Ron gazed into the bedroom and then off to the left, into my study, a small adjoining room where I had not even thought of looking. In there were my own cork bulletin boards with notices and clippings, my own work spread out on the desk and the studio couch. Also in there was a young woman I knew from down the street.

"That's Penelope!" I gasped. She was setting up a loom the size of a harp, which held a half-finished rug in brilliant reds and blues. Other rugs were piled on the floor, their bright colors peeking through brown paper wrappings.

"Oh, do you know that one?" asked Ron.

"Sure, she's a neighbor. A weaver." I chuckled. I had never before connected her name with her trade. "Penelope. A weaver!" I began to laugh uncontrollably. "Don't you get it?"

Ron seemed baffled, but he stared at Penelope with curiosity. I stopped laughing.

Penelope was tall and lithe, with a sheet of straight black shining hair. Her oval face was radiant, possessing a perfection of line seen in Renaissance paintings. Botticellian, but more earthy. She was perennially cheerful, the kind of person who predicts that the sun will shortly come out even on the grayest of days, which was why, though I couldn't help liking her, I avoided meeting her on the street, especially in winter. Her vivacious greetings in that pure, ringing voice were like a shower of ice pellets, and made the cold air crackle around my ears. She believed in raw sprouts and home-baked bread. She had put up Thank You For Not Smoking signs in the lobbies and elevators of all the buildings on the block. Often I had seen her from my window, setting out at dawn in her white satin shorts, not so much jogging as breezing to the park while a wan crescent of moon still hung in the sky.

Still, her presence was reassuring. The others might be her friends. She might have told them of my spacious bedroom, which she had been in once or twice when I was sick and she kindly brought over a jar of pills from the drugstore. The fair was still an outrage, but an outrage with links to the real world. The perpetrators could be dealt with in the usual ways.

"You take it easy. I'll go in and talk to her," Ron mumbled. "See what I can do."

He entered the study and approached Penelope with his guarded savoir-faire. She shone her cheerful countenance upon him and began to speak. Giving an explanation, I presumed—I couldn't hear above the bustle of painters and women. I stopped a young painter just climbing in the window. He had a pleasant face, obscured by an extraordinarily thick black mustache.

"Look here," I said quietly. "I understand that you have to be here because you're working. I wish someone had told me, but okay. But would you help me get rid of these other people? They have no business here. I don't even know who they are." He looked blank. "It's a crime. Don't you see? Trespassing."

He smiled a chilly, close-mouthed smile that altered the shape of his mustache, and replied curtly in a thick and unfamiliar language.

"I'm sorry, I don't understand. Don't you speak any English?"

"It's Greek," one of the young women told me. She was arranging a bouquet of huge paper flowers in a wine flask.

"Greek? Do you know Greek? What did he say?"

"He said he only works here. He can't get involved."

I tried several other painters but they all spoke Greek. If indeed it was Greek—how could I be sure? They gave the same answer; after a couple of times I recognized the syllables.

The black woman with the Afro, evidently a potter, unwrapped smoky-blue mugs and bowls and set them on a table with little cards stating their prices. A pair of women who looked like sisters, with berry-red cheeks and masses of savage black curls, hung silver chains with finely worked medallions from pushpins on a board. Another unwrapped small stained-glass plaques. So it went: from the cartons and shopping bags, as from a cornucopia, flowed batik scarves and silk-screened T-shirts, wall hangings, macramé plant holders, crocheted shawls and purses, embroidered carpet bags, leather belts and pouches, hand-painted ties—a tribute to the fertility of hand and eye. My bedroom abounded in life and color. I had to admit the fair possessed a certain chaotic beauty.

"Where's the grill?" the black woman called loudly, as she pulled a loop of raw pork sausages from a paper bag and held them high in the air. It was a loop so long I could have jumped rope with it. I was a champion rope jumper in my youth, and for an instant I wished I had kept it up, so I could be one of them and jump rope at their fair with the loop of sausages.

"It's outside in the hall. I'll get it," the blond woman said.

"Oh, no! That's the limit!" I tried unsuccessfully to block her path. "You're not doing any cooking in here! This is my bedroom!"

"Take it easy, lady." And she looked at me briefly with menace in her eye, but perhaps it was only indifference. It was clear they had no idea who I was. They didn't read, they did handicrafts. Or maybe they knew and didn't care. It was hard to imagine that they were Penelope's friends. Penelope had always been courteous and observed the proprieties. Surely she would have introduced them, asked permission . . . ?

I tried to see what sort of progress Ron was making. Penelope had spread out a few of her rugs, one over my typewriter. She was standing quite still, close to Ron, her arms hanging innocently at her sides, and was listening to him in a heartfelt and earnest manner. She was practically palpitating with earnestness. Ron was posed stylishly but a bit self-consciously with one foot up on my chair, a hand resting on his knee, and the other hand propped against the wall. Every so often he gave a shy shrug and a little laugh. Penelope smiled in her fresh, vibrant way, and made small humming nods of agreement, meaning, Oh yes, I understand perfectly. Oh yes, it's amazing, I've had exactly the same kind of experience.

The nerve of him! In my house and amid my calamity! On my time, *conquistador!* He worked fast; from this encounter could come another of those whining five-year-old children for me to feed cookies to. Who knows, maybe he was in collusion also. Maybe his coming over this morning had something to do with the crafts fair: he and his children, ah, those sly children, keeping me occupied while the women were slipping in. Of course! He hadn't been bothered by the noise when we were trying to work, he hadn't rushed to help when I called him, he hadn't seemed shocked by the crowd in my bedroom.

I wondered what Penelope, with her counterculture convictions, would think were I to tell her that Ron smoked, drank, ate all sorts of high-cholesterol foods, watched television avidly, called grown women "girls" and used phrases like "fresh flesh," loved money, had no scruples about devising artful tax shelters for big corporations, drove a gas-guzzling Lincoln Mark IV, had been a lieutenant in the army and was proud of it, etc. Most likely she would find sociological excuses and vow to take him in hand. Principles bend easily when mating is involved, I have noticed.

"What's happening?" I called to him sharply. "When are they getting out?"

He turned in surprise, as if he had forgotten all about me. "We're coming along," he said. "We're negotiating." Penelope giggled in a skittish way I wouldn't have thought her capable of.

I wheeled round to face the women. "Everybody out! Out out out!" I shouted as loud as I could. "This minute or I'm calling the cops." Not one of them paid any attention. I shoved into their midst and was about to fling their wares to the floor, but as one woman leaned over a carton I thought I saw something metallic glinting in the back pocket of her jeans. I was alone. They could finish me off in no time.

I would call the police, which I should have done at the start. But not here. On the kitchen phone. Suddenly I remembered the children, left alone for so long, and was sick with dread. Something terrible might have happened to the children. In a story it would have. It would fit right in with the aura of the bizarre and the sinister. What would I do? Ron might not even care—he had defected utterly. I had no hope of extricating him from Penelope's web. Maybe they were not even his children. Maybe they were just props.

In the kitchen all was serene. The three ruddy, robust little boys, sons of one mother, still played cards. Rummy. They had found pencil and paper and were keeping score. When they heard me come in they looked up and smiled in unison. Some children do have a knack of surviving, one way or another. My own did fine without me. The tall slender boy who resembled his father was drawing an abstract, geometric design with crayons on white paper. On the table were three sheets with the same design, colored in the same way. Odd. But children are odd. They do odd, repetitive things. Maybe he was practicing. It wouldn't be so odd if he played the same piece on the piano four times, would it, or repeated, four times, a poem he had to learn? Maybe there were subtle but crucial differences in the drawings, invisible to my casual glance. He seemed content, at any rate. The girl, Erica or Angela, was curled up on the hard floor near the garbage can, her thumb and a strand of damp hair in her mouth. She looked touching and vulnerable asleep, as children unfailingly do. I thought of moving her to a more comfortable place, but she was sleeping so peacefully I didn't want to risk waking her.

I explained to the voice that answered 911, the police emergency number, that my bedroom had been taken over by a band of craftswomen bent on holding a fair.

"Is there an immediate threat of violence?"

"Yes, of course, what do you mean, immediate threat? They're occupying my apartment and I can't get them out. Isn't that violent enough?"

"Is there a *physical* emergency? Are you being threatened with *physical* harm?"

"They might very well have weapons—daggers—how should I know? The point is . . ." And in a voice made thin and high by terror, I gave a cogent little speech on the term "violence," that violence need not always be physical, and so forth. It didn't seem to make any impression on the other voice, which told me to call my local precinct. I did, but the line was busy. I tried four times, at about two-minute intervals, and in between I watched the little boys' card game. They were cunning players. They would pick up cards they didn't need, to mislead the others. I envisioned them doing the same thing years from now, with gray in their hair and lines on their foreheads and big cigars in their mouths, but still smiling in unison.

My local precinct's phone was probably out of order. I walked back to the other end of the apartment. In the study, Ron and Penelope were sitting close together on my studio couch—they had pushed aside three piles of manuscript I had been collating. Their hands were entwined and resting on his thigh, and they played with each other's fingers while murmuring what appeared to be poignant confidences. In the bedroom, the crafts fair was ready. The handicrafts were attractively arrayed, and the green velvet cushions and tall brass urns lent elegance as well as an air of ritual. Happy salsa music came from a transistor radio someone had placed on the windowsill. Rows of sausages were spread on the grill, glistening brown and sizzling; the pungent smell rose, smoky, into the air. The women stood behind their tables proudly and expectantly. The painters had gone, leaving the front door wide open, and through it the public was beginning to arrive, sporting the countless permutations of age, race, size, sex, and garb. The members of the public were boisterous characters, brimming with life. They pushed past me into the bedroom and fanned out to greet what the fair had to offer.

I returned to the kitchen and to the children. I lay down on the floor near the garbage can alongside the little girl, Erica or Angela, and curled my knees to my chest. I dragged a strand of hair into my mouth. I was tired. I fell asleep.

I had a dream, and in it I was the woman I had been more than twenty years ago. I was lying in bed, cold. There were no mystery stories and no mononucleosis. There was no accountant, with no hungry whining children. Naturally—I had done nothing that was accountable. No young women and no crafts fair: I was the young woman, even younger than they, but I had no crafts I could display, yet. It was dark; no, palely dawning now, the darkness sifting into a grainy light. There was the husband I lay with in our bedroom, not twenty-four by thirty, not a place that could hold imagined scenes or a crafts fair, but a small room stuffy with sleep, and there were our ruddy twin infant boys in their cribs a couple of yards off, who would soon be waking, howling to be fed. Already the stench of urine from their drenched sheets rose, pungent and smoky, into the air. That would have to be attended to. My husband would need to be fed and attended to as well, for it was long before the era when he evolved sufficiently to attend to himself. I was still a nice young woman, and yet I wished they would all go away. I wanted the apartment empty.

The pungent smell woke me, not urine but sizzling pork sausages. I found myself on the floor next to Erica or Angela, and I wondered if the young, ruthless women who did not read but did handicrafts were still there, taking over my place, and if the public was still pushing into the space where I had dreamed my mystery stories (for them!) and which I had expected to keep as my private province. I had perfected the work at the expense of the life, and now I couldn't distinguish my fantasies from what was happening to me, or tell which was food for the other.

LIFE IS AN ADVENTURE,
WITH RISKS

That provocative title is a line I often heard tossed out by a memorable, soft-voiced professor who gave a seminar called Problems in Poetic Theory. He said he was quoting Santayana. He would use it, raising his eyebrows and tilting his balding head to one side, with students who were nervous and hesitant about delivering oral papers, or who were afraid to follow the implications of literary or philosophical theories to their logical, bitter ends. He was an astute, generous teacher, beloved by the class; I profited from his abundant wisdom. Except that leaving his seminar the last day of the term, I tripped on the stairs and lost the heel of my shoe. Limping down the street, I collided with a fire hydrant, fell off the curb, and broke my ankle, which needed to be set and bound: I had to stay off my feet for a month.

Recently, alone in a restaurant downtown, rummaging in my

purse for change to pay the check, I noticed that I had lost my eyebrow pencil because of a small hole in my make-up kit.

The loss of a lipstick or a Max Factor $2.99 compact would have meant nothing. These could be easily replaced in the Woolworth's across the street. But the eyebrow pencil had a curious history.

Years ago, I used the familiar shiny red Maybelline eyebrow pencil, until one evening a friend who worked in an advertising agency told me my eyebrows were too dark. She said a soft gray drawing pencil would do better; moreover, she had an ample supply at work. Why not? I said, and so she brought me one, about six inches long. She was right. The drawing pencil did give a much gentler, toned-down line, especially when I learned to use it correctly, in short light strokes. I sharpened the pencil occasionally, but never to a very sharp point, for that would destroy the soft line it made. Because I used it so sparingly, the pencil lasted a long time. It lasted fifteen years, and the day I lost it, it was an inch-and-a-half stub, still serving me well.

It sounds odd to say I missed an eyebrow pencil, yet I did, for it brought back those lost days when I was a young girl and my friend was sketching underwear ads and I was working as a laboratory assistant examining the legs of fruit flies under a microscope. Much later, of course, we both rose in the world. She became a sculptor and I became a copyright lawyer.

Anyway, while I sat in the restaurant brooding over all this in front of my empty coffee cup, I began idly to listen to the conversation at the table next to mine. A young girl of seventeen or eighteen with billowy strawberry-blond hair and a gentle rosy face was talking animatedly to a young man with a dark beard. She told him the following story of lost and found, which touched me and made me smile. I stayed to hear the end, even though the waitress glared at me with her impatient eye.

"Talking about contact lenses," the strawberry-blond girl said, "the craziest thing happened with my lenses last year. I'm not really careful with them, y'know, so one morning I was washing them to put them on over the sink in the bathroom. I was up so late studying the night before, for this history test, y'know, I could hardly keep my eyes open. Anyhow, what should happen but one drops right down the drain. God! I was even afraid to tell my mother, but, y'know, like, I had to.

"So I called her and said, 'Ma, my lens fell down the drain.' I never used to wear my glasses before I had the lenses. I had this thing, y'know, about how I look in glasses? But I got so used to seeing, with the lenses, I mean, that I didn't like not to see. So my mother comes in and tries to reach down the drain, my sister comes in and tries, but no luck. So I wore my glasses to school. I couldn't stand not seeing, once I was used to it, y'know?

"Anyhow, after I left, my mother, she's very mechanical, like, she takes the whole sink apart. And you know, she found it. I swear to God. So she wrapped it up and gave it to my sister and told her to take it to me in school. My sister didn't have a first-period class that day, so she left later, y'know?

"So my sister gets on the bus with the lens in her bag, and when she gets off at school there's this tremendous downpour. Cats and dogs. You could practically drown. So she bends down for something and one of her lenses falls out. I'm not kidding, can you believe it? They say it can't happen, but I'm telling you, it did. So of course in that rain, like, there's no use looking, so she comes into my room and asks the teacher, y'know, if she can speak to me for a minute. And she comes over and whispers, 'I have your lens but I lost mine.' So I said, 'What?' And she says, louder, 'I have your lens but I lost mine.' Well, of course I can't believe it, I mean, and soon all the people around me hear us, and then the whole class is breaking up, because she keeps saying, 'I have your lens but I lost mine.'

"Well, after school we both go home and tell my mother, and she says, 'You girls, stop it, you're driving me crazy with your lenses.' So anyway, the next day we go to school together, she's wearing her glasses this time, and when we get off the bus she says, 'This is where I lost my lens.' So I bend over the curb and I reach down and I pick up the lens, right there. I know, but it's true, I swear. I bent over and picked up the lens. I swear to God."

*   *   *

Some years ago I lost my underpants in the dressing room of a ballet studio.

I was taking a weekly ballet class. I wasn't very good at it, nor was it likely that I ever would be. But my aim was not to do it well, only to do it. I was approaching thirty and afraid the parts of me were beginning to slip and fall. I wanted something to hold my body together in reasonably good shape.

The ironic thing is that I hadn't always taken off my underpants for the class. At the beginning I used to pull my tights and leotard on right over them. Soon I came to see this was very unchic. Most of the others in the class—all younger than I, some teen-agers—took everything off. I wasn't inhibited by the modesty of an older generation. It was vanity that kept my underpants on. I felt I was too fat. Not a great deal fatter than the others, perhaps eight or ten pounds, but those pounds seemed to make an alarming difference in the dressing room. Ballet students are generally flat all over, and an unfair criterion for the average person. Still, I thought my naked self was too much, too much specific woman for our ascetic pursuit. Soft white bulging flanks belonged in a bedroom, not in this bevy of skinny chattering girls who, in their stages of undress, always reminded me of French academic paintings of mythological scenes. Except that these girls were bonier than nymphs.

Then I lost a lot of weight. Not through dieting but through secret heartache, much the easier way, since no conscious effort is required. I became thin enough, in my own judgment, to prance naked around the dressing room. No longer a Rubens, a Titian, a Veronese, I was more of a Modigliani. No one noticed me any more than before; I felt freed.

The sign on the dressing room wall said, "Carry your valuables with you," but I never imagined that "valuables" referred to underwear. Two or three weeks after I began stripping for class, I found the pants missing from the bench where we piled our clothes. I strode brazenly about asking if anyone had seen them. No one had. Fortunately I could wear my white ballet tights under my skirt—that was easy enough. But I would miss the pants: low-cut hip-huggers, white cotton with a scattering of small aqua flowers all about, a half inch of lace around each leg and at the waist. I had bought them as one of several rewards for my new-found slimness. My tribute to a loss was lost.

I lost an opportunity to have a lover.

It began in the Museum of Modern Art, a place where I invariably bump into long-lost friends. Standing in front of the Rousseaus, paintings which have always made me melancholy because they show a lost (or unfound) world, I felt a tap on my shoulder. An old friend. He and his wife and my husband and I had gone through law school together and married right after graduation. He had two small children with him. We sat in the garden and reminisced while the children threw pebbles into the water, watching the circles crest and disappear.

"They're getting restless," he said after a while. "I'd better take them home. Look, why don't you come back to the apartment with me and have a drink? It's only a few blocks."

"Of course. I'd love to see Anne again."

"Anne's not there. She's away for the weekend, at a conference in Pittsburgh."

"That's funny. So is Paul."

"The one on defending juveniles?"

"Yes!"

We both expressed more astonishment at this not unlikely coincidence than it really warranted.

In the apartment, large but modestly decorated, with lush hanging plants everywhere, we drank and strayed into a long, heady but not personal talk. I cannot remember what we talked about; it was the sort of abstract, fervent conversation that is quickly forgotten. Fusing Life, Goals, and Values like foods in a blender, it thickened, frothing and intense, resembling the late-night talks in college dormitories that are eventually supplanted by the pursuit of practical things.

At last my friend rose and came towards me. I assumed he meant to refill the glasses, and I stood up to help. But he took my arm, sat down in my chair, and gently pulled me down on his lap.

We kissed. It seemed quite easy and natural, though I had known him for years and never thought of him in this way. He was extremely thin. I have never thought of extremely thin men with desire. My feeling was pleasant, mild surprise. He placed his hand on my leg, under my skirt. We stood up.

"Let's go to the bedroom," he said.

"No," said I.

"What's the matter?"

"I can't."

He pulled me closer. "What's the trouble?" He asked it kindly, as if I might name something specific, like toothache.

"The children," I said.

"Oh," and he waved his arm vaguely in the direction of the playroom. I didn't know what that wave meant, exactly, but it seemed to dispose adequately of his children.

"I just can't."

We kissed again. I realized that considering my intentions I should have resisted. I felt no urgency—neither, I think, did he— only a warm limp tenderness, and a strong curiosity to see what would happen, as if I myself had no control over the outcome. It was a very warm, mellow day, and the air, from all his plants, had the rich smell of dank soil. Would he persuade me?

I was about to speak again—I shall never know what I might have said—when one of his children came galloping into the room, shouting and waving a doll with a severed leg that needed fixing.

He displayed great equanimity, this suddenly interesting man.

"Well"—he smiled, releasing me—"it looks as though even the children are against us."

We parted cordially. I was disappointed and immediately regretted not seizing that opportunity. What I regretted far more, though, was not telling him my reasons. They seemed too intricate to explain in the simplicity of his embrace. Yet no doubt I had left him with mistaken feelings of rejection.

My reasons were quite pragmatic. We—my husband and I— had decided it was time to have a baby. I had purposely had my loop removed, and last month we had devoted my calculated fertile week to fruitless attempts. Now the right week had come round again. We were conscientiously spending the nighttime hours, except for the two evenings he was away discussing juvenile crime, in pleasurable stabs at impregnation.

I couldn't risk having another man's child. A de Maupassant story flashed through my mind, in which the mother of three children tortures her husband by telling him that one child is not his, but refusing to say which one. It made me shudder.

However, the de Maupassant story really portrayed the opposite of my situation because my friend and would-be seducer was black. Under normal circumstances this fact would not have hindered me, indeed might have served as a spur. But just now it would never do. Should I become pregnant, the suspense of uncertainty, drawn out over nine months, would kill me. And the alternative, getting rid of the harmless, unidentifiable fetus, was equally intolerable. Of course had I been swept away by passion I would not have been able to calculate so clearly and rapidly, nor to envision the shocked faces, and the rest of my life spent in ambivalence, remorse, and pained maternal love, all of which absurdity flashed before me as they say drowning people relive their past in a brief instant. But I was not swept away.

It was distinctly inappropriate to explain this to a friend who was embracing me, gracious and simply frank about what he wanted, though he had had the same training in complex logistics as I had. Paradoxically, it would have spoiled the moment, which was pleasant, if abortive. As I left him I had a vague sense, not for the first time, that in the dynamic of my feelings, a small but important piece of machinery was missing.

I thought about him a lot in the weeks that followed, wondering what it would have been like, nursing an intense curiosity along with a tame desire. I even thought of calling him to explain, but it would be impossibly awkward to make that ludicrous speech over the phone. And then, Anne might answer. Ten months later, I was delivered of a beautiful baby girl. I lost my mammoth belly and gained a child. She took after her father. Looking back, I thought complacently, I had almost certainly done the correct thing.

When my daughter was four she needed to go to the hospital for a very simple operation to straighten an eye muscle. I trusted the surgeon and had no doubt that he could do a good job on her eye. But I worked myself up into a completely irrational state about losing her under the anesthesia. It seemed to me that such a small body, heavily dosed, would have to put up a tremendous struggle to climb through the layers of blanketing ether back up to consciousness. Like a drowning swimmer. Wouldn't she be more likely to slip away, from deep to deeper sleep, gone forever?

Even though I consulted three doctors about this—the eye surgeon, our pediatrician, and an anesthesiologist, all of whom told me it was quite the contrary: a young child with a healthy heart runs far less danger under anesthesia than an older person—I couldn't give up my crazy unscientific terror.

A few days before the operation I got my period, so strongly that I believed I must be hemorrhaging. I imagined all the blood draining from my veins and seeping out between my legs; soon I would be a bloodless, crumpled skin. The gynecologist was unimpressed by the dimensions of the problem as I described it over the telephone. It required, he said, no more than ice packs on the lower abdomen. I should lie in bed with my feet up on pillows.

We lay in bed, my husband and I, watching *The Maltese Falcon* on the *Late Show*. Every twenty minutes or so, during commercials, he would go to the kitchen to freshen my ice pack. Meanwhile, on the screen, the black bird was lost and several lives depended on its recovery. Brigid O'Shaughnessy disappeared and a strange man clutching his heart stumbled into Sam Spade's office, muttered a few words, and died. I felt a surge in my entrails and began to cry quietly.

"What's the matter?" my husband asked.

"I'm going to die from loss of blood."

"Is it still coming?"

I nodded.

"Look and see," he said.

I did. In fact, the bleeding had abated. I took two aspirins and at the end of the movie went to sleep cautiously, flat on my back with my feet up on pillows.

The operation was a success. Our daughter was composed and unafraid, so successfully had we strained to create an air of nonchalance. The only thing she complained of was the bandage over her eye. I told the doctor this when he came around hours later to check on her.

"That's all right. We can get rid of that."

And with a swift, experienced hand he reached out and deftly ripped off the bandage. I closed my eyes, dreading what I might see. When I opened them, the eye looked perfectly normal, except for a large squarish clot of blood floating near the outside corner, which he said would disappear in a few days.

Late one night several years later, I stood in my bedroom getting ready for bed. My husband was already undressed, stretched out full-length in the peculiar cut-down pajama bottoms he likes to sleep in. We were having a serious talk about whether to leave our daughter in the progressive school she attended, which stressed self-discovery and independence but was weak in the three R's, or to transfer her to a more traditional school which gave a solid background in academic subjects. There was something to be said for both; we each felt equally divided. I was taking my things off slowly, shoes, watch, beads, belt, skirt, panty hose, shirt, when it struck me that he was totally unmoved by the cool, evenly paced strip being performed right before his eyes. He was agreeing with the advantages of early self-knowledge, but questioning whether that emphasis might deter or postpone the development of necessary intellectual rigors—accuracy, thoroughness, and the like. We had to make a decision soon, yet I suddenly wished he would be sidetracked by passion, grab me, and pull me down to him on the bed. I could easily have seduced him from his worthy concerns, but I wished it to happen without words or gestures from me; I wished my bare presence to be irresistible. I put on a nightgown and sat down near him on the bed to weigh the issues.

I felt a wry sense of loss. Something shadowy, perhaps not terribly important in the long run, yet precious, was gone, irrecoverable and uncompensated.

We decided to transfer our daughter to the school that stressed academic subjects, on the grounds that a sense of identity with no external nourishment could grow like a choking weed rather than an unfurling flower.

I have always been a strong swimmer, and felt myself more a creature of water than of land. After my daughter learned to swim I used to take her out in the ocean with me, over her head, past the foam. I taught her how to ride the waves, how to surf in on them, how to dive through them, how to lie down and yield herself to them. At first I would grip her arm tightly when a wave came, and hang on no matter how I was tossed. Later on I let her fend for herself, still right by my side. When I surfaced I would find her immediately: she would always be laughing, her thick hair loose and sodden, her suntanned face glowing with drops of seawater. I was very careful when she went in the water by herself. On my blanket, or standing at the water's edge, I never took my eyes off her. I had been told the sea was dangerous. To me it was an ancestor, a refuge, a transcendent embrace. But out of duty, I watched.

Once when she was eight, she went floating on a rubber raft, on a beach with no lifeguard. I turned away for an instant, and when I looked back the raft had drifted too far out. She waved, having a marvelous time. I could see from the pattern of the waves that she was headed farther out. My husband and our friends said she would come in on the next wave, but they did not know the underside of the water as I did. I swam out to her, full of strength and power. Is it possible to be confident and terrified at the same time? The confidence and the terror merged, alternated, and contained each other's images, like those cheap iridescent rings our pediatrician used to give out for good behavior. From one angle you could see a grinning devil, from another a circus clown. If you turned the ring slowly enough you could see them simultaneously, and watch one change into the other.

I caught her and pulled her back to shore, still gleeful on her raft.

She never believed she had been in danger.

One day when she was ten I took her to the beach alone. As soon as we arrived she ran off, leaving me to spread out the blanket and arrange rocks, shoes, and our picnic basket at its corners, against the wind. This done, I looked up to find her running towards me, already soaking wet, gasping and crying. She was so breathless I could hardly understand her words.

"A big wave took me out and I couldn't get back."

"What do you mean?"

"I couldn't get back," she cried. "It pulled me out. It was like a whirlpool."

"But you're okay now. It's all right now. It couldn't have been so bad." I held her, and stroked the dripping hair away from her face.

"I couldn't get back!" She was so shaken that she didn't seem to realize she had gotten back. Yet the time had been so brief. I thought she must be exaggerating, as I often did myself.

We were near the water's edge, with my arms clasped around her. I saw the lifeguards coming towards us, in full force.

"Yes'm," one said. "She had a scare."

They were large and bronzed, and all three had golden hair, one crew-cut, one stylishly shaggy, and one with curls. All month I had watched them with benign amusement: big handsome boys with nothing to do, taking turns up on the chair, the off-duty ones playing cards on the sand. Each wore a tight bright-green bathing suit with white stripes down the sides and a conspicuous bulge in the front. They looked like Olympian gods; they chewed gum and tossed Frisbees; they were such blatant symbols of beauty and vigor, with those vivid innocent good-natured faces, that all the older women on the beach smiled involuntarily and knowingly at the sight of them.

"What happened?" I asked.

"It's a bad ocean today. There's a sea puss out there."

"A what?"

"A sea pussy. It sucks you in."

I have always been unable to keep from grinning foolishly at that kind of metaphor. Even when the electrician gravely refers to the plug and socket as male and female, I must consciously control my face. It seemed terribly inappropriate to grin right now. I tried to disguise my expression as friendly interest, also inappropriate, but less so. I became very aware of my mature, well-tended, ballet-sustained body.

"It caught her," he went on, "and swept her out. It's like a little whirlpool, the shape of the waves does it." He made a V with his hands. "It pulls you, and it's hard to get back. But she put up a terrific fight. She did it on her own."

"We were standing at the edge with the ropes," said another. "We were ready to go in after her. But we like to let them try to get out of it themselves, if they can. It's better for them, in the long run."

"She's a real strong kid," said the third. "Put up a real good fight." He glanced at her admiringly.

I thanked them. I was stunned. The sun beat down heavily. My joints were loosening, and I expected that my arms and legs might drop off and melt into pools on the sand.

"A sea pussy? Is that what you call it?" I asked sociably. Perhaps it was a joke.

"Yeah. Traveled all the way from Fire Island. Gonna be a bad day. Bad sea."

All day long the lifeguards ran into the surf, hauling people out with ropes, one end looped diagonally around their big bronze torsos like banners. Crowds gathered at the edge and listened to the exhausted survivors stammer their tales. Heroic and modest, the lifeguards made up for their summer of idleness. My amusement at them shifted to awe: they retrieved the lost.

Later in the afternoon I took my daughter into the sea once more so that she would not be forever frightened. She was happy in the waves; I was frightened. I had always wanted to die drowning, given that die we must one way or another. For me, going to water

would have been a return more than a departure. It would still be
the ultimate loss, but it would be a recovery too, perhaps of some
state of being that renounces the firm footing and yields to the tug
of the current. I could have gone in her place. The sea might have
known that and not played tricks with me. I felt betrayed, and lost
my trust.

But above all, I almost lost my daughter. Probably, they would
have pulled her in. But I persist in thinking, I almost lost her. My
hands tremble now as I write it, the way they trembled as I un-
packed our picnic lunch. I almost lost her. All the other losses I
can bear. I accept that we are born whole and spend a lifetime
eroding, racing decay. Nevertheless, it is too horrifying to confront
these words on the page: I almost lost her.

THE DEATH OF HARRIET GROSS

She died, my mother told me, in childbirth. She needed blood, they gave her blood, and the blood was poisoned. She died with a stranger's germs cruising through her veins at a startling rate. The baby, a girl, lived. Her husband cared for the baby and in time remarried. Her father kept in close touch with his son-in-law, and took the baby every Saturday. He had wanted a grandchild badly, and he needed to keep the connection in memory of his daughter, who had been an only child. I say her father because her mother's mind was opaque: what she felt or needed we shall never know.

Her name was Harriet Gross. When I knew her, as a child and teen-ager, she was not clever or pretty or distinguished in any way. But she was very agreeable and free of malice, and all those who took the trouble to notice her liked her. She was never too busy with homework or dates, always ready for an impromptu visit or an aimless outing. She didn't add anything special to a group, but you missed her if she wasn't there.

My mother had to tell me twice that Harriet died. She told me
ten years ago, shortly after it happened, and she told me again last
month, when our conversation, lugubrious, was running to sad
tales of untimely death. I forgot, the first time. Harriet was easy to
forget, but it was not that quality that made me forget. I denied.
Harriet was the sort of person to whom dramatic events should not
happen. She should have lived peacefully to be eighty.

I denied that Harriet Gross died. I shredded the news and cast it
out my mother's kitchen window. "But I'm sure I told you," my
mother said. I denied that too. Later, of course, I remembered.

I denied that she had told me because I was horrified and embarrassed to admit even to myself that I could forget such a piece of
news. For in the intervening years I had actually thought of Harriet once in a while and wondered what she was doing.

Harriet's family and mine spent the summer in the same dull
mountain resort, her family because her father worked as handy-
man for the owner, my family ostensibly for pleasure. Her family's
quarters were off the main path, at the back of a low building of
attached units. To get to see her I had to climb through thorns and
brambles, and I felt like a Victorian lady of mercy bringing baskets
of goodies to the slums. In fact their rooms were as spacious and
well-kept as ours, and identically furnished. We had very little in
common, Harriet and I. We picked berries together, and watched
our team's baseball games, and raided each other's refrigerators.

When we were very small girls we caught salamanders together
in glass jars with air holes poked in the covers. You had to go out
after a rain, along the dirt road. The tiny orange creatures hid
there, where the dirt met the shrubbery. We picked them up by
the tails and watched them wriggle, then dropped them gently into
the jars, which had a half inch of water in them. I suppose they
died there, after a while. One afternoon my only salamander died
on our way home. He lay inert at the bottom of the jar, bright
bright orange, but all the life had gone out of him. Harriet said he
wasn't dead, though. She lifted him up and laid him in her outstretched palm to let him dry in the sun, and soon, a miracle, he

began to move again and inch up towards her wrist. "Here," she said. "He's okay. He was just sleeping." I was very grateful, and suddenly felt that Harriet was, perhaps, special in a way I could not name.

One thing we did have in common, later on, was not being paired off with any boys at the resort. It is a mystery how these random pairings and exclusions come about, but I imagine in our case it was because I was awkward and bookish and Harriet was unattractive. Her hair was stringy and brown, her face was oily, and she was quite thin. She had prominent shoulder bones and poor posture.

What saved Harriet's self-esteem was her father. He loved her, as my own father used to say, to excess. He took her along for company from one bungalow to the next on his fixing missions, praising her goodness to all he met. He was gruff, in overalls, always in need of a shave, joking, curly-haired, a wizard with bathroom pipes. "No dope," my father said about him—the highest compliment. Harriet's mother, a well-meaning woman whom nature mistakenly burdened with the face and manners of a witch, scolded and screeched, but Harriet laughed kindly and said, "All right, all right, Ma." Deficient in mind, she managed to cook, clean, clothe her child, and get by. "For that," my mother said, "you don't have to be a genius."

The only things I found unpleasant in Harriet were her voice and speech. She was nasal, a bit whiny, and ungrammatical besides. She had a limited vocabulary and a New York accent. I sought Harriet out daily, for she was the most unthreatening person in the universe, in addition to her other good qualities, but I always wished she could learn to speak better. Then I would think, in her defense: with a mother like that to guide her, it's a miracle she speaks as well as she does.

When we were about thirteen Harriet and I began to see each other winters in the city as well as summers in the country. I discovered, after all those years, that she lived only six blocks away. We attended the same junior high and high school. I brought Harriet home and introduced her to my friends; she brought me home and did the same. Her friends and my friends formed a social club that met every Friday night. We went frequently to Radio City Music Hall and the Ice Palace, and we wore navy-blue jackets with white satin lettering across the back. There were naturally differences between her friends and my friends. Hers were not smart in school, took shorthand and typing, cracked their chewing gum, smoked, had pierced ears, and went further with boys. Mine were in special progress classes, spoke grammatically, read books, played the piano, overate, and with boys did nothing below the waist. We were mutually fascinated.

That is all about Harriet herself. Loved by her father, liked by her peers. In the few years between high school graduation and death she led, I am quite sure, an ordinary life.

The second time my mother told me Harriet Gross died in childbirth I lay awake at night enumerating the reasons why Harriet's death was unfair:

She was too young, my age, and not ready to die.

No one should have to die giving birth.

No one should have to die of another's poison.

She was the only comfort of her worthy father, whose wife didn't do much for him.

Her husband would be wifeless.

Her baby would be motherless.

Mortality in general, like city air, is unacceptable.

But as I rolled over and over in my mind these seven reasons, like smooth round marbles, I kept coming back to the first. I couldn't escape it. She was my age, of my age, my age, not ready to die, and I fell asleep with that song in my head.

That night, I resurrected Harriet in my dreams. A grown woman in her early thirties, she was presiding over a small cocktail party in her living room. Still unobtrusive and quiet, she had transformed her indistinctions into a gentle, reliable charm. The mousy brown hair was a dark blond, with the sheen of frequent washing. She was impeccably and elegantly dressed in a green wool suit and white ruffled blouse. The skirt swirled softly around

her knees. Her face was the same, but without the shine: she had
learned how to use make-up. Her lipstick was the same shade as
mine. Green eye shadow echoed the green of her suit. Ease had
replaced the lankiness. Harriet moved among her guests, offering
trays of oyster canapés, stopping here and there for a low-voiced
remark, a warm, intimate smile, a tilt of the head to show she was
listening.

It was clear that only good things had happened to Harriet.

Her living room was modestly but nicely furnished, with soft
green carpeting, soft chairs, soft lighting—nothing tacky. Like
mine, it had a view of flowering trees and a river. A print of
Seurat's *Sunday Afternoon at La Grande Jatte* hung on the wall. Harriet moved through her room as if it were a larger body she lived
in; I felt she could have moved through it blindfolded.

Her daughter appeared for a moment to get a snack, and was
introduced. Harriet put her arm around the shoulder of the tall,
thin blond girl, and drew her close. The child was bony, but
would be beautiful after puberty. Her features were fine and sharp;
her voice chirped in a nasal twang. Stuffing a cheese and cracker
sandwich into her mouth, standing barefoot in her short plaid
skirt, she let her eyes move serenely over the guests, contented and
accepting.

I, too, was tall and slender and blond, with well-washed hair,
and I wore green. I accepted a drink from Harriet and she sat next
to me on the arm of the couch. Her voice was low and pleasing,
her diction perfect, her facial expressions the mirror of inner and
outer harmony. She was well-satisfied with life. She asked polite
questions about my life since we had last met, which I answered
obliquely. I didn't want to talk about my life but about hers. I
wanted to ask Harriet how all this had come about, how she had
contrived to make this gentle, benevolent life happen to her—perhaps she might help me as she had once before with the salamander—but I didn't get the opportunity. A telephone rang; she
left to answer it. She waved to me with a ringed hand on her way

out, as if to say, I'll be right back, and she was ringed in sunlight streaming through the window.

I woke in the dark and thought, But Harriet Gross is dead. Then, Harriet Gross is not dead. I deny the death of Harriet Gross, and will deny it as long as I live.

GRAND STAIRCASES

I knew a man once—it was like having a disease. He was my
disease. Also the wonder drug that relieved it. I felt grand whenever I had my fix, which could be simply his bountiful presence in
the room, his voice—he was an inspired talker—but terrible coming down after. The worst of it was, he didn't seem to know the
pain he was causing. At least he didn't like to hear about it, naturally enough. Moments when it strained at the leash and I had to
let it loose, he would change the subject to something more entertaining. He was a gifted subject-changer. In truth there was no
telling how much he knew. For all the bounty of his talking, he
had certain remote, inaccessible chambers of secrecy. And he was
smart. Like an idiot savant, smart enough to be dumb when he
needed to.

One night in my kitchen, after it was officially all over between
us, I was telling him in a mild way, over the remains of dinner,
how bad he had made me feel, sexless and ugly and dull and at

times almost evil, when I had been used to seeing myself as just the opposite, as very like him, as a matter of fact. He made me feel that way because he resisted me. First he stalked me and afterwards he resisted. Not from any perverse strategy, I don't think. He felt he had a reasonable position to defend. He was trying to be faithful to an architect he was in love with, but alas she was away in Eastern Europe for six months, studying grand staircases of the eighteenth century. It was during the second month of her absence that we met. I began as his friend and confidante. He would tell me how much he missed her, loved her. He obviously needed to tell this to someone and I didn't mind, then, being the one. He showed me her picture. Well, there was nothing wrong with that either, at that point. More and more he sought me out, more and more he talked about her. He had the idea that she was some sort of goddess or perfect being, that she would save him, I'm not sure from what, from everything in life men require saving from. I should have known enough to be wary—when men talk to women at length about their earlier women . . . But soon we were talking about many other things as well, hours at a stretch like adolescents, telling everything we had ever done or thought or felt. And I let myself drift. I didn't dream of diverting his love from the architect: he seemed a type I could never fall in love with, hale and hearty, good-humored (until I discovered this was only the facade; behind it he was glum and introspective, just what I liked). Though I suppose I was a diversion, in the other sense.

Later on, when we were together every evening, he still talked about her, but less. After all. I remembered the picture and her alleged supernatural appeal. She was pretty, a little prettier than I but not all that much. She looked gentler perhaps, yet who can really tell from a picture? I wondered what enchantment she possessed that I lacked, and decided after much wondering that more than any magical quality it was her having been there first, at a more propitious moment. A couple of things he told me about her I found funny, for example that she cut out recipes and pasted or typed them on five-by-eight cards to be filed alphabetically in a metal box, but I knew the one thing I must never do was laugh at

her. That would be sacrilege. Not that she was any more laughable
than anyone else—a couple of things about everyone are funny. I
found her interesting actually, orphaned young, jolted in and out
of foster homes and so on, which was probably why I first listened.
Though it may have been the way he saw her and told about her
that made her interesting. He had that transforming power; ordinary things would pass through his mind and come out lustrous.
Sometimes I went to movies or read books he had described and
found them less vivid than I expected; then I realized it was all in
his telling, the enthusiasm and the play of mind, those grand and
undulating ascents.

I was picking at the crumbs of the excellent brownies he had
brought for dessert and telling him in a friendly way how he had
made me feel, without bitterness or accusations, because it was all
officially over between us, the torments, the pulling together and
pulling apart (his pulling apart), the endless shuffling over whether
we were to be just friends or lovers as well (whether our being
lovers would destroy him as the decent moral being he claimed he
was trying to be), and if lovers, serious or frivolous lovers, and if
serious lovers, serious enough to disrupt the course of each other's
lives . . . for there was always his true love who should not suffer
any more jolting; all over too was the trying to remain friends in
spite of it, that was no longer in question since meanwhile, apart
from the shuffling (or maybe because of the revelations it entailed),
we had become best friends, better friends, we agreed, than most
people could ever dream of being to each other; we were friends of
the blood and of temperament, we could not cease talking or listening, our words some honeyed elixir passed from mouth to mouth,
and we thought and felt alike on nearly every matter except the
matter of us, where I could not accept why such rare con-
sanguinity shouldn't make us the best of lovers as well, but then I
was not at the same time on an erotic pilgrimage and so could not
appreciate his dilemma, nor the well-organized architect's imminent return from Eastern Europe to continue the work of his salvation from I was never quite sure what. Unexpected and puzzling
events like me, perhaps. For after he made love with me, he said,

he was in torment, but at those moments I could not be terribly sympathetic. Had it not been for her, I would think, there would be none of this torment and no need for salvation from it. I could not accept myself as a source of torment: I too had always thought I was trying to be a decent moral being, and such beings do not cause torment, or so I thought. Much as I disliked hearing about his torment, I knew his revealing it was a kind of testimony to our friendship. Not all lovers are such extraordinary friends; conceivably not even he and the architect, which might have contributed to his torment; it may be, though I would rather not think so, that the two conditions are mutually exclusive. And sometimes it was indeed as if we were two sets of people, a pair of wretched lovers and a pair of benevolent friends who discuss their tormenting lovers over long and homey dinners. Yet with all my complaining I never used so strong a word as torment. It seemed too dangerous, as if that word like a gust of wind might blow down our fragile little structure, a house of cards compared to the grandiose structure he had built with the architect, I gathered.

But all that was over now and we were just friends, as they say. Because he kept turning up, hungry, bearing tributes of food, even after she came back with her wealth of information on grand staircases of the eighteenth century. He said we had something special, I occupied a special place in his life, he even loved me—this he brought out with difficulty—and would hate to do without me though he remained deeply in love with the architect.

My telling him how he had made me feel made him very uncomfortable—for he was, to some extent, the decent moral being he aspired to be; I don't wish to give the impression he was heartless, not at all, the problem was the opposite, he indulged in an overextension of the heart—so uncomfortable that he got up and washed our dinner dishes sitting in my sink, just for something to do. This was not one of his more inspired changes of subject; still, it had its merit. He was a man who took the initiative around the house, never an exploiter. The shapers of feminist doctrine would have approved of him, domestically, at any rate. I leaned against a counter near the sink and watched. Over the running water he said,

"It's funny you should be telling me this. You should really be telling someone else these things about me, someone who could take your part wholeheartedly and give you some satisfaction."

"You have a point," I said. "But it's so convenient. You know the situation. I don't have to fill you in. And besides, you understand me better than anyone else."

"True. It's because we are true friends, aren't we?" He looked up from the sink anxiously. He was always anxious about this, always wanted reassurance of my friendship and my good opinion. Maybe he feared that someday he would turn up as usual and I would not wish to see him. He knew that would be perfectly logical. Maybe someday I wouldn't.

"Yes, yes, I just told you so. Listen, we'll pretend we're talking about someone else, that it's some other man I'm complaining to you about."

"That's a little hard to do when I know that other man is me."

"Just pretend. See what you can come up with."

"Okay." And he sighed heavily. "Okay, I'll try."

We went into the living room. I sat in the easy chair with my feet up on the coffee table and he lay down on the couch with his hands locked behind his head, as he always did. It was a couch we used to make love on, in the era when we were making love, and inevitably when I saw him lying there I could not help recalling that era. On the couch or else the floor right below, partly under the coffee table unless we took the trouble to push it aside, but it was marble and very heavy. The couch was not especially comfortable as couches go, and floors in general are not. . . . But often when it happened it would happen fast and there was no time to spare to get up and walk to the bedroom. It would happen so fast because he had been resisting the impulse for so long, hours maybe, floating high on words, being the best of friends, resisting exactly this happening, and then all of a sudden—he might even be getting up to say good night and priding himself on a virtuous evening—he would have no more resistance. Or maybe it was a game he liked, a private spiritual battle where till the very last moment the outcome is touch and go. It was not my game, but

then lovers do play separate games. And maybe he would be thinking about the traveling architect all through it, but I never asked.
Not that I didn't feel free to, but I was afraid of hearing the possible truth, the complexities of it—how I might have been standing
in for her like an understudy giving so fine a performance the audience almost forgets its disappointment; or more likely how the
architect and I both in body and spirit might have been merging
and unmerging in his mind in some far subtler way like chemicals
or, better still, representations of the real and the ideal, each of us
partaking of both but in different aspects, with now one and now
the other of our images advancing to the foreground and receding;
and, most of all, I was afraid of how interesting he would make it
sound—it was painful enough already. For afterwards he would
hate himself and not be too enamored of me either, since I was the
provocation, merely by existing. But he knew too it wasn't entirely
my doing and so he'd feel guilty for turning away; between his
guilt towards the architect and his guilt towards me and whatever
others dragged along from the past, he had constructed a nice cozy
little cell of guilt where he could be all alone after his indulgences,
which is perhaps what he really wanted. Of course it was not always like that; thankèd be fortune it hath been otherwise, as in
Wyatt's famous poem of love and rage, twenty times better, naked
in my chamber, something in that vein; many times we even made
it to the bedroom, but that was mostly at the beginning. Later it
was as if, given the time it would take to walk to my chamber, he
might change his mind.

He had made himself a cup of coffee and set it on the marble
table, and now and then I took a sip. Coffee makes me sick but
sometimes I get a yen for just a little. I liked to drink out of his cup
and he never minded. He was good that way. A generous soul, not
fastidious. Never chary of those forms of intimacy.

"Okay," he said. "This other man." And he looked at me with
great brown sad dog eyes. "I'll tell you what I think. This other
man you're talking about is a fop, a cad, a pretentious, self-indulgent joker."

He kept staring, and I could see that he meant it. I could see in the lush brown of his eyes the torment he used to speak of but no longer did. And in the recesses of the irises, grand staircases to remote, inaccessible chambers. I couldn't speak. Our bodies had touched each other and interpenetrated in nearly every imaginable way, but I felt this moment was the most naked we had ever had. And I felt vastly sorry for him, more sorry, finally, than I did for myself.

He grinned; it was hesitant and shy, like a boy's grin. "Why are you looking at me that way?"

I told him what I had been thinking, about the nakedness and closeness.

"Do you really think so?" he said.

"Yes, I do. And maybe you're right, what you said. Maybe he is all that. But the thing is, you see, I liked him. I was crazy about him."

THE SUNFISH AND THE MERMAID

Gregory allowed the lines controlling the Sunfish sail to rest loosely in his hands as he looked around with contentment at the placid lake ringed by dark, lush greenery, its shores dotted with cottages partly hidden by shade trees. At one of these cottages he was a weekend guest, and he located it from time to time, to keep his bearings.

The Sunfish was small—simply a flat deck about fourteen feet long and four feet at its widest point, with a shallow well in the center. Its silken, royal-blue sail billowed just now in the wind, making Gregory grip the line and tiller tighter and steer against the air currents. Near him lay an orange life jacket, one strap held down firmly by his foot. Gregory would feel foolish wearing it, yet he couldn't bring himself to go out on the lake without it. The wind calmed; he relaxed his hold. He loved the feel of the coarse line in his fingers, taut or loose, and the sure knowledge that by applying the slightest pressure he could control the motion of the boat.

Steering cautiously, he headed back towards the house. He shouldn't be greedy—Joe or Jean might want to take a sail. The Sunfish was theirs, after all. The Franks were close friends; he had known Joe for several years at the office and Jean had become almost like a sister. Some ten years older than he, they babied him whenever he came to the lake, fed him and watched over him as though he needed special care. While Gregory protested, in secret he liked it. He had been a small boy when his mother died, leaving a void, and though he was not self-indulgent in other matters, he could never have his fill of older women fussing over him.

He was securing the boat to the small dock when he saw a station wagon crammed with people turning into the driveway. Arms waved from the side and back windows as Joe appeared from the house to greet the guests.

"Hi, Greg." Jean, smiling and energetic as always, was setting out lawn chairs. "How was your sail? The Carsons are here."

"So I see. I didn't know you were expecting such a crowd."

"They said they had people staying over, so I told them the more, the merrier." Gregory went to help with the chairs, stifling a pang of envy at how easily Jean could face meeting a carful of strangers. He had been looking forward to a tranquil afternoon with the Franks and another married couple. If only Margaret had come. With Margaret nearby it would be easier—they would make a pair, a safe, closed unit.

"We can do this later. Come—let's say hello." Jean reached out her hand to take him along.

There were six of them, all wearing bright, splashy bathing suits with bright-hued beach towels slung over their shoulders. Laughing and talking chaotically, they piled from the car, tanned legs and arms jumbled up and spilling out. One man wore dark glasses that were mirrors; they caught the sun's rays and became two splotches of flashing light. Dazzled by the glitter and the array, Gregory shook hands, knowing he would not remember their

names five minutes later. Except that one, the last to be introduced, made such a rare and poignant impact, he felt his scalp
tingle as he smiled hello.

She appeared about nineteen or twenty but couldn't possibly be
that young; her soft, candid face showed experience and discern-
ment. She had a mass of wavy, dark-red hair that billowed about
her face and hung down her back. It must make her very hot,
Gregory thought, and he noted how often she tossed her head to
get it off her face or lifted it off the back of her neck with her left
hand, her chin tilting slightly upward. He had never seen eyes like
hers, extremely large and luminous and colored pure aqua, match-
ing the splashes of gaudy flowers on her bikini. She was very suntanned, brown and glossy. He was glad, though he couldn't see
why it should matter to him, that she didn't get pink, like most
redheads—he didn't care for that seared-pink look on fair-skinned
girls. The upper part of her face was gentle and relaxed—wide,
inquisitive eyes and wide brow; the lower part more vivid and
stern—narrow, curving mouth, squarish, assertive jaw and chin.
She focused on him when she said hello as she focused on everything around her, with unabashed penetration and assessment.
Watching her, he felt set apart, lifted out of the procession of time
and in the presence of something he had waited for patiently, in his
usual silence.

Her first words were not extraordinary at all, however. "God,
it's hot here in the sun!" Looking up at the sky, she shielded her
eyes, then flung off her blue denim shirt and carried it by one
sleeve towards the chairs, letting it trail carelessly on the ground.

They sat languidly sipping iced drinks. Gregory, lying on the
grass, stared up at her. She had kicked off her sandals, then
crossed one brown leg over the other and swung it restlessly as she
talked. Hypnotized, he regarded the roundness of the calf muscles,
slack now as the leg swung from her knee, and the flesh of the
thigh underneath, which stirred slightly from the friction. The rest
of her body was calm. One long, narrow hand held a drink and the
other lay flat on the arm of the chair. Only that leg, swinging in

tiny, relentless motions like the flickering of a compass needle, hinted at turbulence. She talked too much, talked and laughed and gazed benevolently at her listeners as though her speech were a personal gift. Her voice was low-pitched, faintly husky, a shade too loud. When she was about to laugh, her tone grew higher and melodious, easing into the laugh like a singer easing from recitative to an aria. He wondered if she was an actress. A life-of-the-party type, he decided as she told an amusing story about how she and Phil—she leaned over and put her hand on Phil's arm when she mentioned his name—got their car embroiled in a wedding party that morning on the way up. There was a convertible with a bride and groom, she said, and a trail of twenty honking, singing car-loads. She and Phil had woven in and out among them, waving and shouting congratulations, until finally they passed them all and felt they had been part of the happy celebration.

Instinctively he disliked Phil, whose face was concealed by the flashing glasses and a beard. He seemed meager and unworthy of her. Gregory suspected that most bearded men were hiding weak jaws or chins. He, of course, was clean-shaven, but he let his dark hair grow fashionably long. He hoped she wasn't serious about Phil, and then chided himself. What business was it of his? For all he knew, they might be married, although he doubted it. Her radiant quality, the smooth texture of her flesh, made her appear pure and unused, unpossessed, despite the loud talk and overconfidence.

She set her drink down and glanced towards the water. "Ooh, you've got a boat!" she exclaimed, and half rose from her chair to peer at it.

"Our Sunfish," Joe said proudly. "Neat little thing."

On impulse, Gregory rose to his feet. He was pleased to be tall and muscular—that always put people a bit in awe at the start. "Would you like to go for a sail?" he asked. "I'd be glad to take you out on it."

"Oh, go with him, Deirdre. Gregory will give you a marvelous sail. He adores the Sunfish," said Jean.

"He's in love with the Sunfish—that's a fact," said Joe, leaning back lazily, puffing on his pipe.

"All right," she said, turning to Gregory directly for the first time since they met. "Why not?" And leaving her shirt hanging from a corner of the chair, she followed him down to the dock.

Deirdre, he was thinking. Even her name was outrageous, too much. Everything about her was overblown and overstated. She took up more space and charged the space surrounding her more than a young woman should. And this nagged at him: unfair that one person should exude such vibrating orange light while others were drawn and illumined inward, crouching, almost, in the dim, spare space allotted. Margaret, for example. Probably a much finer person, all things considered, but her body did nothing to the air around it. Then he felt guilty, making comparisons on such foolish, intangible grounds, thinking this treacherous way about Margaret, of whom he was so fond. Anyway, Deirdre wasn't his type at all; she was a quite dangerous type, he suspected. It would be like playing with quicksilver or juggling bolts of lightning. His interest was mere curiosity, he assured himself: how did a girl get that way?

"It's a little tricky to manage," Gregory said. "You sit over on this end, don't move around, and I'll sit there." Once she was settled, he nudged the boat from the dock and hopped on. It quivered beneath them for an instant.

"We don't need this, do we?" She tossed the life jacket onto the dock. "It takes up space."

They were off, too far to retrieve it. He glanced at the still lake. She was probably right. He would try to forget about it.

"If you like, I'll show you how to sail."

"Oh, good." She started towards him to take the line.

"No, no—stay where you are. I'll hand it to you. Pull on it like this." He explained and demonstrated, then gave her the line and showed her how to use the tiller. "There's nothing to it unless a wind comes up. Then you'd better give it back to me."

"Oh, I'm not worried about the wind. I'll manage. It's great fun."

"I'm not worried either," he said tersely. "I'm only telling you all this because it's a delicate craft and the wind can get a bit fierce without any warning."

"Okay, okay!" She smiled. "Do you want it back?" She held out the line.

She seemed very young at that moment, and he was sorry he had spoken so sharply. "No, it's all right. Tell me, what do you do?"

"Do? Oh, you mean work? I work as an editorial assistant." And she named a mildly liberal political magazine.

Her answer surprised him. He had been sure she would be in show business in some small way. Impossible to imagine her shut up in an office, head bent over a desk, quietly pondering arrangements of sentences and paragraphs.

"And what do you do?" she asked.

He sensed the irony in her tone but didn't know why it should be there. "I'm a securities analyst."

She was silent.

He grinned. "I bet you don't even know what that is."

"Of course I do. You analyze securities."

And they both laughed. She was nicer alone, quieter, more subdued. He didn't feel overwhelmed by her as he had on the lawn. Maybe all that loud talk was an act; maybe she was really timid and covered it by a show of flamboyance. The notion gave him courage.

He cleared his throat. "Do you live alone? I mean, you're not—uh—married to anyone?"

"Married?" She laughed broadly, throwing her head back so the tendons in her neck stretched taut. With the deep throaty laughter she seemed to expand and send out ripples. "No! How did you get that idea? Do I look married?"

"I was only asking. You did come up with someone. . . ."

"Phil? No, he's just a friend. Just a friend."

She chuckled softly to herself. Gregory wasn't sure he liked her at all anymore. The laughter was excessive.

"How about you, since we're asking? Are you married?"

"No."

"That's nice."

He had to smile at her quick response. Then he asked her to turn the Sunfish so they could head towards the far, secluded end of the lake. "Why is that nice?" he asked.

She was sitting cross-legged now, leaning towards him, interested. "Most men your age are married. It's curious—reassuring, I guess—to find one who's not, that's all. Who's perhaps taking some more original route. Though of course I don't know a thing about you," she amended. "I have no grounds for assuming anything at all. Maybe you're a wastrel, a cad." She grinned at him. "Can a man be that and a securities analyst at the same time?"

He had to concede to himself, then, that she might indeed do work that involved thought and spirit.

"What do you mean, my age? How old do you think I am?"

"Oh," she said, frowning, "thirty? Thirty-one?"

"I'm twenty-eight." He was often taken for older and was used to it. He knew he had a somber face, and it was a help in business, in fact. Yet coming from her, the judgment hurt.

"Don't look so sad. I'm never very good at guessing ages. How old do you think I am? Here's your chance to get even."

"Well, to look at you, I'd say seventeen." They laughed together once again. "But seriously, let's see. Twenty-two?"

"Twenty-four."

"I wasn't so far off, then."

She handed him the line and tiller. "Here—you sail for a while. I want to look around. Lord, but it's hot, isn't it?" She stretched her legs out in front of her, brushed the hair off the back of her neck with the familiar, intimate gesture, and leaned back on her elbows, facing the serene shore.

They drifted quietly for a while. Gregory was feeling very peaceful. This girl, this Deirdre, he was thinking, made him feel peaceful. True, she took up a lot of space; yet she managed to leave him plenty of his own. He could possess the whole lake; her presence didn't limit or hinder him. She took what she needed and left the rest alone.

"Why do you love the Sunfish so?" Her question didn't break the calm but was part of it.

"I don't know. I've never thought about it. Maybe because it's so compact and easy to manage. And so open, no secret parts. It's almost the smallest thing it can be and still be a boat. Essence of boat." He smiled, and then added impulsively, in a rare general statement, "Who knows why people love things? It can't be analyzed."

"We're so different. If I got to love it, it would be because it's so close to the water. You can practically feel the water under you, through it. In it and not in it at once. I love the water." She dipped a hand in and let water run through her fingers.

"Do you?" He looked sharply into the aqua eyes. "I don't trust water."

She sat upright and shook out her hair again. Suddenly, with her gesture, the air between them was alive and turbulent. "I do. I'm really a mermaid. Didn't they tell you?"

"Mermaids don't have legs." He glanced down at hers, shining, with sparse, light hairs; they stretched along the deck, her toes a mere few inches from his thigh.

"Oh, that's a minor technicality. You know what, Gregory? I'm going to take a swim." She swung her legs over the side and dangled them in the lake.

"Wait a minute. I mean, we're all balanced here, and—"

"There's no problem," she said kindly. "You move closer to the center and I'll ease off."

He had a flash of hot anger. She spoke as if she understood the Sunfish better than he did, and it was her first time out. Before he could think of a proper answer, she slid down and dived beneath the surface. Rapidly, he edged to the center.

He watched her swim. She moved with long, competent, slow but strong strokes, and her hair, darkened by the lake, was truly like a mermaid's, streaming on the glistening water. A beautiful swimmer. Gregory was in panic. They were all alone in the middle of the lake—if she got a cramp, what could he do? The Sunfish would drift away with no one holding it. And he couldn't save

anyone; he could barely . . . It was exactly as he had first sur-
mised. She was a dangerous girl and did dangerous, impetuous
things. At last, ten yards from the boat, she stopped swimming
and began to play, diving under, treading water, floating on her
back in the dark lake striped by undulating beams of sunlight. His
heart was pounding and he knew it would not stop until she came
safely back. He desperately wanted her to come back but he
wouldn't call to her. And abruptly, summoned up by visceral
memory, by the fierce rhythm in his chest, there appeared other
sunlit scenes long gone, when his heart had pounded in just that
way, and he had watched from a distance while others partook of
the sun and the light. After his mother died, his brother, twelve
years older and away at school, would come home to see him,
mostly in summer, bringing him toys and playing ball. For all his
trying it was an unsuccessful brotherhood. To Gregory his brother
was always a remote, younger version of his father, both big fair-
haired men with powerful shoulders and clear eyes, who negoti-
ated their paths through the world with a sureness and ease he
despaired of copying. He understood even then that it could not be
copied, that copying its outward forms would belie its very nature.
After he was sent to bed his brother and father would have long,
man-to-man talks on the lawn in the warm, waning light. He
looked on, trapped in his darkened window. Now, immobilized on
the Sunfish as he saw Deirdre flip carelessly in the water, he recalled one sunny afternoon, hot like this one, with the same dry,
exciting heat, and his father and brother standing close together on
the lawn, their fair hair shining, their light summer clothes hanging gracefully on their muscled bodies. They were laughing in low
tones and talking confidentially as Gregory approached. He was
small and runty and a whiner, and though they would doubtless
welcome him into their midst, he feared their welcome might not
be genuine and he would be shattering a perfect, mysterious moment in the world and camaraderie of grown men. Ten yards from
them he stopped, watched, and turned, downcast, to walk the
other way. He hoped they might call him back, but there was no

sound; he felt that he would never penetrate the circle of light that enclosed them.

"Hey!" Deirdre called, waving. "Can you leave the boat and come in?"

"I can't. It would drift away," he called back.

As she came swimming towards him the pounding in his chest eased. He was afraid, though, that she might grasp the edge too hard and tip the boat over. The Sunfish capsized very easily. Jean and Joe upset it all the time in reckless play and then struggled to right it. But Gregory hated the feeling of slipping off. He had tried it once with Joe and landed awkwardly on his stomach, gulping cold water.

He was relieved to see that she could be sensible. Treading to keep afloat, she placed one hand lightly on the edge, leaning no weight on it.

"Go on, Gregory. You take a swim now and I'll mind the boat. It's glorious."

"No, I'll swim later. There's a wind coming up—we ought to go back." He reached out and helped her aboard. He liked the feel of her upper arm; it was muscular and firm.

"You know," he said as she settled herself on the deck, "I was a little worried about you out there. The lake is deceptive. It's about a hundred feet deep in this part."

"What's the difference?" she said carelessly, intent on gathering the heavy hair in a coil and wringing it out. "Ten feet or a hundred. If you're on top, it's all the same. Oh, that felt marvelous."

"You're a good swimmer."

"When I was a teen-ager I worked as a lifeguard."

He blushed under his tan, feeling an utter fool for having worried and trembled over her. The girl was a lifeguard, while his orange life jacket had lain like a badge of dishonor on the deck of the Sunfish.

She stretched out flat to dry off in the sun. Her eyes were closed, so he could indulge himself, studying her as he would some wondrous natural terrain. The full curves of her breasts slipped down out of the sides of the scant bikini top; he could see where pale skin merged into suntan. Her stomach was flat and her hip-bones jutted up sharply. Where her bathing suit cut across her thighs he could see a few curly hairs, but he looked away quickly, as if he were taking unfair advantage, looking there while her eyes were closed. Her body was ample, strong and large-boned, but not heavy. Five pounds more and there would be too much of her, but as she was, he found her perfect. Her wrists, an anomaly, were narrow and delicate; he could easily ring his thumb and forefinger around them. Drops of water were poised on the hairs on her knees. He wanted to run his hand over them and feel the damp, warm skin, but he didn't dare.

They were silent till they reached the dock, where she sat up and said, "Thank you. That was a lovely sail."

"My pleasure." He smiled.

As they walked side by side towards the others on the lawn he thought they must make a striking couple. He with his coarse black hair, dark skin, and straight features looked like an Indian, he had been told. Sturdily built now, far from the runt he had once been, he diligently kept his body in shape by playing squash during his lunch hour with Joe and other men from the office. He shouldn't feel surprised that she seemed to like him. Girls did like him. He went out a lot, dinners and concerts and theaters; they liked being seen with him. It was only Margaret, though, whom he was close to. He must remember to drop Margaret a line later on.

They all had another drink, and the Carsons and their friends swam, then said they had to be getting along; they had steaks marinating at home. Gregory wished he might have the chance to say goodbye to her alone, though what he wanted to say he didn't know. It just felt clumsy this way, as if she were merely another stranger shaking hands, as if their shared sail were obliterated.

Surprising him, she took his hand and pulled him aside.

"Call me in the city, why don't you?" She gave him her wide, frank look, straight into his eyes.

He blinked under the gaze. "But I don't even know—"

"Deirdre, come on," the others called.

She turned to go to the car. "Call the magazine," she whispered over her shoulder, then got in, slammed the door, and was gone.

He told Joe and Jean he was going to rest for a while, and closed his door tightly behind him. He lay on the bed in the warm shaded room, intending to sleep, but he couldn't get her out of his mind— her eyes, her wet hair, her outrageous nothing of a bathing suit, the fair hairs on her legs, the feeling of her long fingers on his arms when he pulled her onto the boat. She was exciting him even in her absence, and he resented her for it. He preferred to choose the times he was available for arousal. Her kind of excitement was certainly not for him; it was excessive. He had ordered his whole life to avoid excess. Now this feeling came along, invading him without invitation or permission.

What was she, after all? He didn't know anything about her. He didn't even know if she had been to college, if she had an original idea in her head. Editorial assistant. Most likely a glorified secretary like the ones in his office, plodding through dull tasks all week and craving excitement on the two days of release. Or maybe she was the radical, slovenly type, angry at the world for her own shortcomings. He couldn't tell, hadn't even seen her dressed, except for the blue work shirt everyone wore these days. For all he knew, she went around in tattered jeans or long patched denim skirts. He probably wouldn't want to be seen in a decent restaurant with her.

He sat at the desk to try writing to Margaret. At least he knew who she was. Margaret was the personnel director of a large private hospital. She was steady, nice-looking, well-informed (she knew what a securities analyst was), and a hard worker. Indeed it was because she had to work overtime that she wasn't with him this weekend. Fleetingly he envisioned Margaret here, the convergence of Margaret and Deirdre at the lakeshore, but pushed that from his mind; it was unthinkable. He and Margaret went out every Tuesday and Saturday evening and returned to spend the night in his or her apartment, and when he left her the next day he felt refreshed and contented.

"Dear Margaret," he wrote. He would probably see her before she got the note, but it made him feel sober and virtuous to write, and she would enjoy receiving it. "It's a pity you couldn't be here this weekend. You poor thing, working away in the hot city." He hastily crossed that sentence out; it was an alien voice he didn't recognize, whose equivocation disgusted him even more than its condescension. He would have to copy it all over when he was finished.

"Joe and Jean had some friends over this afternoon and we sat around drinking. Decadent! Naturally I took the Sunfish out again. Twice."

He paused, assaulted by memory and desire. It was no use. A crowd of fantasies stormed behind his tight-shut eyes—what he would do to her, what she would do to him. He would hold her up against the wall a few inches off the floor so that their eyes were level, unavoidable, and ram her ceaselessly, without mercy. He could see perfectly the startled, then melting look in her huge aqua eyes. He would catch her around the stomach from behind as she was stepping into the shower, drag her down the hall and throw her, her red hair heaving, her mouth howling shock and lust, onto his white living room sofa. She would climb on top of him savagely and her hair would slide back and forth over his chest, and her tongue would lick his neck and lap inside his ear, tantalizing. He would lie quite still on the rug while, with burning fingertips and palms, she massaged every bit of him slowly from head to toe. Then he would roll her over and grind her into the floor as she cried out in amazement and clutched him closer. He covered his eyes with his fists to make the pictures stop, and found tears wetting his knuckles.

It was no use. He had wanted her, every damned inch, from the moment he saw her, but surely he would never call. He knew himself, his ways, too well to dream of changing course. There was altogether too much of her. She was too loud and took up too

much space and her hair was too reddish and fluffy. It didn't lie
flat as it should. Girls' hair should lie flat, and if it couldn't, at least
stay where it was put. Hers responded to every slight breath of
wind or stirring of the air, billowed and streamed, so that around
her splendid face was endless motion.

THE OPIATE OF THE PEOPLE

David, when he was feeling happy, used to dance for his children. The war was over, the Germans defeated. Once again he pranced across the living room raising his knees high in an absurd parody all his own, blending a horse's gallop and a Parisian can-can. Lucy, his youngest, would laugh in a high-pitched delighted giggle—David looked so funny dancing in his baggy gray trousers and long-sleeved white shirt with the loosened tie jerking from side to side. His business clothes. He wore them all the time, even at night after dinner. Sometimes at breakfast he wore his jacket too, as he stood tense near the kitchen sink, swallowing orange juice and toast and coffee, briefcase waiting erect at his feet.

When he stopped dancing he would smooth down his wavy dark hair modestly and catch his breath. "You like that, eh?"

Lucy was six. She wanted her father never out of her sight. She felt complete only when he was present.

"Yes. But why can't we have a Christmas tree?"

*   *   *

Lucy was eleven. They had a large family with many cousins, nearly all older than she was, and always getting married. At the big weddings the band music was loud and ceaseless. After the fruit cup and the first toast to the newlyweds, at some point during the soup, the popular dance tunes would give way to a rapping syncopated rhythm with the pungency of garlic and the ringing tone of a shout or a slap. The grownups leaped away from their bowls to form circle within circle, holding hands. Anna, Lucy's mother, was a leader. She was heavy, but moved nimbly. Her head would bounce up and down to the music as she pulled a line of dancers under a bridge of arms.

"You can do it too, Lucy," she called out. "Come on."

And the circle opened, hands parted to let her in.

David did not dance these dances. She saw him at the edge of the circle, his tie neatly knotted, observing keenly, lighting an olive-colored cigar.

He waltzed. He waltzed with her mother, the two of them floating with stiff, poignant grace. His face, sharp-boned, alert, was tilted up proudly, his hand spread out flat against Anna's broad back.

"But why," Lucy asked, "can't we have a Christmas tree?"

"Don't you know yet?" He was annoyed with her. "It's not our holiday."

"I know, but it doesn't really mean anything," she protested, leaning forward against the front seat of the car, flushed with the champagne they had let her taste. "It's only a symbol."

She could see the edge of his smile and knew he was smiling because she had used the word "symbol." She felt clever to have charmed away his annoyance.

In the morning she accosted Anna.

"Why is he so against it?"

Anna did not turn to face her. She was putting on mascara in front of the mirror, and the tiny brush she held near her eyes looked like a flag. "Because they made him wear a yellow arm band when he went to school."

"But . . ." Lucy said. These bizarre facts tossed out at chance intervals made her feel another world, a shadow world, existed at the rim of their own. "But that was in another country."

"It makes no difference. The tree is the same."

She grasped that David was keeping something back from her, something that touched herself as well as him.

"What was it like when you were growing up?"

"We were poor," he said. "We worked, we studied. We lived where your grandmother used to live. It was very crowded."

"No, I mean before that. Before you came here." She whispered the last words shyly, for fear of somehow embarrassing him.

"I don't remember."

"You must remember something. You were the same age as I am now, and I'd remember this even if I moved away."

He tightened his lips and turned to the bridge game in his *New York Times*, sharpened pencil poised.

Saturdays, driving into the city to visit aunts and uncles, they sped through shabby neighborhoods with once-fine brownstones, down streets where men in long black coats and fur hats and unruly beards shambled in the path of oncoming cars. They had hanging curls in front of their ears, delicate straggly locks that gave Lucy a feeling of weak revulsion.

"It's Saturday," said David, "so they think they own the streets. No one should drive." He had to brake to avoid a group of teen-aged boys with unnaturally soft, waxy skin. Rolling down the window, he shouted, "Why don't you stay on the sidewalk where you belong?" Then, "Someone's got to teach them a little English," he muttered at the steering wheel.

"You sound like some ignorant peasant." Anna's eyes followed the group of boys sorrowfully. "Why can't you live and let live? And drive like a normal person?"

"Filthy refs," muttered David.

"What are refs?" asked Lucy from the back of the car.

"Refugees," said Anna.

With an inner leap of glee, she thought she spotted an inconsistency in David's thought, usually so logical. "Well, weren't you one too?"

"That's different."

"How?"

"They have no business looking like that. They give the rest of us a bad name. Lenin was right. Religion is the opiate of the people."

"Who was that again?" Lucy asked.

"Lenin. Vladimir Lenin."

"Oh, what kinds of things are you teaching her!" Anna exclaimed. "Leave her be."

He pronounced Vladimir with the accent on the second syllable. Lucy made a mental note of that.

"What was it really like back there?"

"I don't remember."

But she was fifteen now, strong with adolescence and nearly full grown; she stood over him and waited while he turned the pages of his newspaper.

Finally he yanked off his glasses and looked up at her. "You really want to know? They came around at night and chased people out of their houses, then set them on fire. You were afraid to go to sleep. They sent you to the army for twenty years. They said we poisoned their wells and chopped up their babies. So everyone came here. One at a time. First Saul, he was grown up, then Peter, then Avi, then I came with my parents and the girls, because I was the baby. It stunk on the boat. People vomited all day long. All right?"

"All right, all right." She cringed and drew back from the brittle voice shouting at her. "All right, forget it."

Most of the time, if secretly, David was very proud of the way his life had turned out. Considering. He was proud of having married a good-looking American-born girl he fell in love with in high school. Anna kept a good home and took excellent care of the children, and when they went out to meet people she was just right, friendly and talkative, never flirtatious. He took pride in that wholesome, free tone of hers, so American. She was loving to him, though she might tease grudgingly if she thought he wanted her too often when the children were small and wore her out. Spirited, also: they disagreed often and loudly over petty things, but never over big things like right or wrong or decency or bringing up the family.

He was proud of their children, their house, and their car. He was proud most of all, though he would never have admitted this, of his perfect English, no trace of an accent. At school he had imitated the way the teachers spoke and stored their phrases in his keen ear. Walking there and home he moved his lips to practice, and when other boys ridiculed him he withdrew silently, watching with envy as they played in the schoolyard. He used to play too, back there, but now, after the trip and the ordeals of a new house-hold in an incomprehensible land, he could not launch into games. His father never wearied of saying the four boys must work very hard to show they were as good as the others. They might not have much, but they had brains better than anyone else's. In this coun-try lurked fortunes waiting to be snatched up by boys with heads on their shoulders. After two years of effort David's speech was flawless, untainted, and he hoped that with the language embedded in his tongue he could do whatever he chose, that no one need ever know how foolish and awkward and alien he had once sounded.

His older brothers fared well too, and their English was fluent. More than fluent: they spoke with style and a feeling for diction and phrasing. Luckily, the family was gifted that way. But when he listened to them now, Avi and Peter and Saul, he detected a flavor of the foreign born. He couldn't place it—not any mispro-nunciation or inflection, but something. He wished them no ill, these nattily dressed brothers with flourishing businesses, but se-cretly he was glad to have been the youngest, best able to reshape the habits of his tongue. His sisters, already grown when they ar-rived, and pushed promptly into factories so that the boys might go to school, would always sound foreign. The oldest, Ruth, who had diligently mastered her English grammar, still kept an antique musical lilt, like a catch in the voice. It could take him unawares, even now, and bring unwanted, artesian tears to his eyes.

Their second night off the boat, an old uncle who had come two years earlier sat David's father down at his oilcloth-covered kitchen table. Along with countless bits of advice and lore, he instructed that the paper to read was the *New York Times*, and so David's father bought it daily, sending one of the boys out to the newsstand in the gray of morning with pennies in his pocket. The words "New York Times" were among the first in David's vocabulary.

Each night after ten hours bent over ledgers in the asphyxiating office of a Hebrew school, his father sat at the kitchen table learning English from the *New York Times*. No one was permitted to disturb him while he studied. Every two or three minutes he would look up a word in a black leather-bound dictionary, wetting the tip of his forefinger to turn its pages, which were thin and translucent like the wings of an insect. He was insect-like too, a small man with a small pointed graying beard, lined skin, and a black skullcap on his head. His shoulders were narrow and rounded. The sleeves of his white shirt were rolled up and his arms spread out over the open newspaper as in an embrace. When David recalled him now it was in that pose, hunched in the unshaded glare of the kitchen light, studying as he used to, except back there it was the Talmud and here the *Times*. He remembered how, near midnight, finished at last, his father would gather the family together and summarize for them the contents of the major articles in the *New York Times*. Then they could go to bed. And remembering, David was assailed by an irritating mixture of pride and shame and nostalgia, which he tried to evict from his soul.

David went to law school. He was a dashing sort of young man, he liked to think, and he enjoyed reminiscing about his bravado in taking the bar exam. Hardly studying, for he was busy driving a cab in his spare moments, he passed the first time, usually a practice run. He hadn't even bothered checking the school bulletin board, but waited to find out the results from the list published in the paper. The achievement of passing the bar exam was rivaled only by the achievement of having his name printed in the *New York Times* for all the world to behold. It was while studying law that he came to appreciate and to love—though David was not a man who acknowledged love readily—the peculiar genius of his adopted country, and to feel deep affinities with it. He responded to the Constitution as an artist to an old master. A nonbeliever, in this he believed; he even admitted to feeling awe for the men who wrote it, though again, he felt awe for his fellow man rarely, all expectations and assessments of humanity having been incised on his spirit early on, in the years of the yellow arm band and the pogroms. He learned the Constitution by heart and remembered it—this was another of the achievements he took pride in. And on days when the Supreme Court (pinnacle of his favorite branch of government, for he was, by temperament and heritage, judgmental) struck down or upheld laws in accordance with David's interpretation of the Constitution, he was happy, and on those days he danced for his children.

He and Anna had two boys close together and then, ten years later, Lucy, who received the doting care spent usually on an only child. The boys turned out well, David thought, one a lawyer himself, the other an engineer; they married suitably nice girls, made money, and gave him and Anna grandchildren. And Lucy, he trusted, would be fine too. She had his head, quick and secret and sharp; though her temper flared up easily, like his, she didn't stay angry long. She could take care of herself and she was good-looking, which was important for a girl. All in all, a fine American girl.

Sometimes she made him worry, though. It was one thing to quote Marx and Lenin with righteous indignation—David did that himself—but another thing to take them seriously, especially here where matters were arranged otherwise, and it was just as well, too, for people like themselves. Lucy took it all far too seriously. She joined groups and recklessly signed her name to endless, dubious petitions. When David and Anna refused to sign or even to read those long sheets of paper she waved in their faces—for once you had signed your name who could tell where it would end up, no country is perfect, look at the business with McCarthy not so long ago—she got angry and made passionate speeches. And if David defended the way things were, she retorted that his narrow-minded and selfish mode of thinking was precisely the trouble with this country. Moreover, he and Anna were stodgy, unadventurous, needed broadening. "Why don't you travel? You have the money. Go to Europe. See another culture, how other people live, for a change."

"I've been to Europe," said David with a sneer and a tilt of the head. Then he saw her face turn hurt and ashamed, and he was sorry.

By middle age, when the boys were already young men, he had grown slightly pompous. He could hear it in his voice, but felt he was entitled to it, after all. He had made a certain amount of money, had a certain status, and spoke with an authoritative air, in well-sequenced paragraphs expounding his views to his thriving family on political, economic, and moral issues. Anna, who had heard it all before, puttered in the kitchen; sometimes she would interrupt with a remark or anecdote that she mistakenly thought illustrated one of David's points. But the boys listened respectfully, and even Lucy looked raptly attentive. Now and then he might stop to paraphrase something for her in simple terms and she would nod gravely, but he was never sure how much she understood. His vocabulary was studded with multisyllabic little-used words he enjoyed hearing spoken in his own voice. Among his favorites were "belligerent," "manifest," "deteriorate," "pejorative," complex words he had deliberately mastered years ago, words difficult not only to say but to use accurately, and on occasion he adjusted his thoughts to create opportunities to utter these words, feeling pride at the casual, indigenous way they slid off his tongue.

Sometimes he wished he had made more money. He was never quite sure he had made as much as his father had expected, when he told him, so many long years ago, to learn and show he was as good as the others. But since his father was dead now he would never know exactly how great those expectations had been. In any case, he had made enough. It was only when he thought of his brothers, and of childhood friends who had made more, that such doubts pricked him.

*   *   *

The first day of college, Lucy's roommate, a blond girl from Virginia whose father was in the foreign service, asked where she was from, and Lucy replied, "New York City."

"No, I know that, it was on the list. I mean *really* where you're from." As Lucy stared at her quizzically, she added, "Where you were born."

"New York. I told you." And then Lucy stared, with some unease, at the twin beds, twin dressers, twin desks, all squared off and bland. David had warned that at a school like this one, a "classy" school, as he called it, she would find bigotry, and she had brushed his warning off. For she had never, to her knowledge, experienced bigotry while growing up in New York City.

"I'm sorry," the girl, Patty, said with a harmless smile. "It's just that you have such a striking face, I was sure you were foreign. Middle East, Mediterranean, or something. I have a talent for placing faces—my parents dragged me all over the world, my whole life. Listen, all I mean is some people are lucky, that's all." Patty turned to the mirror in mock dismay, screwed up her ingenuous features, attempted a glamorous expression. "I mean, just look. No one would ever find *me* exotic." They both laughed, Lucy with relief. Patty was no bigot: *exotic*, she thought.

For months Lucy was exhilarated, as if she had discovered an intriguing new acquaintance; each evening she scrutinized her face, searching for what Patty had seen. It was true, a few of her aunts, with their olive skin, high cheekbones, and broad, almost Oriental faces, did look distinctly foreign, but she did not resemble them. Her jaws sloped down sharply to a strong chin. Her nose was straight and perfect, as her friends used to say enviously, her mouth small and finely curved. She had a high, smooth forehead with dark hair falling over it in calculated disarray, and dark, opaque eyes like David's. It was a good face—she was satisfied with it, but had never dreamed it might be *exotic*. She would not mention the incident to David, for she knew instinctively that he would not be pleased. David liked her to look like everyone else, and to wear whatever the girls were wearing that year. Often he asked her if she needed extra money for clothes, and when she came home for Christmas and Easter that first year he appraised her up and down and commented, in his understated way, "You look very nice. What do they call that kind of sweater?" Or coat. Or dress.

The following year she took an individual reading program in the nineteenth-century Russian novel. At the end there was an oral exam given by a panel of professors. She telephoned David long-distance the night before to find out the correct pronunciation of all the Russian names. Her ear was acute. If David said them over the phone a few times she could copy them. And then, in her fantasy, the professors would say, "Where did you get such a fine Russian accent?" and she would respond, with nonchalance, "Oh, my father is Russian."

Smerdyakov, Nozdraev, Sviazhsky, Kondratyevna . . . He resisted at first, but she coaxed until finally he said them for her, warmly, the heavy, earthy syllables rushing through miles of telephone wire into her ear. Saying them, he sounded like a stranger. She penciled accent marks in the proper places and repeated the names after him, but was shy about repeating them as well as she could have done. She sensed David might not like her assimilating the alien sounds too perfectly.

Except the next morning at the exam she found that several of them were wrong. At least the professors pronounced them differently. Lucy felt a shudder of fear, as if the room had suddenly gone cold. Who was David, really, and where was *he* from, if anywhere? And what did this make of her? The fantasy—"Where did you get such a fine Russian accent?"—never happened.

It could never have happened, she realized later. She had forgotten what Anna once told her privately, long ago. "Being Russian is one thing. Being Jewish, from Russia, is something else."

She learned also, in a history course, that it was Marx who first said, "Religion is the opium of the people," not Vladimir Lenin.

Months later, riding in David's car, Lucy said, "All those Russian characters in the books I studied for that course last year. They all had this great passion about life. Do you know what I mean?"

"Yes. Yes."

"Like your sisters. The women reminded me of them. And of me. They were all passionate about different things, but underneath it was the same."

"Yes."

"Do you feel that way sometimes?"

"What way?"

"Passionate. About life, I mean," she added when she saw him shift uncomfortably in his seat.

David moved into the left lane to pass a car. A truck appeared over the crest of the hill, approaching them. Speeding up, David swerved to the right, and in a reflex action, as he used to do when she was a child, shot his arm out in front of Lucy's chest to shield her. Safe again, he settled back and cleared his throat. "They always had much more respect for their great writers than we do here. You have to say that for them." It was understood that they never discussed his rash driving.

"Tell me, what was it like?"

"I don't remember."

"You must remember."

"It's so long ago, I can't."

"You left a brother over there, didn't you?"

"Yes, Mordecai."

"Well, what happened to him? Why didn't he come?"

"He was a grown man, established, with a wife and children and a job. It would have been hard for him to leave."

"Didn't you ever write to him?" She could almost touch it in the space between them, her own passionate urgency pressing him, and his resistance. "Didn't you ever want to know what happened to him?"

"He's probably dead now. Or else a very old man. Chances are he's dead."

"But why didn't you ever write? You could still try to . . ." She was warm and full of energy; like those women in the novels, she could set out on a sacrificial trek to trace this lost brother or his descendants, if David would only ask.

"How could we write? There were wars and pogroms. You think it was as easy to correspond by airmail as it is now? . . . Well, we did write, at first, then we lost touch. There were . . . incidents. Killings. Didn't you learn any history? Didn't you learn about that famous ravine? That was our city." He pulled into the garage and leaned over to open the door for her. "You can afford to have passion." He smiled and patted her hand. "Come into the house."

Lucy was twenty-six. The last of her many cousins was getting married and she was taking Allan to the wedding. She had met him during a trip to Mexico, at an outdoor market in a dusty village. He was buying oranges. The way he stood at the fruit stand, tall and lanky, in faded blue jeans and work shirt, handling each orange thoughtfully, tenderly even, before dropping it into his net sack, appealed to her. She moved nearby, hoping he would notice her and start a conversation, which he did. But first he held out an orange. She always remembered that, how even before he spoke he offered her something.

No doubt some of the aunts and uncles would comment teasingly about Allan's beard. Men like David and his brothers shaved fastidiously, beards being part of the detritus they had left behind them. She had also prepared him for their sly remarks about marriage; he had a gentle face and they would take liberties: "So what are you kids waiting for? See, it's painless!"

For surely David or Anna would not have told anyone that they already shared an apartment. That fact was a thorn to David, and she was sorry to inflict it on him in his vulnerable years. Anna didn't seem to mind as much. She kept up with changing times, wore pants suits now, read articles in magazines about drugs and venereal disease, and even thought the ponytail on her oldest grandson was cute. But David's views were ancient and changeless.

"This must be the place," said Allan wryly. He found a space in the crowded parking lot. "Simplicity itself."

"I warned you, didn't I? We don't do things in a small way."

Inside, all plate glass and draperies and potted plants, they were ushered past a chapel, a ballroom for the dinner and dancing to follow, and onto a terrace overlooking a bright green lawn. A bar was set up at one end; at the other a band played a waltz. Men in dark suits and women in long gaily colored dresses flecked the grass in the sunlight of the early June afternoon. A few couples danced on the terrace.

Lucy caught Allan's hand and pressed it. "It's beautiful, though, isn't it? A garden party."

"Very nice," he admitted. "All right, let's plunge in. Lead me to the slaughter."

"I'll start you on the young ones—they're easier. Then you can work your way up."

"Save me a dance."

"What kind of dance do you want?"

"Oh, any kind," said Allan. "I can do them all."

David rushed up to where they stood talking with a group of cousins. His walk had slowed lately, but just now he strode with the energy of his youth, reminding Lucy of the vigor of his absurd dances. He took her hand and held her away from him, appraising.

"You look lovely. What do they call that funny business up on top?"

"An Empire waist."

"Very nice." His eyes traveled the length of the dress, wine-colored, down to where it shimmered out in folds. "Come, I want you to meet some people. Excuse us, Allan, just for a few minutes. I'll send her right back." And he tugged her off by the hand excitedly, through the clusters of guests, the way she used to tug him in the zoo to show him some rare species she had found.

They stopped at a table where a few gray-haired people were gathered.

"This is my daughter, Lucy," said David, pushing her before him. "My scientist," he added, with his special blend of pride and mild mockery; she never could tell which was dominant.

There were a married couple, Victor and Edna Rickoff, with kind worn faces, and a tall man standing up, Sam Panofsky, broad and dapper, his thin white hair combed straight back from his forehead and stylishly long. Panofsky smiled all the time, leering beneath bushy white eyebrows. From the set of his jaw Lucy knew he thought well of himself and his appearance. In his navy-blue suit adorned with a wide orange tie, he moved rigidly, like a man much older than he looked. His body had a well-kept yet tenuous solidity, as though he stayed firm by artificial means, by laborious hours on machines in expensive health clubs. He watched Lucy; his lips closed, then opened, and he wet them with his tongue.

"A scientist?" he echoed.

"Damn right," replied David. Then, turning to Lucy, "We grew up together. Victor's house was right next door. We all went to school together."

"Sure," said Rickoff. "Did he ever tell you, Lucy, the crazy things we used to do?"

She shook her head.

"Oh, did we have times!" Rickoff's milky eyes lit up behind thick glasses. "Remember that back yard where we played bandits, how we dug in the dirt for bags of gold? And those poor chickens we chased?"

"You chased everything that moved." Mrs. Rickoff was fair and frail, and smoked with a long black cigarette holder. "Such wild boys. Like wild animals, bobcats."

Lucy sat down with them. "So you were childhood friends? This is amazing."

"Friends!" cried Rickoff. "More like family! At a wedding, like today, we used to sneak under the grownups' feet to get in the dance. You should have seen your father jump around. Some little dancer, that one, they used to say."

"And what else?" said Lucy.

"Your father was some smart-alecky kid. Remember, David, one morning you broke the ruler the teacher used to smack us with?" Rickoff tossed his benign and balding head. "So he smacked us with half! And sent us out to stand in the freezing cold for an hour!"

"Those winters were so bitter," said Mrs. Rickoff. "Snow up to your eyes. You had to melt ice to wash. But the summers." She leaned towards Lucy in a sudden surge, her voice deepening. "The summers were gorgeous. That sky, not like anything here. Very wide, with a funny yellow light on the trees. There was a certain time of day, four, five o'clock, when even those old houses had a golden look, from the light. We went around barefoot, jumping in puddles. The ground was hot under our feet."

Lucy was transported. It was just such privacies she had craved, like something out of a book, alien, exotic, transcendent. If only the Rickoffs had been her parents, she might have tasted that vanished spicy air. . . . Then turning to David, who was lighting up an olive cigar, his face bland and impenetrable, she felt a traitor.

"Barefoot, sure," Rickoff said to his wife. "Who had shoes?"

"Yes, you're leaving out the best parts," said Panofsky. "Sky, puddles! Why don't you tell her about the czars? Tell her what fun our boys had in the army." Panofsky moved stiffly towards Lucy and laid a hand on her shoulder. "But a pretty girl like you isn't interested in such things. Would you care to dance?"

She hesitated and looked at David again, foolishly, as though he could tell her what to say.

"Well, maybe a little later. I just got here." She gave a diffident laugh. "I want to hear some more." And then she felt embarrassed for wanting so obviously to possess it the easy way, the way she had taken possession of the old novels, reveling in the abrasive names that exercised her tongue, and in the improbable lusts and sufferings.

"You like this old stuff, eh? Sounds like a TV special, from this end. Right, David?" Panofsky snorted. "But she's lucky. Nice straight nose, good face. No one would ever take her for . . ."

"What do you mean? Take me for what?"

"You could be right off the *Mayflower*. . . . You know you have a few gray hairs already? Why don't you cover them up? A young woman like you with gray hair—no need, in this day and age. In this country, especially, you can change yourself into anything you want. Let me see, I bet you're not a day over . . . twenty-three?"

"Twenty-six."

"And not married yet? What's the matter?" He laughed and

turned again to her father. "The young boys not good enough for her, David? You spoiled her?"

David stood up. "I'm going to go and see how your mother's doing." He paused a moment by her side.

"Go on. I'll be right over." She turned away from Panofsky and towards the others. "Is it so foolish to want to know something about your own history? I mean—" Then she stopped and thought once more how hopelessly naive she must sound. She saw her past as swaddled in secrecy, infused with a vast nostalgia for something she had never known, something which perhaps had never even existed, except as a mystery she herself had created and nourished. From the corner of her eye she noticed David walk briskly away; she felt both abandoned and yet finally free to unearth what she wanted. She gazed at the Rickoffs as though they were artifacts, archaeologists' finds, and then dropped her eyes, reproaching herself: they were ordinary people, and she was tongue-tied.

Mrs. Rickoff must have sensed her discomfort. "Tell me something, Lucy. Did you ever see your father eat a banana?" she asked with a grin.

"A banana? I don't know. I don't remember."

"Fifty-five years in this country," she said, nodding towards her husband, "and still he won't eat a banana. Because they didn't have bananas where we came from. He eats only what he ate as a child. That's how it sticks."

Everyone laughed, and Lucy relaxed. "Caviar," she said. "That's what my father passed on to me. Caviar every Sunday morning."

David went to sit with Anna, but over his shoulder he kept glancing at Lucy, still with the Rickoffs. A beautiful girl, it was undeniable, and the maroon dress suited her. She had turned out well. At school, first she had studied languages, then unexpectedly changed to biochemistry, more practical anyway, he decided. Now she had a job in a laboratory, working on an epilepsy research project and making good money, for a girl. Only the business with the boyfriend grated on his heart. Not Allan himself—he was a fine young man with a future, exactly the type he would have picked out for her himself. The beard was not worth making an issue of. When she had first brought him home to meet them David was pleased, and assumed it was only a matter of time.

"So," he teased the next day over the phone, "will we be seeing more of him?"

"I imagine so," she replied in the same tone.

"Good. I presume you see a lot of him?"

"Oh yes. As a matter of fact he's sharing the apartment. I was going to tell you, soon."

He hung up. In the kitchen he found Anna and shouted at her in a rage made worse because she went on quietly chopping onions while he flung his arms about and ranted.

At last she said, "What did you think she was doing with him? Times have changed. Maybe it's better."

He couldn't fathom Anna's attitude. It gnawed at his insides that Lucy could turn against him so. In his mind he had to stop himself from calling her filthy names in a foreign tongue; alone, he would cover his ears and nod his gray head back and forth like an aged man grieving. Back there, women who did that were called those names, and when respectable women saw them they crossed to the other side of the street.

Anna advised him to say nothing about it to Lucy. His pain dulled, or he became accustomed to it. At least the boy was Jewish, he consoled himself wryly. The other he couldn't have been able to tolerate. She continued to visit with Allan, and David got through these visits by behaving as if they were married. They seemed so, in every way but the license. He would have liked to take her on his arm and walk down a flower-scented aisle, leaving her in the middle for Allan to fetch. And be host to all the relatives, showing what a fine wedding he could give. Surely he deserved it, after all his efforts? Yet this fantasy might never happen.

"But what will happen?" he would ask Anna petulantly.

"What will happen," said Anna calmly, "is that one fine day she will accidentally or on purpose get pregnant, and then they'll get married like everyone else, and you will have nothing to worry about."

He smoked and watched her at the table a few yards away. They were all talking and laughing loudly, except for Panofsky, who sat a bit apart, staring at Lucy as David himself was doing. Rickoff was telling some story, thrashing his arms about wildly, tossing in Yiddish and Russian phrases, and Lucy threw her head back and laughed. Then she leaned forward eagerly to ask him something. Rickoff sobered and gave her a long reply, his facial muscles moving in an old, foreign pattern, in a language counterpoint to his spoken English. Mrs. Rickoff joined in, also waving her hands, and as the three of them talked at once, it seemed to David that Lucy was taking on their old-fashioned expressions and gestures—extravagantly raised eyebrows, pursed lips, rhythmic shrugs and nods, lively winks and puckers and thrust-out chins and jaws. She said something with a swift dramatic flick of her hand that suddenly brought his mother back to life. David could not hear most of their words, but he imagined she was taking on their rough-edged foreign accents as well, her voice falling into a nasal, singsong intonation. He felt a chill: it was as if she were being transformed before his eyes, as if he had delivered her over to the very powers he had been shielding her from all these years, and she was all too willingly drawn in, drawn back. For a split second he glimpsed her not in her stylish silky dress but in heavy shapeless skirts and shawls, a dark scarf wrapped around her shaved head, her fine features coarsened by endless childrearing, scrubbing, cooking, and anxiety. When he blinked the image vanished.

He saw Panofsky lean forward to whisper in her ear. Lucy looked confused, then rose, reluctantly, it seemed, and let him lead her by the elbow to the middle of the terrace, where he swung his arm around to pull her close for the dance. His large hand pressed into the small of her back; her hand rested on his shoulder lightly, barely touching. Panofsky was more than a head taller than she, and he looked down at her, grinning. From David's distance Lucy seemed fragile and helpless in the flimsy dress with the bare back, though he knew she was neither. Still, Panofsky was holding her tightly, and she looked uncomfortable. Panofsky, that old lecher, burrowed his face against her hair for a moment, and David leaned forward as if ready to spring from his seat. Could Panofsky know, by any rumors, that she was living with a man, not married? He had made that nasty crack about her being too spoiled to marry. An old panicky tremor rose in David's stomach, a sickening tremor he knew from years ago on the boat, and later in school. Panofsky's face was red, his eyelids drooping, as he tightened his arm around Lucy's waist.

David was sick to his stomach and had to put out his cigar. The very air, dotted with the aging, familiar faces of transplanted people like Panofsky trying desperately, uselessly, to be carefree and self-assured, to be new and free and American, suddenly smelled fetid to him. And it seemed that in the idiotic, the nearly senile yet firm embrace of Panofsky was everything old and reeking of foreignness that he had labored so hard to protect her from. For himself he accepted it, it would cling to him no matter what fine words or clothes or houses masked it. But for his children, especially for her—ah, he had wanted them new, untainted, bred without that ancient history.

Panofsky gripped her hand and bent his cheek to her hair again. David saw Lucy draw back so that his head jerked awkwardly. Panofsky shifted and pulled her against him with the pressure of his thick wrist. With relief, David watched her push at his shoulder and extricate herself from his hold, leaving him standing ridiculously, arms open in dance posture, in the middle of the sunny terrace. Would she come to them or go over to Allan, standing at the bar with the young people? He could not bear the thought of her shaming him in front of Allan, telling, in her voice which could be so harsh and mocking, about his crude, his unredeemable friends.

But she was coming towards him and Anna, sweeping over royally, head high, face flushed, holding up the bottom of her dress to walk faster. Before she said a word she whisked Anna's drink off the table and gulped it down.

"Christ, that one is the original dirty old man! Who let *him* in?"

"He's still a friend of your uncle Peter's," said David remorsefully. Unable to look his own daughter in the eye—was this what it had all come to?

"He was unbelievable! Blowing in my ear, practically. What a nerve! If he weren't an old friend of yours I would have told him exactly what I thought of him." She sat down and lit a cigarette.

Anna, the perenially serene, said, "Panofsky's always been like that, with anyone he can get his hands on. Once he got me out on the dance floor and I told him off good and proper. It's nothing to bother about."

David was relieved to see Lucy's frown beginning to turn slightly amused. Only an outburst of the moment, perhaps, a summer storm. She would forget it.

"Gray hair," and she laughed. She pulled a random hair from her head and studied it, then flicked it away. "Silly old fool. But seriously," and she put her hand on David's arm, "I liked your friends. The others." She paused and looked straight into his eyes, her anger spent. "It meant a lot, meeting your friends. They were wonderful. They told me your father was famous as a scholar. I never knew that. I never knew he managed an estate, either."

"For one of *them*," David sneered.

"That's not the point," she said.

"What is the point? You want to feel you came out of a book by Tolstoi? That's what you want? You didn't."

"Oh, Dad," she groaned. She turned in despair and looked at Anna, but Anna's face was closed and absent, as if she had witnessed this many times before and grown weary of it. Lucy sat silent for a few moments, then said, "They told me I looked like your mother. Is that so?"

"There's a resemblance." He shrugged. "For a few months in her life, maybe, she had a chance to look like you."

The band was playing a slow and stately waltz, the kind he used to dance with Anna. He could still do it well enough, he was quite sure. He edged forward in his chair, glancing first at Anna, then at Lucy, and hesitating. He saw her face brighten, but it was for Allan, who was approaching from across the terrace. Before he could reach them Lucy leaned up close; her hasty whisper was like a hiss. "Would it have cost you so much to tell me some of those things? Would it?"

David's face burned hot with shame, with an unspeakable confusion, just as Allan stepped up, smiling broadly, innocently, to take her hand. He wanted her to waltz.

EPISTEMOLOGY, SEX,
AND THE
SHEDDING OF LIGHT

"Guess who I saw in a Chinese restaurant in Washington," Harry asked me. He had just returned from offering expert advice on disaster relief to government officials.

"Henry Kissinger."

Harry's eyes narrowed and his smile of anticipation vanished. "How did you know?"

"I don't know."

"Well, guess who he was eating lunch with."

"Liv Ullmann."

Harry stopped combing his hair and regarded me with some bitterness. His eyes had that disappointed look Rachel's had when, a few years ago, she left the dinner table to go to the bathroom and returned to find Harry had finished her hamburger. He assumed she was done. She has never forgotten. "How did you know?"

"I don't know. I'm sorry. Tell me how they looked, anyway." That was not the whole truth. I had read several reviews of Liv

Ullmann's autobiography and learned that she had once dated Henry Kissinger. Still, that doesn't account for my knowing.

I wasn't reading Harry's mind, either, as often happens. For example, five years ago he looked longingly at a box of saltine crackers on the supermarket shelf. "Do we need these?" he asked.

"We have saltines at home."

"Oh."

"Take them anyway. It's the box you want, isn't it?" It was a large square cardboard box about five inches high, with rounded corners. There were colorful flowers and curlicues painted on its sides. The metal lid in its center was round with raised edges, the kind that would have to be pried off with a spoon.

He looked distressed. "How did you know?"

"I know what you like. That's your kind of box. Take it. We'll dump the crackers into a canister."

He was tempted, but his upbringing was too powerful. "No." Harry is not self-indulgent, especially about spending money. Cash, that is. He prefers to write a check, or better still, whip out a credit card. As a result he buys big expensive things more willingly than small, cash-and-carry things. Penny wise and pound foolish, one might infer, except here the issue is not wisdom or folly, only the degree of abstraction of the money.

With the saltines my knowledge, though seemingly uncanny, might have been traced to certain fleeting perceptions stored in my brain cells. It was quite different with the case of Henry Kissinger and Liv Ullmann, a true epistemological mystery.

Similarly, I have unaccountable lapses. In the Central Children's Room at the Donnell Library two weeks ago my dear friend Emily from California, my daughter Rachel, and I admired a Gila monster on display in a jar of water. (Rachel was in the library to do research for a social studies report on Thomas Alva Edison.)

"Isn't it beautiful," I said. It was light orange and black, thick, powerful, coiled on itself. I felt an electrical charge of affinity with the Gila monster, though physically we have nothing in common, except that orange is my favorite color. After a while I added wistfully, "I think it's dead." Emily and Rachel burst out laughing.

"How could anything live in a jar of water?" Rachel said to me, with her twelve-year-old's stare of incredulity at my stupidity.

I was stupid indeed. I heard myself say in self-defense, "I guess I thought it was like a fish." I wonder how and why I could have assumed the Gila monster was alive. Apart from wishful thinking, I suspect it had something to do with the surprising appearance of Emily, whom I hadn't seen in over six months.

Emily was in New York on a flying visit; we spent an hour drinking in a bar near the Donnell while Rachel hunted for books about Edison. I was shocked when I first saw Emily, for she had cut off her hair and lost about fifteen pounds and was dressed in long black flowing garments.

"I'm thirty-eight years old," she explained. "I decided it was time to stop looking like a sophomore at Music and Art."

"Well, you've succeeded," I said. "You look like a lady."

"Do I look like a lady poet?" She is in fact a poet.

"I think so. Definitely a lady, anyway."

The transformation of Emily was so unexpected and disconcerting that perhaps it jolted something in my nervous system that subsequently made it possible for me to assume the Gila monster in the jar of water was alive. Perhaps.

At Hunter College the other day I asked my freshman students in Expository Writing to write an impromptu essay on a contention by Erich Fromm that education gives children a fictitious picture of reality. I made quite sure to put "fictitious picture of reality" in quotes on the blackboard so there would be no doubt they were Erich Fromm's words and not mine. One learns caution when teaching freshmen. I suggested they support their assertions with examples from their personal experience. After a half hour of quiet writing, a boy with braces on his teeth came up to me and asked, "How is the word 'fictitious' used here?"

Surely the answer "as an adjective" was not what he sought. "What do you mean, how is it used?"

"I mean, well, what does it mean?"

One also learns, teaching freshmen, not to show surprise or any emotion that might discourage progress. "It means made up, not true, like a story."

"Oh. Thank you." He smiled happily and returned to his writing. I discussed this incident with a psychotherapist friend, who said that for her the real interest of the story was not that the boy did not know what "fictitious" meant, but that he did not know how outrageous his not knowing would appear.

My own education, if more thorough, was equally unbalanced. As is the custom in schools, the teachers ignored connections and stressed facts, particularly facts regarding the Boxer Rebellion, Alexander Kerensky, the nature of scalene triangles, the names of the inns frequented or referred to by Chaucer, Shakespeare, and Dr. Johnson, the principal exports of Uruguay, and the names of cabinet departments (St. Dapiacl, an acronym now an anachronism). Up until the age of twenty-five I remembered it all, then slowly, like a sandy, weather-buffeted slope of land, it began to erode, except for the Tabard and the Mermaid. The Tabard and the Mermaid, like seeds luckily blown to more fertile meadows, took root elsewhere in my brain, where I watered and nurtured them because I cared.

When Rachel first went off to be educated I used to go to pick her up every day on the Riverside Drive bus, taking along Miranda, two years younger. Once in a while our trips were graced by the glorious double-decker bus, whose erratic schedule we could never master, unfortunately. But most days, silent and absent, Miranda would gape morosely out the ordinary-bus window, with a finger in her mouth. I naturally inferred boredom and resentment. When Rachel learned to come home by herself I said to Miranda, "I bet you'll be glad not to take that bus ride every day."

"But I won't get to see the statues."

"What statues?"

She confided that she had a private story explaining the freestanding statues dispersed along the drive between 120th and 81st Streets, which she regaled herself with every day, going and coming.

The first statue, a man on a pedestal, is a king, she told me.

Beneath him, a soldier with a flag is holding a woman who is on her knees. The woman is really a princess but she's in rags. She is going to be put in jail and she's crying, "Let me go, let me go!" (113th Street, erected in 1928 "by a Liberty Loving Race of Americans of Magyar Origin to Louis Kossuth the Great Champion of Liberty"; below Kossuth are a flag-bearing soldier and a long-haired old man in flowing robes; they are gripping hands).

The next statue, Miranda related, is a man who looks like Abraham Lincoln, with a pedestal next to him. He is the father of the prince, and he is going to get a drink of water (112th Street, Samuel J. Tilden, "1814–1886, Patriot Statesman Lawyer Philanthropist Governor of New York Democratic Nominee for the Presidency 1876 I Trust the People").

The third is a man on a horse. He is the prince. He has heard the news about the princess and is going through the forest to rescue her (106th Street, an equestrian labeled tersely, "Franz Sigel").

Last is a lady on a horse. She is the same princess as in the beginning and she got rescued and that is the end (Joan of Arc, 93rd Street, armed with a sword, mounted on a rearing horse, "Burned at the Stake at Rouen France May 30, 1431, Erected by The Joan of Arc Statue Committee in the City of New York, 1915").

I was disturbed by only one omission. "Why didn't you use the Buddha at 105th Street?" (The "Buddha" is Shinran Shonin, 1173 to 1262, founder of the Jodo-Shinshu sect and presently adorning the doorway of the New York Buddhist Church.)

"Oh, him. He was too big." Seeing my dismay, she added, "I did use him once. He was a magician. He was trying to stop the prince, who was going through the forest. He's wearing a frown because the prince got the princess." She hesitated. "But he's really too big for the story."

"And I thought you were bored."

"I was, sometimes."

I asked Harry at dinner, the night he returned from Washington, if he had thought of going up to Liv Ullmann to tell her he enjoyed her performance in *A Doll's House*.

"Oh, no. They were looking for obscurity."

"What's 'obscurity'?" asked Miranda.

He told her. "Anyway, I eschew celebrities."

We laughed.

"What is 'eschew'?" asked Rachel.

"An obscure word meaning avoid," he said.

"I don't believe you."

"It is."

"That's ridiculous." At twelve, her only pejorative adjectives are "ridiculous," "gross," "disgusting," and "weird." "I don't believe there's such a word. It sounds weird."

"Go look it up in the dictionary." Harry spelled it for her.

"All right. But don't eat my dinner. I'm coming back."

"She'll never forgive me," he said. "She's like the elephant."

"Because you still do it," said Miranda. "You ate the M & M's I got from Willy's party."

"They were out on the table. I assumed they were common property."

"You should ask before you assume anything," said Miranda.

Rachel was chagrined to find "eschew" in the dictionary.

"While you're there," I called in to her, "please look up the Gila monster."

"God," she moaned, very put upon. She read me what it said about the Gila monster. Of course I have forgotten most of it. I do remember that it has a "sluggish but ugly disposition," because I found the phrase, with its assonance, extremely suggestive, and I was intrigued by the choice of the connective "but." I also remember that there exists a "closely allied form" in Mexico named *H. horridum*. I shall doubtless remember *H. horridum* forever. These facts made me love it more.

After Rachel returned to the table I reached for my purse, which I had set down in the center of the kitchen floor when I returned from giving my class the essay assignment on Erich Fromm's educational theories. As I picked it up, somehow its entire contents spilled out. Harry glanced over at the array of objects scattered on the floor. "Where is your eye of newt?" he asked.

Every now and then he says something that makes me recall with jubilation why I married him.

"Eye of newt!" I laughed, crouching on the floor. "How do you know about eye of newt?" He reads mainly the *New York Times* and books on the structure of society and how it can be improved.

He shrugged.

"Come on, where do you know that from?" I challenged him. "Tell me where that comes from."

He paused, frowned, looked vaguely at the children for help not forthcoming. "Shakespeare?" he asked finally. "*Macbeth?*"

While I was putting my purse back together he said to Rachel, "By the way, how did you make out with the report on Thomas Edison?"

"Okay. Did you know that Thomas Edison was deaf?"

"Yes," said Harry, and "No," said I, simultaneously.

"Was he born deaf," I asked, "or did he get deaf?"

"He got deaf, when he was around twelve or fourteen."

"How?"

"Thomas Edison," Rachel began in warm didactic tones, "had a job on a train, selling candy and stuff like that. When the train pulled out of the station he would grab hold of an open car above the wheels and pull himself up. One day he couldn't pull himself up so he was just hanging, and he knew that he could be killed, so a man standing in the car pulled him up by his ears. And Thomas Edison heard something pop in each ear and his ears really hurt for a while after that." She paused in reflective sympathy. "They really hurt a lot, and he began to get hard of hearing. And then his parents took him to a doctor, and the doctor examined him and said he couldn't do anything and he was going to get deafer and there might come a time when he would be totally deaf. And then when he was grown up another doctor offered to improve the situation but Edison refused, because he said he liked living in his laboratory without outside noises distracting him, and he was used to it."

I said, "That is fascinating." Rachel smiled proudly, as if she had made the story up herself, which, given my ignorance, she might have done. "Could he hear anything at all?"

"Yes," she replied. "He wasn't totally deaf; part of the time he could hear if people talked loud. Later on he could read his wife's lips but it was easier for her to tap Morse code into his hand. He was married twice."

"Which wife tapped?" asked Miranda.

"The second. He taught her Morse code and asked her to marry him in Morse code and she tapped back yes."

I was growing ecstatic over this memorable information.

"Also," Rachel went on, "when he was about six or seven he went to this small school run by a man and his wife, and it was very crowded. They had kids of all different ages and didn't have time to talk to each kid alone. He came home one day after three months and said to his mother, 'My teachers say that I'm addled.' So his mother took him and went to the school and she said to the teachers, 'This boy is smarter than you are.' Which in Edison's case was true. After that he never went back to school. His mother taught him and he taught himself and he was reading college books when he was about ten or nine. But he wasn't good at math."

"What is 'addled'?" asked Miranda.

"Confused," said Rachel. "Like you don't know what is going on."

"Did you learn anything else important about Edison?" Harry asked hopefully.

"No. I don't know. I don't remember." She stood up. "I'm finished. You can have that if you want it." She pointed to the remains on her plate.

Harry looked disturbed as he slid Rachel's plate towards him.

"Miranda," I said, lest she feel overlooked, "you'll never guess what nice thing happened to me on the way home from work."

"You caught the double-decker bus," she promptly replied.

THE MAN AT THE GATE

He stood in the shadows, as usual, as Charlotte had come to expect. He was a part, by now, of the quiet late afternoon street that gathered her in when the working day was over. It was dusk, early spring. The air was warmish, and as Charlotte rounded the corner she could smell the honeysuckle, rising like incense. If she leaned over close, the honeysuckle was smothering, like an anesthetic. Such a powerful, rich scent—she imagined if she bent too close, its vapors might make her swoon with forgetfulness, or cause numbness or sleeping sickness, like some strange tropical herb. But this way, passing a few feet away from the hedges that lined the front yards, she could revel briefly in the sweet-scented air. Then she drew a quick breath, for he loomed up too near. Charlotte was so preoccupied with the thought of the Harrises coming over later for coffee that she had forgotten to cross at the corner to avoid him. She hated to walk right by him, yet crossing the street abruptly might be too obvious a move. She went on, head down, legs trembling. She wanted to look up into his eyes, but she wasn't brave enough. When she reached her own gate, she turned furtively. He hadn't stirred.

Every evening the man—she always called him "the man" in her thoughts—stood at the wrought-iron gate in front of the house directly opposite hers and Fred's. She never saw him come, never saw him go. But he was always there, evenings, when she looked out the front window, or if she passed by alone or with Fred. Mostly she passed by alone. He was a thin man, not young, not old, and dressed in an old-fashioned way, in a light-brown hat, a tan belted raincoat, and dark pants. The top buttons of the raincoat were usually open and she could see his white shirt, also unbuttoned, with no tie. His long bony face appeared vague: lit by the street lamp it was waxen and expressionless. The jutting chin, hollow cheeks, and tan raincoat reminded her of a puny gangster she had once seen in an old movie on the Late Show. She couldn't remember the actor's name, but he too had kept his hat brim down low and his hands deep in his raincoat pockets. The man at the gate was sinister yet pitiful in just that way.

He had done nothing to frighten her except stand, evenings the year round: still, she was afraid. Coming home from work (she worked at a women's magazine, where she assembled household hints and amusing fillers for her boss's monthly column), Charlotte was careful to walk on the other side of the street. Fred once suggested ironically that she should greet him, stop to chat. But then Fred was full of outlandish ideas. From across the street she would steal looks at the man before lifting the latch of her own gate. Once inside she would peer out the window.

It was a peaceful green neighborhood of three-story houses in a sleepy section of Philadelphia. The houses, old and narrow, with kindly, worn facades, were set well back from the street. Nearly all of them had wrought-iron gates and small flagstone walks dividing the meager front lawns. Charlotte and Fred rented a top floor. In the yard of the house opposite, where the man stood, grew a magnificent dogwood tree that flowered lusciously pink in late April. For two years Charlotte had watched it bloom and quickly fade;

this would be the third. It lasted so short a time, she thought sadly every spring: eight, maybe ten days. It waited all year for its brief blaze of pink, and then sank back into dullness to wait again. At night the street lamp gave the dogwood a lurid plastic sheen that made it hideous. But she loved to see it in the mornings. She would linger at the window sometimes before leaving for work, to take in the sight of the glowing pink tree. It helped prepare her for the day, while Fred lay sleeping, snoring and cumbersome. With his head barely showing out of the brown blanket, he was like the great leatherback turtle she had once seen washed up on the beach, staining the sand around with dark blood.

She climbed the stairs slowly. "He's still there," she told Fred.

Fred didn't answer right away. He was sitting on the couch in his T-shirt and undershorts, tinkering with an old broken alarm clock which he said could be fixed. He had taken it apart; bits of shiny metal were scattered on the coffee table. Charlotte didn't care about the clock: she didn't need an alarm clock to wake up on time, and Fred didn't have to get up at any special time, but it was his latest obsession. He looked as though he had recently gotten out of bed. Charlotte didn't know why she was so sure of this. Perhaps it was his puffy, dazed expression or the dryness around his lips.

"Of course, what did you expect? He's always there."

She sighed, and set down her bag of groceries on the coffee table. She must remember to tell him about the Harrises, but not right now. "Did you look today?" she asked.

"Yes," he said. "Nothing."

Fred had been job-hunting for two years. He had quit his old job soon after he moved in with her, just three months after they met. He had been working for an airline, doing something called "dealing with the public," but he was unhappy there. His bosses were fussy and gave him a hard time. Charlotte never knew which airline, or where his office was. It had seemed quite unimportant then, in the early days. There were other things to talk about. Now she found herself wishing she had known.

The airline was only a stopgap, though. His real work, he told her, was acting. He came from Chicago, where he had performed with several small theater groups and even had bit parts in two films, but they were obscure gangster films Charlotte had never heard of. She asked him, the first week they met, why he wasn't acting any longer. He cocked his head in that appealing way he had and smiled his rueful, paternal smile. "Ah, well." Things had gotten messed up, he explained. After his parents' death, money problems—probate court, his investments screwed up by a crooked broker, now in jail. It was all too much. He had needed a job quick, any job, when he fled East. Luckily the airline job came along, but it was not the sort of thing he wanted to stay with.

Charlotte imagined he must have been a good actor, even though he wouldn't do any of his parts for her when she begged him to—not in the mood, he said. He was big and handsome in a rugged beefy way, though just a tiny bit fat around the middle when she first knew him. That would never do for an actor, she said, and she recommended a diet. And just a tiny bit gone to seed, she thought, feeling disloyal as she admitted it. That was from hard luck, but it could be fixed. Amazing what a little confidence, a little success and good luck, would do for him, when it came. Her father had looked that way once, she remembered, when he was out of work, and then he had perked up when he found a job.

He told her he was thirty-five. He appeared older to Charlotte, but if it made him happy, poor fellow, to say thirty-five, then let him. It was hard to tell a man's age anyway. His voice sounded like an actor's voice, deep and resonant, and he spoke well, probably because of his training. It was that voice and speech that first attracted her. No one had ever spoken to her in those low, deep tones. Compared to Fred, the others she had known were boys.

And he was funny, too. He had an offhand, bizarre wit. At least he made her laugh, and God knows she had needed to laugh. She was twenty-four then and living with her widowed mother, who scarcely let a day go by without reminding her that such a big girl would have trouble finding a suitable man. Charlotte didn't mind being so tall; she accepted it as she accepted most things in life, only her mother harped on it so. She was five foot ten and solidly built, never overweight. Statuesque was what people called her when they wanted to flatter her. Well, she had found a big man, and she displayed him proudly to her mother like a trophy. Charlotte reached just to Fred's lips. Big enough? she wanted to ask her mother. And you said it couldn't be done. Only it was too bad that when Fred met her mother he had been so quiet. Not funny at all. That was the first time she experienced one of his silences, and it was chilling, but she chalked it up to nervousness. Afterwards her mother said, "A hulk, but what else? Can he talk?" That was the end of that. Charlotte moved out and took an apartment, and soon Fred joined her.

She had great plans for him when he quit the airline. He would go back to the theater. He might not be a star, but he would work steadily, and cultivated people would recognize his name. She would help him. Charlotte was energetic; her healthy exuberant face shone with life and motion. Before her father died, when she was twenty-one, she had had many friends and was full of ideas for adventure. She was never lonesome, never neglected. She had been on the point of moving into her own apartment with two friends, but she took pity on her mother, left alone, and remained. She became quieter, would spend long hours at home doing nothing. Like a young child, she longed for a sister or brother to keep her company. At last she met Fred and summoned the energy to leave her mother. It was a relief to talk again, to live with someone she could talk to. Soon she felt like her old self. She was lively, her spirits expanded, she made plans for trips they would take and pleasures they would share, and Fred listened good-humoredly, not saying much, but that was his way. She bought theater newspapers and magazines for him, and on the bus going to work she would read them and underline anything that looked promising. For a few months he took her advice and went to auditions. He would tell her about them in the evenings, how he had done his prepared bit, a monologue from *Who's Afraid of Virginia Woolf?*, how the director had looked him over in an appraising, offensive way, how silly the other auditioners had been. Fred made those stories very amusing. Sometimes his sarcasm bothered Charlotte, though. The others couldn't all have been that bad, she thought. But then she knew nothing about the theater, really. It was a terribly cutthroat and competitive field, and it was no wonder Fred sounded bitter.

He was down on his luck, that was for sure. As he described it, there always seemed to be something against him. One day he had almost gotten a part, but the man who auditioned next turned out to be the son of a long-lost friend of the director. Another time they had needed an Italian accent, and Fred's wasn't good enough. Some actors have a ready flair for accents, but he wasn't one of them. With a little time to prepare, of course, he could have done it well enough, but according to Fred they didn't judge by innate talent, only by superficial things. He started going to auditions at night. Sometimes when he came home he smelled as if he had been drinking, or he looked rumpled. Charlotte always waited up for him with coffee. Often she would be waiting in Fred's bathrobe; it made her feel less lonely. He would say he had gone out for a drink with some other actors; once he said he had been in a fight. "Why don't you bring your friends home? You can all have a drink here, and I can meet them." But he never did. The phone never rang for him. All she knew of these friends were their names: Phil, Jeff, Mike. They could be anybody.

About a year and a half ago was when they had first noticed the man. "There's a man standing across the street," Charlotte said from the chair near the window.

"So?" He was watching *Kojak* and didn't like being interrupted. He kept the TV on all the time. This bothered her at the beginning, but gradually she got used to having lively voices in the background. She even got to like it herself. Fred didn't always watch it, he simply liked to have it on. Sometimes after a detective story he would grunt and say he could have done the main part better.

"I mean, he's just standing there against the gate, staring straight ahead. He's been standing there for fifteen minutes."

"And have you been watching him all that time?"

She fell silent. It made her feel so foolish. But after a week or so

Fred caught a little of her interest. When dinner was over they would check to see if he was still at the gate. Once Charlotte determined to wait up and see how long the man stood there. But she fell asleep in her chair at twelve-thirty; when she woke at a quarter after two he was gone. The weather grew cold; it was dreary November, and still he came.

One evening Fred went out to the corner store to bring back a pint of strawberry ice cream, and when he returned he told her, "I spoke to your friend out there."

"No! What did you say?"

"Nothing much. 'How's it going, pal?'"

"Oh, no! I don't believe you."

"Suit yourself," he teased. "I told him to look up at our window if he wanted to see a sexy item."

"You didn't." But she drew the curtains anyway.

To pass the time they sometimes sat on the couch and made up stories about who the man might be and why he stood there. Charlotte's were not pure fantasy; they were what she half believed.

"He's planning to rob our apartment and he's developing a very careful log of our comings and goings. Except you're at home so much that he's been frustrated so far."

"I see. And what valuable article in this apartment does he want?"

"I don't know. The TV. Me." She laughed awkwardly.

Fred gave her an odd look. "No, he's a Russian spy," he said. "He's looking past our building to the big apartment house on Walnut Street. There on the top floor is another spy who sends him signals with a flashlight through the curtains. And these signals spell out the details of our next space flight, which is why the Russians are always a step ahead of us."

"Oh." She put her arms around him. "You have so much more imagination than I do."

Fred grinned. "Try again."

"All right. He's an ex-con, just out of jail after ten years for embezzling. But he was innocent. It was a frame-up. The guilty party who framed him lives down the block. The man is waiting for him to pass by on a dark night—no, wait, that would only land him in jail again, and he doesn't really have a criminal temperament. He's haunting him, so that the guilty one will eventually be driven mad by his own conscience."

"Interesting," said Fred. He poured some more beer into his glass and thoughtfully watched the foam rise. "He's a dealer in heroin. The heroin is in tiny plastic bags, hidden in the branches of the dogwood tree. Maybe tied with little strings. Or, better, in the leaves of the honeysuckle. The connection comes by in the daytime. The man is there to guard it from a rival gang."

"Maybe," said Charlotte, "he's unemployed and hoping someone will come along and give him a job. . . . Sorry, I shouldn't have said that. It just came out. But really, don't you think we should call the police?"

"What for?"

"He's a suspicious character."

"What could you charge him with? He hardly moves a muscle; he's not drunk and disorderly."

The nights Fred was out Charlotte double-locked the door and drew the curtains tight. Once she woke at three in the morning. Fred was not back yet. It was bitter cold. She hugged her arms, shivering, then put on his heavy robe and walked barefoot to the front windows. The man was gone. And she felt the strangest sensation of being abandoned and unsafe.

Fred stayed out at night more often. And he slept during the day, she was sure of it. He had stopped looking for acting jobs over a year ago. It was a rotten time for theater, he said. It seemed to Charlotte that the papers were full of notices of small theater groups springing up everywhere. It seemed odd too that Fred never suggested going to see the new plays these groups were putting on. But, she thought, he must know what he's talking about. What could she presume to know about the theater? Perhaps it all depended on the right connections.

He began making appointments to be interviewed for office jobs. That went on for months. She couldn't keep track of the places he

said he applied to, and if she asked too often he got touchy. Some
mornings he would get up when she did and put on a suit and tie
for an interview. It was so comforting on those mornings. They
were like two ordinary people getting dressed for work together.
But nothing ever came of it, and Charlotte stopped asking. Life
was dreary. She would get home, tired from the long day and the
crowded bus ride and the grocery shopping, to find him undressed,
playing chess against himself with the expensive ivory chess set he
had bought, while the television spewed out *Gilligan's Island* or *I
Dream of Jeannie*. Sometimes they wouldn't even greet each other.
She would simply walk into the kitchen, unload her groceries, and
start dinner.

One evening she got so exasperated she couldn't control herself.
It had been an awful day at work. They were painting the office
and she had had to move all her things into a tiny space in the hall,
and her boss had rushed her about reading the galleys, which she
couldn't find until nearly lunchtime because of the general chaos.
She hadn't gotten a seat on the bus going home; it was raining, and
a man's umbrella handle poked into her ribs during the entire trip.
To finish it off, as she entered the kitchen her damp paper bag tore
and oranges and cans of tomato sauce spilled out and rolled across
the floor. Fred must have heard the clatter; surely he heard her cry
out when a can fell on her toe, but he didn't budge. She ran out of
the kitchen, shouting, "You could at least cook dinner, goddammit,
you've got nothing better to do! You sit here watching *Batman* with
all the twenty million other kids in America, it's some life, isn't it?
Don't you think I'm worn out, working all day to support us? I
don't know why I stand it, I really don't. Why don't you learn to
cook and make yourself useful? You think you're some kind of
stud? That's all you're good for, and let me tell you, you're not all
that great at that either."

Then she was terrified. She had never shouted at him before in
the two years of their life together. She had never shouted at anyone that way. He looked like the violent type. What if . . . ? But
apparently he wasn't the violent type after all. He didn't say a
word, merely slunk off to the bedroom and pulled the covers over

his head. As she ate her dinner alone Charlotte thought bitterly, Of course he wouldn't, he needs me.

She began to lose control more often, now that she knew it wasn't dangerous. They spoke less. Fred kept the house tidy; she couldn't complain about that. He repaired things promptly, and built cabinets and bookshelves. He even began to cook: two or three times a week she might find dinner waiting when she got home. Charlotte wished he would tell her on the mornings when he was planning to cook, so that she could avoid the daily shopping and anticipate the rest. But he never did—he must do it on the spur of the moment, she imagined—and she didn't like to push him too far. He was really rather sweet, she thought, and pathetic. He gained weight, and when he sat in the big morris chair watching TV and drinking beer, his belly rolled over the top of his pants.

Last month, March, the man hadn't come at all for a whole week. Though she knew it was absurd, Charlotte missed him.

"Look, Fred, it's the second night in a row he's not there."

He was watching *Mission Impossible*. "Maybe Godot finally came."

The fourth night she said, "It's ridiculous, I know, but I'm worried about him."

No answer. Well, Charlotte thought, that really didn't deserve an answer.

On the way home from work she would round the corner cautiously, glance sideways, then walk by the empty space. She knew his precise spot and could picture him in it, hands deep in his raincoat pockets, hat brim pulled low, eyes staring straight ahead, unseeing. His space was blank, like a niche without a statue. She had a sudden glimpse of the static quality of the world, with everything fixed eternally in its accustomed and foreordained place. The man belonged there, just as she belonged on this daily trek from the bus stop carrying her paper bag, just as Fred belonged upstairs in front of the TV, taking apart the blender to see why it didn't work on the puree setting. She paused at her gate to lean down and smell the honeysuckle, and remained there for several moments till she was dizzy and almost faint from the perfume. Her head was swimming, but she relished the feeling of oblivion. When she stepped back, it was almost like rising from a deep sleep. She took a breath of the clearer air, straightened her shoulders, and walked into the house.

The next night it was close to dawn when Fred returned. She rushed to the door at the sound of his key in the lock.

"My God, I've been frantic. What happened to you?"

His eyes were bloodshot. He shoved past her and headed for the bedroom.

In a rage of relief she went after him, pulling at his sleeve. "Oh, no you don't! You don't just fall into bed as usual. Oh, no! You're going to tell me what you've been doing. No more silent treatment. Open your mouth and speak!"

He started to undress. "Lay off, will you? I'm tired."

She tore the shirt off him. "How was she? Any good? Did you just pick her up or have you known her a long time? But she doesn't work for you, does she? Oh, no. Not that. I notice you're always around here at mealtime. Like a dog."

"Stop it," he wailed. "So what? So what? You manage everything else I do, can't I even do that on my own? Can't I get a little relaxation somewhere?"

"Oh my God." She sat down on her side of the bed, which was still warm. She hadn't really believed it, only said it to taunt him. The words seemed to come out of an unknown place, uncontrolled. She had imagined he was out drinking, walking, anything but that. "My God!" What a fool she was. She had had opportunities too, and passed them all up. For she had always felt that Fred would straighten out one of these days. Things would go back to normal. He was down on his luck. He needed time, patience, understanding.

They sat far apart, at opposite edges of the bed.

"I manage everything you do! What a joke. It's you—you've got me on a string. I jump for you. I jump out of bed every morning at seven-thirty for you. Do you think I love to work? I could have saved. . . . I could have gone to Europe. . . . I could have— I . . .

Tell me," she whispered, so low that she hardly recognized her own voice, "tell me just one thing. Were you ever really an actor?"

She knew he was pretending to be asleep.

"Fred, were you ever really an actor?"

He didn't move, so she began to scream and shake him. Grabbing his hair and his pajama top, she shook him back and forth rhythmically, violently, in time with her shrieked words, over and over again: "Were—you—ever—really—an—actor?"

He sat up and dislodged her fingers. "You'll never know," he said viciously. Then he lay down again.

Charlotte got up early for work as usual the next morning. Fred was in a deep sleep. He looked so worn out, she thought, and sad, really. Not vicious, only sad. She had a great pain, like a lump, somewhere in her body, but she couldn't localize it. She drank a cup of coffee to wash it away. After work she had a hamburger at a luncheonette and went to a double feature, so that she wasn't home till nearly eleven. The man was still not there. She wondered nervously what Fred's reaction would be; it was most unusual of her not to come home, not even to telephone. He was watching *Cannon* with half-closed eyes.

"Hello," she said.

"Hello."

They were quiet to each other, and polite.

The man came back the following night. Charlotte and Fred agreed he must have caught the flu that was going around. Fred had had it two weeks before. Why shouldn't the man be susceptible, like everyone else, thought Charlotte. He too must live somewhere, eat and sleep and trudge to work like the mass of men. She went back to crossing the street every evening to avoid him.

It was calm in the house for several weeks. Fred finished repairing the blender, and he hung up some old silent-movie posters that made the living room more cheerful. They began to play lengthy games of Scrabble in the evenings, games filled with dense silences, after which Fred would come up with recondite words. Charlotte admired his cleverness. Meanwhile she made a few small gestures she felt were daring. Like inviting the Harrises over for coffee tonight.

They never had friends over. Fred didn't like most people. People always talk about what they do, he said, and he didn't do anything. But, thought Charlotte, you get tired of spending every evening alone with the same person. She was a little nervous about telling him. Yet she paid the rent, didn't she? She bought the coffee. She could invite people over if she wanted to. If he didn't like it, well then . . . So when she met Gloria Harris on the street this morning and they got to talking, and she realized again what a pleasant person Gloria was, Charlotte said, on an impulse, "Why don't you and Arthur come over tonight for coffee?" The words felt odd on her tongue—she remembered it had been more than a year since she had invited anyone to the apartment.

After she put away the groceries she went into the living room to tell Fred, waiting patiently for a commercial before she attempted to speak. She tried to present it casually, as an ordinary event. The thing to do, she had decided, was subtly, gradually, bring their lives back to the ordinary. Since their quarrel she had come to see how far out of the ordinary they had drifted. Perhaps with the Harrises she could get a better idea of what the ordinary was, what she had a right to expect.

"You must have seen them around," Charlotte said. "They live two doors down from the house with the man. Gloria and Arthur. She's a teacher and he's a—well, that doesn't matter. He's stocky and blond, you'll recognize them. They're very nice people. I see them on the street all the time."

He was in a good mood tonight. "Okay. What time?"

"Eight-thirty. Listen, Fred—uh—will you talk?"

"What do you mean, will I talk?"

She tried to speak gently. "I only meant, you know, will you talk to them?"

"Maybe you'd like to prepare a short script for me."

Charlotte went to the kitchen to get dinner ready. The dogwood, she thought, will bloom any day now. Tomorrow morning, even, she might have a glimpse of pink before leaving for work.

Gloria and Arthur Harris were congenial guests.

"I'm glad you asked us over," said Gloria. "You know, I've really wanted to get together, but every time I meet you on the street one of us is rushing off somewhere."

In the kitchen, scooping vanilla ice cream over the pie, which she had warmed in the oven, Charlotte listened anxiously. Thank heaven the Harrises weren't talking about their work. Arthur Harris was describing their camping trip in Maine last summer. They had had two weeks alone in the woods. Arthur said, "It was great. We're both so busy all year that this was finally a chance to, well, get away and concentrate on each other for a change." Then Gloria talked about her family, how she had four sisters scattered all over the United States. Fred asked a few questions. He mentioned his sister, far off too, in Detroit. It was going smoothly. Charlotte, after settling down with her pie and coffee, tried not to lead the conversation. Let Fred see how pleasant it could be, spending a little time with friendly people. They got to talking about articles in magazines and about current novels. That was good. Fred spent whole days reading, which he could do even while the TV chattered. He sounded somewhat scornful of everything he read—she hoped that wouldn't put the Harrises off—but at least he was talking.

Later, while they were having brandy, Charlotte said, "By the way, have you ever noticed the man who stands in front of that house near yours at night?"

"Noticed!" said Arthur. "How could we miss him?"

"Then tell me, what on earth is he doing there? I've been wondering for over a year."

"It's one of those peculiar stories, Charlotte," said Gloria hesitantly. "It'll depress you."

"That's all right," said Charlotte. "We're dying to know."

"Well, he used to live in that house. Some of the older neighbors even remember him from back then, which always strikes me as weird—he's not someone you can picture as young. Anyhow, his wife ran off one day and took the kids. One of those ghastly stories. I don't know the details. He moved out. No one knows where he lives now."

"But why . . . why is he standing there, after all this time?" As she spoke, Charlotte noticed that Fred had picked up a magazine and was starting to leaf through it.

Gloria shrugged. "Kind of an obsession, I suppose. You know how these things are."

Charlotte set down her glass carefully. She was faintly dizzy from the brandy. "But what about the people who live there now? Don't they mind him just standing there night after night?"

"Oh, there's no one there now," Gloria said. "The house is empty. Didn't you know? It has been for years. He never sold it. Hung on to it."

Charlotte's whole body was trembling. She looked over at Fred again. He had let the magazine drop and didn't appear to be listening. His hands were clasped loosely over his stomach and his eyes were half shut.

"Do you mean to say he stands in front of an empty house?" Her head was pounding. She was remembering all the stories she and Fred had invented about the man, and how far off they had been. They had never thought of the force of memory, of habit, of yearning, nor of madness. And yet she felt it was not really yearning, or madness either. It was something for which she could find no name, a kind of dogged, rooted, purposeless sticking. . . . She felt herself starting, childishly, to cry, and felt, too, that she must say something to explain her tears or she would be mortified. "That's . . . that's the saddest story I've ever heard."

"Ha ha ha," roared Fred suddenly. His fat belly shook and the bottom button of his shirt strained, threatening to burst off. "Ha ha! What an ending!" He laughed raucously, stomping his huge feet on the floor and bouncing his head up and down. He laughed on and on, as if he could not stop, as if he might go on forever.

Charlotte leaped to him and grabbed the glass out of his hand. It was sloshing liquor all over the rug with every jerk of his body. "Fred, stop it. It's not funny. What are you laughing at?"

She saw Gloria and Arthur exchange a shocked look. Arthur's formerly bland eyes were alarmed.

"Ha ha! Not funny!" Fred gasped. "It's the funniest thing I've ever heard!" He slapped his thighs and threw his head back. Old gold shone from his wide-open mouth. Subsiding, he wiped his eyes, and then his shoulders began quivering with another swell of savage laughter.

"Fred!" cried Charlotte. "Don't laugh like that!"

Gloria Harris put down her brandy glass and stood up.

Charlotte, sobbing, a fire streaking through her chest, ran downstairs, outside, and buried her face in the dark of the honeysuckle. She wanted to forget the last half hour, forget the dreadful story about the man, forget the years with Fred that had thickened around her like a dense layer of fat. She wanted to be transported back to the time before she ever knew Fred, even before her father had died, when life had stretched before her full of possibility. It was hopeless, she knew, and yet she took deep gasping breaths and dug her teeth into the leaves, trying to bite off and swallow the deadening sweetness.

ACQUAINTED WITH THE NIGHT

Alexander Smith woke to find himself sitting up in bed. The bedside wall lamp was on. His glasses were still on, and a book lay open on the blanket, two middle pages peculiarly upright, swaying in the faint fall breeze from the nearby window. The digital clock said the time was 2:47. Odd how the last two numbers were his age, a reminder in the dead of night. "Shit," he muttered. He hated to doze off reading, which had been happening to him about twice a week lately. He had trouble getting back to sleep, and mornings after, felt jolted out of sequence, as if two days had passed instead of one. A small click sounded; it was 2:48. There, he had aged. Staring at the straight-edged, unfriendly numbers, he vaguely recalled a Robert Frost poem that said a solitary clock proclaimed the time was neither wrong nor right. Yes. That was exactly how it felt in the middle of the night. The time was just a meaningless number with no attachment to events. Alexander felt stranded and forlorn.

He put aside his glasses, switched off the lamp, and got down under the covers. He felt the warm back of his wife, Linda, turned away from him, her contours familiar and soothing. He hadn't thought to look, when the light was on, to see if she was there. But where else would she be at two forty-eight? A click; he made the correction, forty-nine. Just so, it went by.

Sleep eluded him. To make matters worse, he discovered something quite strange nagging at him. A small shape, dark, yet standing out against the deeper dark, danced behind his closed lids. It looked like a bacillus. Alexander's eyes had been strained lately, since he used them constantly in his work as an architect. Perhaps he needed stronger glasses. Perhaps he was getting old. Undoubtedly he was getting old. He watched the bacillus dance about, and found that if he rolled his eyes from left to right the spot moved with them. If he rolled them up and down the spot went along too, but the up-and-down motion hurt.

Minutes clicked by, and it would not go away. It made his skin tingly and restless, as if his insides were struggling to escape from their container. He knew what it was, though, and knowledge was reassuring. The spot was an aftereffect of sleeping for two hours with the light on and then waking up to the dim glow and going abruptly back into darkness. It was some optical phenomenon he couldn't explain precisely, but whose broad outlines he felt he understood. As a matter of fact, he felt that general imprecise understanding about a great many things, he realized: the tides, rocket ships, airplanes, rainbows. Maybe he really didn't know anything thoroughly. What the hell, though. He managed, didn't he? Now sleep.

Alexander opened his eyes in the dark. He could see nothing. It was too soon. You had to lie awake for a while in the dark before you could see everything. He saw only the spot, dark against dark, floating through the void like a flying saucer. No longer shaped like a bacillus, it was a small circle with undefined edges, rather like a planet seen through a telescope, with a halo around it. Or a gray star with a gray glow. He closed his eyes; it remained, spinning, creating a haze, a wake of its motion. Horrible. He opened them. He could begin to distinguish the furniture now. The room was spacious. There was his armchair against the far wall. Then his bureau drawer on the right; Linda's was on the left. Above Linda's was a mirror, illumined in places where moonlight glimmered in through the window. The spot went everywhere Alexander's eyes went, relentless. It flickered in the jagged beams in the mirror. He couldn't get rid of it. A UFO with a message. Glaucoma. Retinitis pigmentosa. Impending death, beckoning. To ease the panic he moved closer to the warm body of Linda. She was wearing a thin silky nightgown that excited him mildly as its smoothness brushed against his chest and thighs.

He realized he was trembling with fear. Maybe he ought to make love to Linda. That would at least be something to do while he couldn't sleep. She was still turned away from him. He put his arm around her and pulled her closer, testing the strength of his desire. It was nice making love to Linda. He pressed against her. She was usually an eager partner, and if not always totally eager, if some vague, ancient tug seemed to hold her back, she was at least amenable. He put a hand on Linda's breast and eased a knee between her thighs. The spot in his eye throbbed, zoomed forward and back to tease him, taunt him, like the cavorting spot at the end of an invisible laser beam. Did he want to make love to Linda? He queried his body. Actually not very much. He was tired and distressed by the frustrating day and longed to sleep.

But maybe he should do it anyway. It might make him forget about the thing in his eye. Once he started he would want to. He moved his palm around Linda's nipple but she did not stir. God, what a deep sleep! He envied her. His eyes rolled involuntarily with the motion of his hand, and he noticed that the speck rolled too. It was terrifying. Trembling, he turned over on his other side, leaving Linda. The clock said 3:04. The right-hand numbers of the clock stopped at sixty. Maybe he would die at sixty. Or the next sixty. Actually they stopped at fifty-nine. There was no 3:60. The spot was on the clock, on the upper-left-hand tip of the four. Five.

Alexander began to experiment with the spot. If he could not get rid of it he could at least play with it, tease it back. He stretched out flat and looked up at the ceiling. He blinked. The spot disappeared for the fraction of an instant that his lids fluttered down and up, but immediately reappeared to jiggle on the ceiling. He began to blink to the rhythm of the first movement of Beethoven's Seventh Symphony and the speck obediently danced. But the fast pace made his eyes ache, so he lowered his lids to rest them. He didn't feel like playing with it. He was exhausted. There was no comfortable way to arrange his body; his pores seemed about to burst open. The speck was an intrusion, undeserved, unbearable. He wanted to cry out in protest, as he would protest to the police if a thief entered his house, but there was no one to protest to. It was his very own speck. He thrashed around in the bed, viciously kicking the covers about him. Then he pressed his fists hard to his eyes and for a moment found relief. Gone! But when he released them it was back, surrounded by colored flashing dots. They went away gradually but the spot remained. Alexander started to sweat. He hated the spot savagely. It was not in his body—it seemed located in distant space, yet it controlled his existence like a vital organ, heart or lungs. Then he quieted in surprise, for the way he had just described the spot, distant yet part of him and controlling, sounded like the idea of God that was taught to children. The speck was God. God was paying him a nocturnal visit. A vision.

Alexander couldn't believe it was himself having such alien thoughts. His brain was softening. Premature senility. He ought to laugh; he must be delirious. But it was not funny. Very possibly this was the way people went insane. God. Shit, he thought. He would never read in bed again. His forehead was cold with damp sweat. He went into the bathroom for a drink of water and looked in the mirror, but couldn't really see himself because of the mote in his eye. There was only a haggard, generalized familiar face: anyone's, a good-looking model for expensive Scotch in the pages of a slick magazine, caught unawares in his pajamas, with a hangover. The mote was in the mirror, on the pupil of his right eye. It was a gross distortion of figure and ground. He was the ground and the mote was the figure. Blood surged through him. Furious, he lifted his fist in a violent gesture to smash the mirror, but stopped himself in time. He really must get hold. Maybe he ought to read for a while. But he knew that the speck would move along the words of the page; he knew exactly how it would look, gray, bouncing along the white page, a replica of his eye's movements, and he didn't want to try.

Back in bed, he pressed the pillow hard over his eyes. Thank God! It was gone. Maybe now he could sleep, if he could find the right position. Soon it would be morning. He peered out: 3:58. The hour was aging. Linda lay calm; she hadn't stirred. Linda was forty-one. He experimented with the pillow; at last, lying on his stomach with his face pressed into it but turned slightly to one side, he could keep the mote away and still breathe.

Sleep did not come, but he was more peaceful. He tried to think of nothing, but events of the day, blueprints, drawings, the faces of his associates, ran through his mind. It had been a troubled day: a contract they believed they were sure to get was at the last moment given to a younger, rival firm. Alexander had been ruthless, shouting at his staff and threatening to fire people for not working hard enough. He had felt weighed down with the burden of the business pressing on the front of his head. He thought of women he had seen in Caribbean islands moving gracefully down dirt roads with huge, heavy baskets on their heads. They sailed along, proud and erect. He staggered, clumsy and in pain, beneath the burden. Now he could see that the contract was less important than it had seemed. Perspective. The firm was in no real danger. He shouldn't have carried on so. All right, so he had made a mistake. So he had behaved like a bastard; more like a frustrated child, actually. Was that a reason to be punished so harshly by this . . . thing? Nothing like this had ever happened to him before. He was a reasonable man, after all. But at least now he had it under control. He thought, in a while, that he might try a little test. Maybe the whole horrid episode was over, gone as mysteriously as it had come, and there was no longer any need to remain uncomfortably in this absurd position. So very gradually, as if afraid of being noticed, he raised his head from the pillow. Christ, it was still there! In a rage, he pounded his fist into the mattress. He wasn't going to get any sleep at all and he would be a wreck in the morning.

How could Linda lie there sleeping so calmly while he tossed in agony? It wasn't fair. She was his wife. She was supposed to share his pain.

"Linda." He shook her. "Linda," he called loudly in a hoarse voice. "Please," he added more softly.

"What?" She was still sleeping, he could tell. The word was a reflex.

"I can't sleep. . . . I have this . . ."

She rolled towards him. "What is it?"

"I have something in my eye."

"Go to sleep. It will go away."

"Linda, this is terrible. It's this thing. I can't stop seeing it. I can't sleep."

"Murine." Her eyes never opened.

"What?"

"Put in Murine. Drops. Bottom shelf."

Could she do all that in her sleep? Women were amazing.

"Listen to me. Wake up. It's not that kind of thing. It's something I keep seeing. I can't stand it."

There was no answer. She was sleeping. Alexander was enraged, but when he looked at the pretty curve of her shoulder he relented. What did he want from her? She hadn't sent the mote, and she certainly couldn't make it disappear. The mote rested on the peak of her shoulder's curve. He put his hand there; the mote was on the back of his hand.

"Alex," she murmured unexpectedly.

"What?"

"Hold me. I'm cold. And close the window."

Grumbling, he rose, shut the window, returned to bed and held her. The spot was still now. His eyes were tired and not moving, and so the spot was still. It obeyed his eyes, a marionette of his eyes. Perhaps he was making a kind of peace with it. Perhaps he would have to live with it for the rest of his life. How would he manage that? He could spend the rest of his life staring directly in front of him, never moving his eyes, only his head. People would certainly think him odd. But seriously, he could get used to it. People got used to worse things. His brother wore a hearing aid. One of the junior partners at the office had had a toe amputated. A friend of theirs had had a breast and a large part of her upper arm removed and had to wear her arm in a sling for the rest of her life. That must be very annoying. Of course, much worse than annoying, but for the purposes of this survey, annoying. Linda had a slight stammer when she got nervous. She knew just when it was going to happen, she told him. But she lived with it. It was a small thing, when you put it in perspective.

Thinking of all these things, Alexander was more wide awake than before. He detached himself from Linda, tucked the blanket around her and rolled over, hugging himself tight. The mote was acting up again, bouncing back and forth like a Ping-Pong ball. He wasn't getting used to it at all. A person could get used to a sling— of course it was terrible to have cancer, but a sling was something you could accept after a while. You would be grateful simply to be alive. He would willingly wear his arm in a sling for the rest of his life if only this torment would go away and he could get some sleep. But that happened to women. Most likely he would have cancer of the prostate one of these days, he was nearing that age. Would he be so willing to give that up? Your mote or your balls? Wait a minute, I'll have to think that over. He remembered Esau, who sold his birthright for a mess of pottage. Ah, he understood now how men could make these foolish bargains. The speck winked at him; it was tiny, infinitesimal, a molecule. Maybe he was the only man on earth to have seen a molecule with the naked eye. It darted about wildly, flickered, floated, vibrated. He broke out in a sweat again, and yearned to die suddenly, right here, with no pain. He pushed his face in the pillow, but it stayed, even with the pillow. His last resort was gone. He wanted to cry from hopelessness. Maybe if he cried, some chemical reaction would take place in his eyes and it would go away. He rarely cried; all he could manage now were a few weak tears that had no effect.

All right. It was going to stay for a while. He would accept it. Be reasonable. He tried to lie still, though his skin stung with frustration. He would think it through. The mote must be more than a mote. It must be a symbol. It represented something about himself that he refused to face. That was how it worked: you buried something, and it came back to haunt you in strange ways. He loathed self-examination. He really didn't believe the meanings behind things mattered very much. Action mattered, not motives. He supposed he was rather obtuse that way, at least Linda said so. But women in general were better at that sort of thing; it was their upbringing.

Still, maybe there was some awful secret about himself that he didn't know. A friend of theirs, telling them the sad account of her recent divorce, had presented the theory that everyone had a secret, a secret secret they didn't even know themselves. Her husband's secret, she said bitterly, was that he hated women. "Ron is a latent homosexual," she murmured. He and Linda had been shocked. Alexander was willing to accept that Ron hated women, but did this make him a latent homosexual? It didn't seem logical. "Linda"—he spoke quietly into the dark—"do I have a secret?" She slept on. He hadn't really meant to wake her.

Maybe he was a latent homosexual, Alexander thought. Anything was possible. He was willing to accept it if his acceptance would make the spot go away. He thought of several men he knew and juxtaposed them alongside the idea of his own possible latent homosexuality. Nothing happened. Did he secretly crave their hands stroking his body? He tried to imagine it, and felt neither disgust nor excitement. Lack of interest. "Linda," he said again. No, he could not ask her that. She was sleeping, and if by chance she heard she would surely laugh or else think he had gone out of his mind. He dismissed the idea of latent homosexuality. What next?

He thought of all the bad things he had ever done in his life and never confessed to. Once he had accepted a three-thousand-dollar bribe and distorted some figures in order to get a contract. He would not do it again today, but eighteen years ago they were hungry. He did not think, even now, that it was so terrible. He had done an excellent piece of work on the job, better than anything the competing firms would have turned out. Alexander searched on. He had not paid enough attention to his parents in their old age. He had been very busy at the time, getting the business on its feet and raising the children with Linda. He had let the distance between him and his parents grow until when they died it was almost as if he were burying strangers and had buried his real parents long ago, little by little, without ceremony. Yes, all right, that was bad, but they were dead now, in any case. He was sorry. Before that, when he was in college, a girl he slept with three times begged him for money for an abortion. He was poor and gave her all he could get together, seventy-five dollars. He didn't think he was the father; she had a reputation for sleeping around. For days she phoned him, weeping, begging for more money, afraid to tell her parents or anyone at school. Finally in disgust he shouted at her, "It's not even my fucking kid. Leave me alone and get it somewhere else. From what I hear you have plenty of contacts." Was that so bad? She had indeed found the money elsewhere. Alexander felt he had a pretty good case. He rubbed his eyes; the mote bloomed astonishingly, then retreated to its familiar size, a speck, a seed. He shouldn't have said, "From what I hear you have plenty of contacts." That was gratuitous. I'm sorry, he screamed inside. For Christ's sake, it was ages ago. He had two more children now, grown. He had raised and cared for two children. Wasn't that enough? Now go away. But it didn't go away. It bobbed, like the little white spots used to bob along the lyrics of songs flashed on the movie screen years ago.

Once when his daughter, Sandy, was five years old he flew into a rage because she defied him, refused to pick up her toys from the floor, and he hit her hard all over, face, shoulders, arms, back. He stopped himself when her screams finally penetrated to him. No one else was home. He was alone in the house and abusing a child. How could that happen? It was something he read about in the papers with horror. He stopped and cried, "Oh my God," and held her in his arms, weeping, and apologized. It was agonizing. That was the only time he ever hit her. But was that so terrible, in perspective? Didn't many men hit their children, more often, and did they suffer for it fifteen years later? It was very unjust. Sandy probably didn't even remember. He could ask her next time she was home from college, but he was sure she wouldn't remember.

He had slept with a number of women during his twenty-one years of marriage, mostly when Linda was in the final months of pregnancy and the early months of motherhood—that was understandable—but at other times too. He met them in bars or at parties, saw them once and never called again. He wasn't proud of it, but he had never thought it was so terrible. Nobody was hurt. Linda never knew. It was simply a need he had at the time, he didn't do it anymore. All right, the women were hurt, he admitted. They were decent women, not whores. He always said he would call them and never did. As he was leaving he would say, "I'll give you a call in a few days." An easy way of saying goodbye. The words made him wince. "I'll give you a call in a few days." All right, that was pretty bad. It made him feel pretty low, remembering. But on the other hand, he had to be fair to himself, he never hurt them. Physically, that is. He knew that lots of times when a man picked someone up in a bar and got her home he used the opportunity to do awful, cruel things, really atrocious things. He had the chance, but never did anything like that. He was very nice with them in bed. He was as nice as he would have been with his own wife. Didn't that count?

The spot did not relent, even as Alexander dredged up all these things from the past that he never thought about anymore. It swirled in zigzag patterns, mocking, torturing. His body ached from tossing. Confessing his sins was no help. He felt more depressed than guilty. What was the use of dwelling on his own ugliness? So he was a worm, all right. Wasn't everyone? He was no worse than the next man. If everyone were to confess everything we'd all be in jail. Adultery, he thought, is a crime in this state. Possibly he could go to jail for it. He could also go to jail for child abuse, accepting a bribe, being an accomplice in an abortion. As a kid he and his friends used to steal miniature cars from Woolworth's. Theft too? This was becoming absurd. He pictured himself in jail, wearing a striped suit and cap, lining up with a tin bowl for nauseating meals, hacking away with a pick in a rock quarry, and he gave a small laugh in the dark because his image of jail came from old James Cagney movies. The man in the next cell would tap out a message in code on the wall, asking what he was in for, and Alexander would tap back, "Adultery." The other inmates would laugh at him. Would the mote follow him to jail too? Sleepless nights on a hard cot, watching a speck dance on the concrete walls of his cell. It would feel pretty much the same as now, except the bed here was soft and the room was large and well-furnished. Yes, he thought, he was a good provider. He had provided his own cell and not made himself a burden to the state.

God, he moaned, help me! When Jack and Sandy came home from college at Thanksgiving they would find their father a changed man, aged, weak, fragile, and delirious. His children. Tears leaped to his eyes. The mote shimmered. He crushed the pillow between his fists.

There was one thing he had neglected to mention. All right, all right. For a year he had been madly in love with a girl named April. She was an art historian who worked at a museum, and he met her at the opening of a friend's show. He had remembered her afterwards only because he thought it was a ridiculous name. Then he met her on the street. They had a drink. And so on. He came to adore the name. After they made love he would sing her to sleep with all the songs he could think of that had April in them. April in Paris. April in Portugal. April Showers. He hadn't seen her in six years. The month of April was still a torment to him, though, writing the date all the time. He usually wrote "4" instead. No, he really must not think about her or he would go mad. Just the thought of her name in the dark filled him with sudden craving. Lord, what was a man, at the mercy of a name. He looked over at Linda. He could wake her. You miserable bastard, he told himself. If you could do that . . . Hadn't he done enough already?

He remembered how Linda had confronted him with it. It was all over him, how could she miss it? They talked for a long time at the kitchen table late at night, rationally, considerately, about what they could do and what this meant in their lives. There was an air of unreality over their talk.

"It's not that I don't love you," Alexander was repeating calmly after an hour. "Don't misunderstand. These things happen."

"Yes," she said. "I can understand that."

She got up, took a pair of shears from a drawer, and cut off a great hank of her long dark hair.

"Linda!" Alexander stood up.

"It's all right, it's all right, don't worry," she said. "Sit down."

She put the hair in an iron pot and poured vinegar over it. It smelled foul and ugly. Then she lit a wooden kitchen match and set fire to the hair. Alexander could not speak or move. Civilized English had left him. He felt they were living before civilization began. This was a primitive rite that made him paralyzed and mute with awe. The hair sparked and crackled and soon the kitchen was filled with a hideous acrid smell that brought him to his senses.

"Linda . . ."

"Shh." And she smiled with her lips closed, and blinked her glinting eyes at him. "When it's all done I'm going to eat it."

He leaped up and shook her hard by the shoulders. "Stop!" he yelled. Her head wobbled back and forth. She looked terrifying, with half of her hair tossing and the shorn side jagged. "Stop!" he yelled again. He grabbed the sizzling pot and ran cold water in it. Dark hair overflowed into the sink.

She sat down quietly at the table. "You're sending my beautiful hair down the drain."